ENTER
THE
AFTER

PATRICK KEITHAHN

ISBN: 978-1-7323882-1-5

Cover design by Brandi Doane McCann/Ebook Cover Designs.

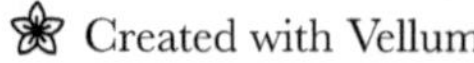 Created with Vellum

CONTENTS

1

INTO THE DARKNESS

I never imagined being here. I've been ripped from my life and tossed into a dark place. Sometimes we live in our nightmares.

I'm packed in an ambulance swaying on a stretcher, siren from the outside parting traffic, emergency medical technician inserting an IV and sticking electrodes to my chest. I'm just trying to breathe, but that one task is overwhelming.

The ambulance is a portal for the barely living, the destination straddling survival or death. Along its inner walls are machines and supplies to fight for life, all of humanity's most vital medical wisdom stuffed into a truck. People suffer here, and today it's my turn. The EMT, a muscular black man, is calling ahead to the hospital, conveying my condition in baritone as if ordering a pizza: "Forty-four-year-old male complaining of shoulder and neck pain, shortness of breath, blood pressure one sixty over ninety-two, pulse is . . ."

The ambulance interrupts with a jolt over a pothole. It's like the driver is trying to hit ruts just to antagonize me. My body constricts like I've been crushed by a boulder, and I groan through pursed lips.

"Morphine?" I ask the EMT, but he tells me no, it could close off my airway. He continues his report to the hospital.

But I digest what the man just said: Close off my airway? That would be worse. At least now I know. I grip my pant legs with both hands, my next best option to ease the pain, the nerves in my shoulder spraying impulses like a drunken outlaw spends bullets. There's nothing I can do but ride the pain and wonder how I got into this mess.

I'm dying. This is how all people who face horrible death have to deal with it, grab onto something and hope the end comes quickly. Some face it with grace, others with terror. I'm much more prone to terror and always have been.

But I'm not going to die. I can't allow it to happen to my young family, not like this, due to a complication from neck surgery. I'm going to die in my sleep when I'm 87, after I've done and seen it all, when the loose ends are tied up on a cold winter's night after Christmas when everyone expects it. Not like this, suffocating in my own skin. But I also admit that's an impractical fantasy, and it's far from what I'm trending toward. I can idealize my future all I want, but my life has problems—too many to list. Futility is my dominant trait, and that part of me believes dying might actually be merciful.

I reach for my left shoulder with my right hand and feel the huge lump. The bulge is an angry dachshund, and it's consuming the skin on my neck as if a black hole has opened on my collar. An hour ago I was in my bed waking from a nap, a day removed from the hospital. That's when an invisible anaconda of surgical complications took hold of me in my sleep.

"Ten minutes," the EMT says as he touches my arm. "Almost there."

I look out the rear window and think how many times I've seen an ambulance and wondered what was going on in there. I would much rather be the rubberneckers in traffic watching the ambulance pass than being jostled in here. They don't know how good they have it stuck in gridlock.

Longest ten minutes ever. I feel like I'm counting the seconds, but each second takes ten hours. It's as if I've been here for weeks, sweat pouring over me like it's raining. I squeeze the most from every horrific second, dwelling on the passage of time because there's nothing else to do. I might be in this ambulance for the rest of my life.

So I'm legitimately surprised when we make a turn into the hospital lot, driver swinging the ambulance around and backing in before we stop and wait. The rear doors open and the EMTs unload me.

I'm wheeled inside the hospital to emergency room

chaos. The ER is an open room where people in scrubs attend to patients experiencing a really bad day. I feel as if we're soldiers just recently swept from the battlefield, and our collective prognosis is poor. I'm given a bay on the end while a team of nurses and doctors descends upon me.

Here come the simple questions I'm too incapacitated to answer: How old are you? When was your surgery? How's your pain? Are you having trouble breathing?

My responses are confused, it's not even me talking. I can't concentrate, and when I speak it sounds like I'm on helium. I'm Alvin the Fricken Chipmunk. I'm terrified how screwed up my voice is. How long until my windpipe is squeezed out totally? The doctors and nurses confer with one another, plans are formulated, then I hear that my surgeon is on the phone and wants to know what happened.

I know the answer. What happened, Doc, is I'm being squeezed to death. There's an invisible anaconda choking me, and someone just needs to pull it off, lure it away with a rabbit or a squirrel. Why did you do this to me, you malpractice hack? Did you even go to med school? But the doctors will tell my surgeon in more suitable clinical terms. Just as well.

I start to gag, and I think this is it, my air is gone. I produce a cough that sounds like a troll living in my chest is supremely cranky. A nurse puts a salmon-colored basin to my lips and asks if I want to spit. Don't mind if I do. I spit something white and sticky, and she clears a trail of spittle from my lips with a towel. This isn't a dignified activity to do in front of other adults, but I have to think they don't mind, that they've seen much worse.

I ask if I can have pain medication, but once again I'm told it's too dangerous. I'm sure my expression shows how disappointing that answer is, and I cough and spit to give it an exclamation point. For the next couple of hours, I will become a master of coughing and spitting, my spews rivaling any Big Leaguer.

The ER staff clears out, and I'm left with the nurse whose job it is to hold my spittoon. She's older than me, a veteran of the ER, plain but pretty, and I wonder if she's ever envisioned putting this on her resume. If I had any self-respect, I'd stop cough-spitting and spare her, but I don't care and can't help it anyway.

"How's your breathing?" she asks after a while. I shake my head and say in my Munchkin voice that it's not good. She's probably been told to keep checking on this, and it's another thing for her resume. I'm sure she thinks it's funny to hear a grown man speak like an elf, but she's very professional.

"Do you have family nearby?" she asks, and I nod. I have a wife and two daughters, I say. I don't complicate it by telling her we're separated. I don't add that my wife decided she had had enough of me and told me to move out some months ago, to give our marriage a break and see what happens. I don't need to get into it now, although I guess I have, to myself.

"Just hang in there, okay? The doctors are figuring out what to do."

I nod. Of course they are, that's what doctors do. They just take their time doing it.

I notice there's a large man in a shirt and tie wandering the ER like he's bored. He's not a doctor, he just doesn't look like he could be that smart, and he's not doing anything medical, he's just here to observe. He must be some sort of security guard, and for some reason he's taken an interest in me. He stands by the door out to the nursing station with his arms folded, just looking at me, and I cough and spit.

My unstable mind is trying to tell me that the guy isn't a security guard at all. Then who is he? No one says a word to him, it's as if he isn't there to them, but I see him all too well. That's because he's an Angel of Death. I convince myself of this. He's here to take me away, waiting for nature to take its course.

Well, that's just silly. I'm not that demented to believe this. My mind is just being a jerk, telling me lies because the part of the brain that maintains rational thought is overloaded.

Then why does the guy keep staring at me? He should look at his phone or go get some coffee. Why does the sicko insist on watching me die? It must be quite the spectacle.

I'm not dying! I have to stop thinking that. Because if you start thinking those things, they can really happen. I try to think of something else, but what? There's nothing else to think about except how much this hurts.

"Sir?" It's one of the doctors. He's wandered over to me without my noticing. "So here's the plan. We're going to get someone in here to insert a breathing tube. He's an ENT—ear, nose, and throat doctor—and he's coming here under police escort. Should be here in less than an hour. How's your pain? How's your breathing?"

I'd like to tell him I'll go bonkers waiting another hour, or that I'll suffocate long before then, but instead I say I'm fine. Why do people say they're fine when they're not? The doctor nods and leaves.

I don't have a clear enough head to pray well, and I'm not much of a praying type anyway. But two words come to mind, and they bring me comfort: "Please, God."

If God is real, and I'm pretty sure he is, he'll know what I mean with such a truncated plea: Don't let me die like this, don't let me suffer, don't stand there and watch like the security guard Angel of Death.

For the next hour, I cough and spit and think "please God" a hundred million times. The nurse is silent and dutiful, catching my spit in the basin. They're not paying her nearly enough, whatever it is.

An hour later, a new doctor enters, a dapper man with olive skin and a tie, the breathing tube guy, and he looks unfazed to see me in my condition.

"Sir, I'm Dr. Mendez. How is your breathing?"

Oh wonderful, my breathing is top notch, like I'm an

Olympic athlete inhaling the mountain air. I tell him my breathing is poor and I hurt like he can't imagine, and I realize now that I can barely talk.

"Okay, we're prepping the operating room now. I'm going to insert a breathing tube, put you under, and send you downtown in an ambulance so your surgeon can attend to you there. Okay?"

It's a solid plan, and the way the doctor speaks gives me confidence that this might work. Until he offers more insight than I'm prepared to hear:

"Of course, inserting the breathing tube has some risk. Your airway is very tight. If I can't insert it, we'll have to do a tracheotomy to clear your airway. There's risk of discomfort . . . and in the worst case, death."

Please God please God please God.

Did the man just say what I think he said?

Yes, my mind tells me, he just said that. The security guard, who really is the Angel of Death, I know it now, is still looking at me, arms folded. He'll stay there as long as it takes, but he knows it won't be long now.

"Do you have any questions for me?" the doctor says.

I have a million questions, but I shake my head, no. What's the point?

"Okay then, sit tight and we'll take care of this." He pats my arm and leaves.

I feel the object in my pants pocket, my phone, and I consider reaching for it. Until now I didn't see the need to call my wife, it would just alarm her to hear my voice like this. But if the doctor's warning comes true, this will be the last time I can talk to her and my daughters.

No, screw that, I'm not going to call her, because I'm not going to die. Calling her will be admitting that I'm going to die, but I'm not.

All too soon a gaggle of nurses and doctors comes for me. They have masks tied to their necks and wear blue hats, battle gear for the medical professional. But the nurse who had handled my spit stays in her normal scrubs, and she's the one who wheels me out, my head at the front of the gurney so I can see her pushing me to the OR. I feel a connection with her, she's been there with me throughout much of this ordeal, and she heard what Mendez said. I can't help but think she's on my side in a way none of the other hospital people is.

"You'll be all right," she says to me, and I really believe her. Maybe she's heard doctors tell their patients they might die, and she sees through the liability verbiage, knows I'll be all right, and is acutely aware that I need to hear that right now. I'm so taken by what she says that I can't respond, though I want to tell her thank you.

At the OR door, the nurse's job is done. She passes my gurney off to the OR staff, and she watches me as they open the door and bring me inside. I want to go back and be with the nice nurse some more, not in the operating room, but soon she's out of sight and I'm inside.

They've dimmed the lights for some reason, and it's really dark in here. There's a crowd of hospital staff waiting, so many that it makes me understand just how much trouble I'm in. They've called in everyone to help, and I'm on center stage.

They bring me to the operating table and lift me onto it, pushing out my gurney, saying things to each other that I don't understand.

Please God please God please God.

"Okay," Mendez says. "We're ready to insert the tube. I'll put it in on the count of three, and then we'll put you to sleep. Ready?"

No, I'm definitely not ready. I want to go back out to the nice nurse and spit. But in my mind, I remember her reassuring words, and the pain is still ferocious, so the sooner this gets done the better.

"Yes," I croak.

Mendez counts really fast. "One, two . . ."

Wait, no, I really am *not* ready, I was lying, you're counting too fast . . .

"Three."

There's a sickening squishing sound, like a boot being shoved into mud, and something is crammed down my throat. Oh no, I can't breathe! But it's okay, they'll fix it, everything is supposed to be all right, it will just take a second or two.

"Breathe," Mendez commands, and I try, but it won't work. This isn't working. I know because people begin talking, taking action, doing things to me that I can't see.

But it's all over quickly. They've put me under like Mendez said they would, except something has gone terribly wrong. In my mind, as vividly as if it were real, I see a tattered yellow door. It creaks open in front of me, revealing only chilly darkness inside. I don't want to go in there, but this isn't a choice I can make. Something propels me through the doorway, and the yellow door slams shut behind me. Everything in my world disappears as I sink into a disturbing unconsciousness.

2

THE AFTER

It's a remarkable sensation to float through the air on your back as though in zero gravity, knowing it's an impossibility. Yet this feels as natural to me as if I'm a dandelion puff caught in a spring breeze. I sway with the whims of nature's exhale, like being rocked in the arms of some invisible goddess.

Impulses overwhelm the idleness inside me, and my eyes flap open. I'm on my back, and there's a grand puzzle overhead, too intricate to interpret quickly through drowsy eyes. I stare up to make sense of it. Angry tree branches and shriveled leaves form an imperfect awning to a backdrop of hazel sky. It's a dying forest entirely foreign to me, dreary light poking through gaps in the boughs. My view scrolls past as if the forest is a lonely procession moving on by. Then I realize it's me that's drifting past, dragged by an unseen force.

I sit up and look around. What I see solves one

mystery straight away. I'm not floating mid-air, I'm in a wooden rowboat that's splintered and frail with age. I'm astern on the floor peering over the transom at the swirling wake. The boat is wobbling down a narrow river that cuts through dense woods, light scarce enough that it feels like being in a cave.

I hear a creak behind me, followed by a watery slosh. I flinch and turn to see a man seated in the middle of the boat, his hands gripping wooden oars. He's rowing the boat, back facing the bow so that he's looking right at me. I struggle to identify him in the darkness, but when I recognize who he is, I recoil, my back butting the relative safety of the transom.

It's the security guard. Same shirt and tie, same expression he had when he was watching me die in the ER. He's looking at me like I'm both his possession and his burden. He's taking me away, to where I can't bear to know. Even though he can see I'm terrified, he looks incurably bored.

"Who are you?" I ask. "Where are we?"

My words don't matter to him. His rowing matters to him, and even that's passive, the river's current doing most of the work. He dips his oars just enough to keep the boat on course. If you told me his muscular arms got that way from rowing people down this river for an eternity, I'd believe it. He's a brawny veteran of this task, and my questions are nothing he hasn't heard a million times. He ignores me because my questions are of no consequence.

I can't help myself; I ask another question. "Where are we going?"

But he has no intention of answering. He won't tell me or can't, and he sighs away this nuisance.

But nature provides some semblance of an answer. There's a gradual acceleration of the current as the river widens and the forest thins. The flow urges us toward an orange horizon, and I squint into its brightness. The security guard plunges his oars to keep us straight, the rickety boat bobbing through rougher waters. Up ahead is a lake saturated in the orange light. The glow obscures the lake's size, but it appears enormous. We're going there, wherever *there* is.

The security guard rows us forward. He even picks up the pace despite the swift current, and the shore passes by like we're in a motorboat. The light increases in intensity with every stroke, and I shield my face with my hand, my eyes burning as if I'm peering into a bonfire.

Here it comes, the point where the river pours into the open water and the belly of orange light. The river's current and the rowing propel us through. We jostle when the two masses of water collide, spray hitting my face, then we settle into the lake's powerful grip.

The river's current gone, the security guard digs in deeper. He rows with such passion that it jerks me back with each stroke. Out farther the lake becomes placid enough that the rowboat glides across with relative ease, pushing ripples out, oars creaking in their locks, paddles slicing into the black water. The security guard is astutely efficient at rowing, though he grunts with every stroke, and sweat begins to weep from his brow and pits.

My thoughts veer toward the operating room, my last memory before this place. I'm sickened at the horror of that predicament. I'm equally repulsed knowing that being here means something profound has happened. I notice that my neck no longer hurts—the anaconda of pain is gone. At least that's something like relief, but it's hardly a consolation. Where's the hospital? Where the hell am I?

The intensity of the orange sky is baffling. There should be some impression of the sun, but I can't pinpoint where it is. The brightness would suggest it's hovering only feet above us, yet I don't feel its warmth. I feel nothing. My body is here, but I don't have a connection with it; everything is numb. Am I on drugs? Did the doctors finally give me pain meds?

"What is all this?" I ask. The security guard is a rock of silence, and he won't budge on that. His job isn't about talking to me, it's about rowing the boat. I really am aware of that, but I have to speak for my own sake.

Still, I know the answer to my question. I can sense it. My existence is very different now. I feel almost nothing, it's as if I'm existing in my body but not how I once did.

"Am I dead?" I ask. I'm asking myself the question, since the security guard is only going to ignore me. I'm nonetheless bothered by his apathy. It's just poor manners to ignore a person, isn't it?

"Are you always so chatty?" I say, but I know the

answer to this, too. Yes, he rarely speaks, if at all. His job isn't to speak.

I'm apprehensive about how strange this all feels. I look at my hands, and they appear normal enough, but it's like they're not really mine anymore. I'm wearing the clothes I wore into the ER, but I may as well be naked, because I don't feel the fibers against my skin. I have no thirst or hunger, no fatigue or pain. Nothing. I'm dead. Oh God, I'm dead!

I notice the bulges in my pockets. I still have the things I brought into the ER. I reach in one pocket and remove my wallet. I stare at it like it's a relic, rubbing the brown leather with my thumb. Inside it are credit cards, money, and photos of my family. There's evidence of life and responsibility in there, what once was, but I don't want to think about that now. I stuff the wallet back into my pocket and run my fingers over the bulge in my other pocket. It's my phone.

Hey, wait a minute! Why didn't I think of this sooner? I take out my phone, turn it on, and watch the screen illuminate. I call my wife's cell phone, hold the phone to my ear, and look at the security guard, who still rows like a machine. I'm hopeful when I hear the call start to go through. Then there's a click and an eerie buzz, and the line goes dead. The security guard shakes his head, he knows it won't work. Of course a call won't go through from here. I'm dead, and so is my phone. It's still disappointing. I slam the phone onto my leg. I want to heave the phone into the lake, but I resist and return it to my pocket.

The rowing becomes hypnotic with the rhythmic jerks followed by long glides across the water. The security guard has hit his groove, he could do this forever. I'm certain we consume miles and hours across this never-ending lake, but I have no way to gauge our progress in the midst of the orange light.

Eventually I see shoreline ahead. The security guard is guiding the boat there, and I wonder what awaits us onshore. I begin to feel uneasy about that, because this is an entirely new game I've been forced to play, and I don't know the rules.

"What's over there?" I say, even though I know it's pointless to ask. But the security guard surprises me by nodding over his shoulder. Even though Captain Obvious is indicating to me what I already know—that we're going ashore—at least it's a start.

"I'd really prefer to just go home," I say. He ignores me again.

As we get closer to shore, I see the long stretch of rocks and sand, and beyond it a tree line of dense forest. The security guard keeps his rowing pace until he sees we're almost to shore. He gives one last tug on the oars and allows the boat to glide the rest of the way. This is followed by the sound of the bow scraping the rocky shore and a gentle lurch as we come to a stop. He looks at me, as if I'm expected to know what to do.

"Get out," he says. I'm frightened by the authority his voice commands.

"Okay, but you haven't told me what we're doing here."

"Get out," he repeats, and I stand before I really anger him. The man could take one of his oars and pummel me to a paste with it. No one would stop him out here, and somehow I think he'd like to do that very much.

The boat rocks as I stumble past the security guard toward the bow. I leap from the bow onto the shoreline and turn to watch what my strange companion does. He stands and removes an oar from the lock—for a moment I think he really intends to beat me with it—and I step back as he stabs the oar into the sand and shoves the boat away from shore. He sits, reattaches the oar, and begins to row away.

He's leaving me here?

"Wait, what are you doing? Where are you going?"

I'm getting tired of this guy ignoring me. I want to start ranting about how indecent all of this is. He has to be the worst security guard ever. But then I consider that. He was a security guard back in the ER, but here he's someone else. He's an Angel of Death, a grim reaper without the hooded cloak. His job isn't to make me comfortable, his job is to bring me here. Even though I'm still afraid of him, I lose my temper somewhere in my fear.

"Come on! Say something! What am I supposed to do here? You just bring me here and dump me off, not telling me anything? You're a . . ."

I stop short of a potentially dangerous insult, not because I've come to my senses, but because the man has stood up in the boat again. He glares at me as if to consider returning to shore to pound me into the sand.

"I can't help you," he says instead. "But there are some here who'll try. Find them. There are others who will harm you. Stay away from them, far away if you can. And stay away from the little lights."

I don't understand what he's telling me, and since I've irked him enough, I shut up as he returns to his seat and begins to row away.

"Thanks for the ride," I say. Then under my breath, softly so only I can hear: "Thanks for nothing."

REGRETS

Well this is just perfect. I stand in befuddlement for what must be ten minutes watching the boat disappear into the orange light. As much as I hope the security guard will return for me, I know he won't. There's no point in just staring at the lake, so I move.

All I can think to do is walk along the shoreline. This provides a purpose and direction, and I crave both right now. The forest along the shore is entirely uninviting with its giant trees concealing boundless danger. No need to go anywhere near there, thanks.

I remember what the security guard said, about how there are people here who will try to help me. So who are they and where can I find them? With my luck, I'll come across the bad ones first. I try not to think of the others who will harm me, but that's an ominous prospect to ignore. Who would want to harm me? What did I do to them? I don't even know them! Anyway, those types would certainly hang out in creepy forests.

The security guard also told me to stay away from the little lights. Which lights? If he meant the orange light in the sky, I'm not doing a good job of avoiding it. How can I? It's everywhere. I don't think that's what he meant, but I don't know what other lights there could be, much less why I should stay away. He should have been clearer about what he meant. He's much better at rowing than communicating.

I stare at the ground while I walk the shoreline among oval pebbles, coarse lake sand, and sun-baked driftwood. I like rocks, and I have a small collection at home, sort of a beach-combing hobby I share with my daughters. I can't resist picking some up to examine them, tossing them down once I realize collecting seems irrelevant now. Whenever I see a perfectly flat rock, I pick it up and zing it across the smooth lake water so it skips.

Soon I have enough of walking and rock-picking. The shoreline could go on for thousands of miles, for all I know. Where am I even going? This seems like a complete waste of time, but just what is time anymore?

That gives me an idea. I pull my phone out of my pocket and look at the time. It says 00:00. The date, which usually appears on the calendar app icon, is blank. Time has stopped, or else I'm cut off from it. Somehow that feels all the more isolating: I'm so far removed from life that time isn't in the equation. That figures. I resist the desire to chuck my phone into the water again, and put it back in my pocket and keep walking.

I feel like I should be hungry or thirsty, but I'm neither. Not even close. I have many vices, but by far my worst is alcohol. It's caused so much trouble for me over the years. Yet here, in this place, I have no cravings, no physiological needs at all. Still, I stop to take a drink from the lake, maybe out of curiosity. I cup my hands and dip them in, lifting up water and pouring it down my throat. I taste nothing. It's neither warm nor cold, and it's not salty nor fresh, and it doesn't do anything for me. That makes sense, since I'm dead.

So there it is. I've admitted once again that I'm dead, and it doesn't feel far fetched. What else can explain this? I have no other theories. Many of the living would be shocked to see an afterlife like this. People expect pearly gates or fire and brimstone, an order to things: you go where you belong and either live in paradise or suffer in the underworld. Maybe those places are yet to come for me, but for now it's neither. This is a forsaken land with no hint of what's supposed to happen next. There's no system here. I've just been dumped off by an antisocial security guard and left to my own devices. Right now, my own devices are idle.

I walk for what must be hours more before I stop to rest and think. I take a seat on a stone that looks like a flattened armchair and stare out at the lake. I don't know for how long I gaze, hoping I'll see something—a boat, a plane, some reminder of the world I once knew. But there's nothing out there.

"Just what is the point of all this?" I ask myself. Maybe there is no point. Maybe death has no objective.

I try to pass the time by thinking about *Robinson Crusoe*. I love reading, always have. *Crusoe* is among my favorites, a castaway learning to survive on his wits, growing crops, raising wild goats with his African buddy, Friday. But now that I'm the castaway, the story sounds much less pleasant. I have no companion except for this uncomfortable rock I'm sitting on, and I'm nowhere near as resourceful as Crusoe. I decide that I'd make an awful castaway. At least there are no cannibals here—yet. I try to think of something else.

I retrieve my wallet from my pocket and look inside. I flip open the plastic picture sleeve to a spread of two photos. Grinning at me from the picture on the left are my twin six-year-old daughters, Kaitlyn and Lacy. They're midflight on swings from their wooden swing set that took me an entire weekend to assemble. The girls are tiny facsimiles of their mommy: flowing dark hair, thin eyebrows topping amber eyes, grins that puff out their cheeks. If I look hard enough, I can see bits of myself in them: pointy chins, lanky frames, sharp noses. In a world in which I created very little, those two represent my finest work. On the short list of people I didn't want to leave behind, those two are square on top.

In the opposite picture is my wife, Angie. It's an outdoor shot from our wedding day, floral arbor in the background. Her white wedding dress contrasts with her dark features, pure bliss in her smile and her shining eyes, smooth skin soaking up the sunshine. Marriage and children haven't aged her; she looks the same today as she did in that picture. She's beautiful, even more so on the inside. She's shy, but intelligent, fun-loving, and compassionate. I think I've been in awe of her since the day I met her.

I married well, but Angie did not. It's complicated.

I am (was?) Zak Bixby, professor of American literature. Well, I was a professor until I quit my job a year ago. I had my reasons for leaving, none of them all that good in retrospect, but they seemed legitimate at the time. When in the middle of what you deem a life crisis, you react without working out the fine details.

The simple fact is, I wasn't enjoying my work. For that matter, I wasn't enjoying much of anything. My life, it seemed, was a dusty trail of mistakes and losses, going all the way back to when my father died when I was eight. Sure, as an adult I had my family, a job, and a house, and I was proud of all three, but somehow it wasn't enough. It's human nature to want more, to never be satisfied, but I took that a bit far. My distaste for everything seemed crammed into a locked compartment in my head, its door bursting to let it all out.

Hiding in the background was alcohol. Or possibly it was the culprit from the beginning. Drinking was a reprieve, even a crutch, if I'm honest. Usually I showed up to my classes a little tipsy. It was my way to liven up my job, and also my imperfect strategy to get out of my shell for my students. I had done it for years, hiding it well, never intending for it to go beyond minimal self-medication.

But the deeper I dove into my depression, the more reckless the drinking became. Students and colleagues took notice. It swung toward a climax when the department chair confronted me over complaints from students of my drunkenness in class. I didn't deny it, and instead tried to downplay it. He wouldn't let it go so easily. After a lecture about professionalism, he put me on paid leave for a couple of weeks to think about it. In retrospect, that was fair, even compassionate compared to being fired. But at the time, buried in the humiliation of being caught was rampant anger at yet another societal slight against me.

While on leave one night, deep within the hold of alcohol, I hatched a plan without thinking it through. I drafted a letter listing everything I had sacrificed for the college, declaring how all of it had been thwarted by betrayal at the first sign of trouble. I documented everything wrong with the college, the president, the department chair, the students, the faculty, the staff, and even the facilities. It evolved into a toxic letter of resignation, and I held nothing back. Finishing it over my last drink of the night, just before passing out, I emailed the letter to all faculty and staff at the college.

The next morning, I barely remembered writing and sending the letter. Had it all been an alcohol-induced nightmare? A quick login to my email revealed the letter sitting in the sent box addressed to everyone, and the reality of my mistake plunged me into a panic. I began weighing my options. I could say I was hacked by a vengeful student, but would the college investigate and find I was lying? Maybe I could just say it was all a big mistake and ask for forgiveness? Yes, that would be honest. I could apologize and affirm that I didn't really want to resign, even go right to the president if that would help.

Yet it felt like I had gone too far to talk my way out of it. I had said too much and been too detailed to just sweep it all away. Beyond that, there was actually something that felt good about what my drunken self had done, like a huge burden had been lifted. That's why, when the department chair called later that morning to figure out what in the world I was trying to do, I stood by my letter. We agreed that it was for the best for me to move on. I burned a really fine bridge that day.

Angie understood, at least at first. She trusted that I had it in me to find another job, but she didn't know I didn't want another job. I didn't know that, either, until I allowed the months to pass without even looking for a replacement. By the time I did, I realized that getting a new job would be difficult with the disaster I had left behind at the college. Who would recommend me now that I had berated almost everyone at the college? It wouldn't have been terrible if my job wasn't our only income, but with two young kids, we had committed to my wife staying home.

So what does an unemployed, unmotivated college professor do with all of that downtime? He drinks a lot, at least this one did. Boozing can become a full-time job, if you let it, but it's hardly a stable profession. I guess this was my way of searching for answers, ruminating about my next move, denying that I didn't want a next move. We had savings for a while, time on our side, effective enablers of misery.

When did Angie start to give up on me? I know the precise moment. The money eventually ran thin, and so did my ways of coping. She suggested counseling. I was open to that, but also taken aback by the suggestion. Was I not in control of the situation? Maybe not. So I went to counseling.

I hated it. Oh, it was fine for a few sessions, talking about my problems to someone genuinely interested in them. But it also opened doors I would have rather kept closed. My fears, my anxieties, my indifferences, my addictions, my troubled childhood. It showed me that my problems were more complex than I had feared, close to insurmountable. Shouldn't therapy fix problems, not magnify them? Maybe it helps some people, but not me. During one session I had just had enough, and like my job, I walked out.

When I came home from that, Angie didn't hide her disappointment. She was seeing an alarming trend in me, exiting when things got hot, leaving her to suffer for it. We had an argument that night, the worst one we'd ever had. With that, I had lost her, I'm sure of it. It was a month later that she asked me to leave. She told me it wasn't a divorce, just a temporary separation, but I knew divorce was on its heels. She asked me to go to a hotel, to my mother's house, even to a cardboard box—anywhere but with her and the kids.

I went to stay with a friend of mine, a college buddy who traveled all the time and didn't mind me hanging around temporarily. It wasn't the worst living arrangement ever, but it felt all wrong, rash, final. How could I have let it happen?

Then I got sick. Thyroid cancer. That was quite a moldy cherry on top of a yuck sundae. God just figured he may as well pile it all on me at once. No job, no family, no home, no money, no health. I couldn't have made up a more grisly closing chapter myself.

So there it is, the wake of my destructive path, leaving nothing behind but wreckage and regret. I've lost everything. And now, even my life.

This is the first time I realize that I'm not going to see any of my family again. I don't know where I am, but it's clear that I'm here to stay, and that thought almost knocks my breath away. I lie back on the rock, still clutching my wallet, closing my eyes to the orange light. I guess emotions are still possible, because I feel my throat tighten thinking about my family. I wasn't ready to leave them, and I wonder if they already know that I'm gone. Kaitlyn will be hit especially hard. The separation had hurt her most. She's shier and needier than her sister, and we had a special bond because of that.

I curl up on the rock, thinking the words over and over again: *I'm sorry*. All of this was my fault, I should have fought harder to live. I should have fixed things before they got out of hand.

Nowhere to go, I lie there for hours. I just want to sleep, because at least that will take me away from here for a while. But I'm unable to sleep, my body no longer needs to. Instead I just force my eyes shut and daydream of *Robinson Crusoe.*

4

OTHERS WHO WILL HARM YOU

I can't really call it waking up, since I was never asleep, but I open my eyes and it resembles emerging from a nap. I rub my eyes to wet them in defense of the orange light, sit up from my resting place on the rock, and look out at the lake. There's still nothing out there but water.

So this is how it's going to be. I'm forced to inhabit a strange place with no idea why I'm here or what I'm supposed to do. I begin to fear the crush of boredom.

I leave my spot at the rock and begin to walk again. I suppose I'll walk around the entire lake at this rate. I have the time to do it, and it seems like a worthy goal in my quest to find someone else, even though it may take days.

I stop and look ahead to see the sandy beach that marks my path. It really is quite picturesque, but this is all lost on me. I'd rather see someone friendly walking toward me on the sand, someone who will help me, someone who will have answers. But all I see is the vacant shore looking like it has never been explored by human beings. I sigh as if to exhale it all away, or to challenge something to happen, for someone to appear.

Nothing. Still, I wait and watch the shoreline, imagining that I can coerce movement. The effect is I see something way up ahead, a kind of wishful thinking that has transcended into subtle motion. I've yearned to see someone, so something has materialized in my mind. Real or not, I squint down the beach toward it. More movement. I can't disregard that there's something there, and I can't verify it either. I hear myself react: "Hmm."

Something moves again. There really is something there! It's alive, and it's walking across the sand toward me. I study its form. It has to be human because it's walking upright and has arms and legs.

"Hey!" I yell. I wave toward the person, who stops. I've gotten the person's attention. The relief of connecting with someone gives me hope. But wait. Is what I'm feeling something other than excitement? There's an instinctive warning cry underneath my enthusiasm.

There are others who will harm you.

I can hear the security guard's words as if he's standing right next to me, and the realization that I may have just made a critical error overcomes me.

Now wait a minute! I'm always so negative. My first reaction was that this is a friendly person, so shouldn't I trust that? After all, it's impossible to determine friend or foe from such a distance. I need to give circumstances the benefit of the doubt for a change.

I wait. The person starts moving this way again. I might be mistaken, but the person seems to be approaching faster now, possibly running. This could mean the person is eager to see me. Maybe the person is just as desperate for company as me.

Whoever this person is, he's huge. I'll call him a *he* for now, he looks male. He's definitely running toward me because I can see his arms swinging and the sand kicking up from his strides. The speed of his advance begins to worry me, but I have to see who this is. What other choice do I have?

What comes into view is unimaginable. Am I really seeing what I think I'm seeing? For a second I think my desperation is misleading my senses, because creatures like this only live in sick nightmares. But it's here, and coming for me—poor, helpless, college professor me.

Running toward me is a huge man, more like a beast, gray skin, gigantic ram horns protruding from both sides of his bald head, fat belly flopping, bulging arms pumping, one arm holding a club as big as me. He stomps up to within thirty yards of me and stops, lowers his head, and stares at me with green eyes, a mouth full of teeth like shards of glass, filthy goatee flowing below it. He roars at me like a squealing boar.

"Oh," I say to myself. I feel my legs bend like anticipating impact from a steamroller. "Oh no."

The beast begins to glow green. From his body comes an electrical hum, like the buzz of a downed power line, interrupted at intervals by deafening thump-thumps like an amplified heartbeat. It's as if the monster is his own electrical thunderstorm powered from within.

"No!" I shout, shoving my arm palm out toward him. Somehow I think this thing can be dealt with like a stray dog. It's all I can think to do. "Stay!"

He takes a couple more steps toward me, crouching, unafraid of me and incurably interested. He roars again, even louder this time. Then he slams his club onto the shoreline, sending rocks and sand flying.

I take a step back and trip on driftwood. I fall into the sand and begin a backward crab walk of retreat. This creature is no dog, and he's definitely not here to help me. I'm almost too afraid to look at him, but I have to assess the danger, like staring down an approaching tsunami. He's watching me with the intensity of a predator. Worse, he looks incensed by my very presence. I'm something he wants to extinguish with appalling brutality. That expression is also one of ecstasy. I'm easy prey to feed his sadistic soul, and he'll enjoy each moment.

I have to get out of here, but where can I go? My first thought is to run into the water to my left and swim. But what if he can swim, too? Even if he can't swim, how far can I go? I'm a good swimmer, but I can't swim to the other side of the lake, I can't even see across it. He could just wait on shore for me to tire, then get me when I have nothing left. No, I need another plan. I could turn and run back down the shore, but judging by how quickly this thing has reached me, he would be upon me in seconds if I retreated. That's even a worse idea than the lake. That leaves one more option: the dreary forest to my right. I could stumble through the thickness of trees better than this beast could. But can I beat him to it?

I'll risk it. Mind made up, I sprint for the forest. The beast storms after me with a howl. His speed is phenomenal, instantly breeding doubt that I'll make it. I decide not to look at him and just focus on the trees to find where I'll penetrate the tree line. But I hear him huffing and growling behind me, and I can't help but look back at him gaining. He's a furor of claws and teeth and his club, all of them out for blood. He'll club me down and rip me apart, so at least it will be fast. Or will he toy with me first, make it long and painful? Yes, I think that's more his style. I run faster.

It's going to be close. I locate a small opening beneath the gnarly branches and head toward it, my trajectory angling away from the beast and buying me another second. I dive in, branches ripping and scratching my skin as I fall into a bed of leaves.

The beast hits the tree line at nearly the same moment. His surface area being much greater than mine, the branches stonewall him as he screeches in frustration. Conversely, I roll and crawl and fight through the shrubs and branches, pull myself to my feet, and sprint deep into the woods.

But the beast refuses to be thwarted. Behind me is so much wailing and snapping that it sounds like an elephant has plowed his way into the woods, the strange humming from the beast making my ears hurt. I have no time and no desire to look back now. The branches whip my arms and face. A twig pokes me in the eye, and I instinctively close it. Although I have trouble seeing, the violence from behind urges me to go faster.

Despite my injuries, my plan is working. Being smaller than the creature, I'm putting distance between us. I'm dodging trees and bushes like a natural, the terror transforming me into a decathlete. The terrain angles upward, slowing me, but I know this, too, will slow my pursuer, so I lean into the slope and summon the energy to keep surging onward and upward.

At the top of the slope the forest thins, and I reach the edge of a thicket. Ahead of me is an open stretch of beige grassland. A hundred yards across, the woods begin again, but to me, this represents a dead end. I'll be a sitting duck out there away from the protection of the trees.

The creature is steaming up the hill behind me, the buzzing and thump-thumps announcing his arrival. I see trees snap and collapse from his surging, his baleful approach forcing my hand. Good lord he's strong! I'm not going to escape. But I have to try, and my only option now is forward, out into the thicket toward the tree line on the other side.

I run out into the light of the open ground. On a kinder day, it would be an ideal place to spread a blanket for a picnic. But this chase is no picnic, this is life and death. But wait a minute. If I'm already dead, why am I worried? What's going to happen, am I going to die again? That makes no sense. I'm not a cat, I don't have nine lives.

I hear the beast break out of the woods into the thicket behind me. Although I know I shouldn't, I look back. He's raging into the open, a lion and I'm his gazelle in the bush. Dread flushes through me when I realize I'll be overcome well before I make it to the other side. I'm screwed.

Then I trip. It was foolish to look back at him. I've taken my eye off my path and something has tripped me, a root or a rock. I fall hard into the grass, my face slamming into weeds and soil. The fall disorients me, but I'm unhurt, yet that's about to change. I sit up and twist toward the beast and I'm surprised to see that he's stopped. He's toying with me. He's enjoying the fact that I've fallen because it signals to him that his chase is over and the fun part is about to begin.

I stand, knees bent, in a daze from such strange danger. All I can cling to is maybe I can't die again, which would mean there really is no danger. But when I see the beast hurtle toward me again, one last rush to finish the job, I don't believe that. I think I can be harmed again, even killed, and then what? What horrible place will I end up the second time I die? I don't want to find out, and I don't want this hideous thing to trample and claw me to death, so I do one more thing to evade him, my last card to play.

I'm a matador and the beast is a maniacal bull, the thicket is my arena. The trees surrounding the thicket are my cheering patrons, wondering if I'll get the bull or if he'll get me. I have no sword, no red cape, but I make the best of things, waiting until the monster is so close that he's committed to his target. At the last moment, I dive to my right, and the beast charges past, clipping only my legs, but that sends me twirling like the nipping of a bowling pin.

The beast is surprised, momentum carrying him onward while he howls from my deception. I've delayed the inevitable, bought myself a few more seconds, but I land hard and roll in the grass. I can feel that I'm badly injured.

Then all logic quits. Darkness unfolds everywhere, like God has a dimmer switch and he's turning down the light. Am I losing consciousness? My body is swimming in trauma, but I feel aware of my surroundings. I can see the thicket and bordering woods go dark, darker, black. But I still hear the beast stumbling and roaring, and I can hear the pounding hum coming from his body.

I blink my eyes three times, four, five. Each time it's the same. I can't see a thing. I don't know how I know this, but I sense that I don't see anything because nothing is there. The darkness has swallowed me whole.

5

DEENA

Imagine a glorious sunrise, but instead of the sun gradually peeling open the sky, the transformation from dark to light is instantaneous. Darkness that had consumed the thicket is replaced with soothing light of peach and crimson.

As I squint into the light, I'm dumbfounded. I'm no longer in the thicket, I'm somewhere else altogether: on a cliff ledge atop a jagged mountain. The darkness has lifted me up and the light has transported me elsewhere, all in seconds.

"Wait, what?" I say. I wish I had some idea about what's going on.

But I have no time to ponder it, there are more pressing issues. I'm lying on my side, one leg mangled and useless from being smashed by the monster. The ledge I'm on is as wide as a small street with a gradual slope to the edge. Between me and the edge is the beast, who has been carried here with me. He has righted himself from his stumble, yet he looks as mystified as I am. But as he recovers and looks at me, his confusion sizzles into animal outrage. His shriek tells me I'm going to suffer horribly for my little trick. I hope somewhere inside the creature there's mercy, but I doubt he even knows the concept.

He steps toward me onto what should be firm ground, but his leg buckles and sinks. Something cracks underneath him, and he looks to the ground and grunts. A grinding pop follows, and he begins to wobble as the ground he stands upon collapses. He's a skyscraper mid-demolition, his legs crumbling first, his hips swaying from the lost footing, his arms flailing, club falling from his clawed grasp, the anger in his eyes suppressed by choking fear.

A hole opens beneath him, sucking him through. I hear him screech as he plummets. Although I can't see from my vantage how far he falls, I know it must be a long way because I hear his bellows go down, down, down until the only sound is the mountain wind. Dust swirls up from the enormous hole that swallowed him. His weight was just too much for the ledge.

I let out a breath of relief, or maybe it's an appalled sigh that I've watched the beast fall to his death. I watch the hole as if expecting to see something climb back up, but I know nothing will. The creature is gone, and I've survived by dumb luck. But now what will I do?

I inspect my leg and I'm sickened by the sight. My right shinbone is protruding from my pants, glossy blood flowing out like from a drizzling spigot. I reach for the wound, but don't want to touch it, so I just let my shaking hand hover over it, which is no help at all. I clench my teeth and hiss at the wound like the injured animal I've become.

I'm surprised by something though. A broken leg should be excruciating, but it's not. Maybe I'm in shock, and my body has closed off the pain for the moment. Aside from a dull ache, I feel nothing, yet the gruesome sight has pushed me into a clammy state of nausea.

I lie back, close my eyes, and try to breathe past the queasiness and panic. Even I know that you can't survive trauma without some semblance of calm. I'm not very effective at this though. All I can think about is that bone sticking out, and I'm on a mountaintop in the land of the bizarre. No amount of breathing can quell my level of distress.

I decide I need to act instead of stewing. I have to put my nervous energy to use. I want to look around, to figure out where I am. I don't know how I got here, but maybe there will be people nearby to help. But before I do, the frustration and terror built up since being sent to this strange world spill over. I take it all out on the security guard.

I sit up. "Hey!" I yell. "Where are the people who will help me? You said there would be those who'd help me! Liar! You just drag me here and dump me? You big dumbass oaf!"

I don't know what I'm trying to prove by taunting the

security guard, it's not like he's around to hear me. But my complaining makes me feel better. Besides, I'm alone out here, so what does it matter if I vent a little? I call him all sorts of colorful names until I can't think of any more. Then I'm silent, as if waiting for repercussions for my words that won't come. It feels like no one is within a million miles of me.

But the effect of my rant is my head feels a tad clearer. I decide to crawl, carefully dragging my dead leg behind me. I inch to the edge of the hole where the beast fell and where I can see better. I'm on the ledge of the most massive and desolate mountain I've ever seen, crest rising behind me. The peak is gray and rough, like something you'd expect to see on Mars with sharp and twisting points and accents of brown. The view beyond the ledge shows me that nothing alive can be seen in any direction, just the rocky deadness of mountains, an endless supply of them peaking through the clouds.

I peer down the hole where the beast fell and confirm that the thing dropped from a horrific height. The bottom is so far below me that I can't make out any details. He's a goner for sure, and I almost feel pity. Then I remember how ungodly evil the creature was, and I accept his fate without another thought.

I roll away from the hole and lie on my back, looking up at the sky, taking deep breaths because I can't stand heights. Just being this close to the edge gives me the creeps, as if I'll be flung over by the wind, so I retreat a few feet back.

This is it. I'm going to lie here on top of this mountain and bleed to death. I suppose I could decide to toss myself over the ledge and end it that way instead, but the idea terrifies me. I've often thought, given the choice between burning in a high-rise fire or jumping to my death, let me burn, my fear of heights is that great. So there's no way I'm going to toss myself over. If I bleed to death, I'll just pass out and go. There are far worse ways to die.

But first I have to try to rescue myself. How? I'm going to yell and scream again, that's how. It's all I can think to do.

"What am I supposed to do now!" I yell. "Climb down this God-forsaken mountain with a broken leg? There's nothing even down there! Is anyone listening to me? Is anyone out here? Hello? Help! Help me!"

Of course no one is listening. Who would possibly be listening?

Here comes the pain in my leg, and I brace myself for it. There's a throbbing sting at first, then the intensity increases. I wince, pull myself up so I'm sitting with both legs extended out and try to think away the pain. To my amazement, this helps. The pain decreases, but I don't dare move, and instead lie on my back again, arm over my eyes to block out the sunlight. There's nothing else to do but be still and think of a plan better than screaming.

No plan comes, so I just lie in the warmth of the sunlight that even my deadened senses can feel. This takes my mind off my leg, and I soak in the light like it's a mental anesthetic. If I'm to die, at least I can enjoy warmth one last time while my soul is swept away.

Then a new sensation seeps into my consciousness. I can't pinpoint the feeling at first, but it's there. The body is amazing how it can detect subtle changes your usual senses won't. In time I decode the unmistakable sensation that someone else has joined me on the ledge.

I pull my arm away from my eyes and look into the blinding light. When my vision adjusts, I see someone kneeling over me. I flinch and roll away to protect myself, my leg stinging from the commotion.

"Easy!" says a voice, firm and feminine. "I won't hurt you."

The voice has an unnatural echo, as if she's speaking in a vast auditorium. My reflexes continue on the defensive, but steadily I'm seized by a calming energy coming from the stranger. Sinking deeply into the tranquility, I focus on the most peculiar woman I've ever seen.

Her face and hair are the palest white, the color of snow, and her eyes are sparkling light blue, like blue topaz ovals on a white velvet pillow. Her body below her neck pulsates with swirls of blue, light green, white, and gray iridescence, making her human form look like she's wearing a skin-tight suit of light. Her hair, too, seems to color-shift before my eyes, going from white to red to yellow before it settles back to white.

"I'm listening to you Zak," she says.

"Huh?" I ask. Somehow she knows my name.

"You asked if anyone is listening to you. Well, I am."

"Do I know you?"

"In a way," she says.

"What are you?"

"You can call me Deena."

"Okay, but *what* are you?"

"That doesn't matter," she says. "I'm here for you now, and that's all you need to know."

"Oh," I say. I think she senses I'm not satisfied with her response.

"I know all of this seems disorienting Zak. Don't let it get to you, all right? There will be a lot you won't understand, I'm afraid."

I wince when the pain in my leg returns. I venture a look at the horrible wound and see that I'm sitting in a pool of blood.

"I've hurt myself. I need a doctor."

"You won't find one here," Deena says. "And anyway, a doctor would be of no use to you. Not here."

"Why do you say that?"

"Things work differently here. I want you to lie back now. I'll fix your leg for you."

She moves toward me and pushes on my chest gently as I lie back. But when she reaches toward my leg, I begin to fret.

"What are you gonna do?"

"You have to trust me," she says. "It won't hurt."

Why should I trust a bizarre-looking woman in the middle of nowhere who wants to fix my broken leg? Well, because, at the moment I have no better options. Besides, she speaks so gently to me and somehow she knows my name—those have to count for something.

"All right," I say. "Just help me if you can."

She touches my broken leg. The iridescence in her arm sends white light into my leg, so bright that I can't look at it. I look away as I feel a soothing warmth in my shin. Her body lights up pink and red and orange, then blue, then it returns to what it was originally.

"There," she says. "Can you stand?"

"Stand?" I say. Is she nuts? "No, I tried earlier. It's broken."

"Then try again."

I'm confused, especially because she's smiling at me, showing neat white teeth. Then I look at my leg, and the bone that was protruding can no longer be seen. The blood has stopped seeping. I'm astonished.

I pull myself up to a delicate stand, expecting at any moment that my leg will buckle and I'll tumble. But my broken leg is completely healed, and I'm standing on it as if nothing is wrong. I even venture to stand only on the bad leg, and I do it without any trouble.

"How did you do that?"

"It doesn't matter Zak. Do you feel better?"

I nod.

"Listen to me then."

I don't think there's anything I'd rather hear than her gentle voice, her words so soothing and her face so beautiful. Listening to her is no chore, but I nod again anyway.

"You have an important task ahead of you."

"I do?" I ask.

"Yes. You're not supposed to be here. But you're not supposed to be where you came from either, not at the moment."

"See, that's just the thing," I say. "No one has even told me where I am. So if I don't belong here, then I'd like to go back home."

"It's not so simple as that," she says. "As I said, you're not supposed to be where you were. You're not supposed to be home."

Being told that I'm no longer supposed to be in my life disturbs me.

"Am I dead? Is that what this is all about?"

"Yes Zak," she says. "I'm sorry. But you deduced as much earlier. You just need to accept it for what it is."

"My family," I say. "I'll never seen them again?"

"Nothing is forever. You will see them again, in time. Try not to think of anything as permanent."

"I miss them," I say. "I wasn't ready to leave them. And they weren't ready for me to go."

"Few people are ever ready Zak."

I think about my wife and kids and wonder where they are now, what they're doing, how they're feeling.

"I know it's difficult, but you need to focus on other things now. Your current existence is a special one. You're lost."

"You got that right," I say. "That's the most logical assessment I've heard in this place. What I need is a map or instructions. I'm pretty good with instructions."

Deena frowns. "To be honest, there are no such things for this place."

"Then you'll help me? You can take me where I need to go?"

"No Zak, I'm sorry, I'm not able to do that."

I shrug. Of course she can't help me. Why would I think anyone could help me?

"You have it within yourself to figure out how."

I'm getting tired of not understanding.

"And how does that work?"

Deena smiles. "I'm going to leave you now."

"Leave? Wait, you have to get me out of here. I'm on a mountaintop, how do I get down? And I have lots more questions for you. Where are you going?"

"There will be others who will help you," she says.

"Yeah, so I've heard."

I turn away from her to look out at the mountains all around me, and the thought of climbing down myself gives me the willies.

"I sure hope they have a helicopter because . . ."

I turn back to look at Deena, but she's gone. "Hey! Where did you go?"

There's nowhere for a person to hide up here. She just vanished, and I begin to wonder if I've made up the whole thing. But my leg, still good as new, reminds me that she was here.

But now I'm alone again.

6

KAITLYN

Somehow I have to get off this mountain without falling thousands of feet to my death. Despite Deena's vanishing act, at least she fixed my leg. But there was a more profound benefit from her visit. I could write a thesis trying to decipher what she told me, but underneath it all is that my existence here has some sort of purpose. I'm at least morbidly curious to discover what that is.

I formulate a plan to follow the ledge around the crest and look for a passage down. With the peak watching my progress from above, I walk the ledge, measuring its stability with each step. I have no interest in plunging through like the beast did, but it feels stable under my weight.

My plan seems like a good one until the ledge narrows. This isn't a problem at first, but soon the ledge tightens to a two-foot pass. I consider turning back, but I'm feeling brave enough to hug the base of the crest and shimmy along. This is not to say I'm comfortable being so close to the edge. Each time a gust blows, I stiffen and embrace the base tighter and wait for the wind to wane, then inch forward. The narrow pass is temporary though, and soon enough the ledge widens again. I feel a sense of accomplishment once I realize I've made it to the other side of the peak.

I go to the cliff edge and search for a way down. It's nauseating to stand at the edge, but the cliff is less vertical on this side. I walk along the edge, studying each route down but dismissing them all as though I have the luxury of being choosy.

I reach a point where part of the ledge has dislodged and crumbled down the mountainside. Boulders dot the way down like spines on a huge serpent's back. With enough imagination, I envision myself trying to get down this way, but the thought gives me the creeps. I can't see the whole way down. What if I reach a point where I can't go down and I can't get back up?

I need to just do it. I'm climbing down the mountain the only way I know how, like reading a book one page at a time, digesting each word to find the greater meaning. I step, stop, calculate, and step again. My pace is jelly creeping down the crags. If someone with climbing experience could see me, he'd probably stomp me with his crampons for desecrating his sport, but I'm just trying to survive here. I wiggle down the boulders on my rump, close my eyes and try not to hyperventilate between steps, and I'd be crying like an infant if I thought doing so wouldn't make me fall. But I'm actually making it, and that's really all that matters.

But when I reach a flatter slab of granite, the more level terrain makes me overconfident. I'm blind to a collection of loose gravel underfoot, and when I step the gravel rolls under my shoe, throwing me into a baseball slide. Like thousands of tiny wheels, the gravel works in unison to carry me forward, and I'm careening down the slab like a toddler on a playground slide. Ahead I see the slab drops off, and I'm sliding toward the edge to be flung into the abyss. I flail my arms at my sides and try to grab something, anything, to stop my slide. But there's nothing to grab, the slab is too smooth. I roll onto my stomach, slowing the plunge a notch, but it's not enough. I'm going over. Then my foot hits an outcropping just before the edge, jolting me to a near stop, but the gravel still fights to send me down. I catch the same outcropping with both hands and grip it like it's the most precious thing I've ever held. Stopped at last, I find myself half dangling over the mountainside.

I'm not very strong, but panicked energy is on my side. I heave one leg back up to the flat surface, then pull my torso up with my arms and roll onto my back. Safe, I just breathe, longing to be on flat ground where all people should be.

"Sure wish there were stairs," I say to myself.

I gather myself and stand. I hold out my arms and bend my knees like I'm searching for balance on an icy pond, studying the gravel like it's alive and trying to kill me. I'm rattled, but this is just reinforcing that I have to keep going. I go back to my strategy of taking one step at a time, even slower now, not caring if it takes me days to reach safety.

I maneuver down the ledge that almost claimed me, then pick my way through the rocks that follow. Here the boulders begin to thin out, and I allow my pace to quicken. Then I reach an even more hospitable stretch where the terrain makes the transition from cliffs and boulders to smaller rocks. Farther yet and I reach sloping, grassy foothills, the wonderful smell of grass, and relative safety.

I've made it down. God only knows how.

I collapse into the warm grass, relishing the stability of the pastoral hillside. Lying on my back, I look up at the peak that held me hostage, not quite seeing the top through the clouds, the ledge on which I once stood indiscernible. Can I add mountain climbing to my list of experiences? Maybe, but I'd really rather forget it altogether. I never want to see a mountain again.

An icy wind floats across the foothills, rippling the grass in chaotic waves. For a moment there's a melody to the whipping grass, kind of a mournful cry. I listen, as if trying to translate what it's saying, but the sound wanes when the wind changes direction.

I'm up again, driven to find a way out of the foothills. Getting this far is progress, but I want flat ground, and nothing else will do. I take a few steps when I hear the wind's melody again, but it's different this time. The call sounds more human. It really is a voice, and I could swear it's one I've heard thousands of times before. I listen for it again, and it doesn't disappoint:

"Daddy?" it says.

"Kaitlyn!" I yell.

It can't be possible to hear what I hear, but the voice is unmistakable: my daughter. But how? Is she here, in the mountains with me? I stand still and listen. When I hear nothing I begin to think that the wind is fooling me.

"Daddy!" Kaitlyn says again. Her voice reminds me how she used to call me at night from her bed when she was afraid. She always had nightmares. The voice sounds like it's coming from down the hill on the other side of a ridge.

"Where are you honey?" I call.

"Daddy?" she says again. I run toward the sound, possessed by paternal instincts. But when I pass over the ridge where I'm certain Kaitlyn will be waiting, I'm met with more emptiness of the foothills. I look in every direction, spinning around in case I've missed her somehow, but she isn't here.

"Daddy."

Kaitlyn's voice is coming from directly in front of me. When she speaks, a solitary blade of grass glows with blue light. I walk toward it, wanting to understand but I really don't. The light disappears, and I wonder if I ever saw it.

"Kaitlyn, I'm here," I say.

The blade of grass ignites again. "Help, Daddy," Kaitlyn says. It rips at my heart that my daughter's voice is right here and she needs me, but I can't see her. I crouch in the grass and reach toward the delicate sprig. I touch it with my forefinger.

"Snuggle me Daddy," comes her voice again, like Kaitlyn is the sprig itself. The blade illuminates while I'm touching it, and I feel a tingle of energy from it. I think I should pull away, but I can't or I won't. I'm a moth incurably obsessed with the light, running my finger along the sprig, naive to any danger.

Again I consider pulling away, but it's too late, I'm caught. The blue light spills onto my skin, consumes my fingers, hand, and arm. It takes seconds to spread over my shoulder, chest, and abdomen, covering my whole body with an affliction of light. With that my surroundings are smothered as though I've been immersed in murky water.

The next thing I see is the nightlight of Kaitlyn's bedroom. I take in the familiar sights of pink and purple, anchored by armies of stuffed animals and dollies. There she is, my little blade of grass, Kaitlyn huddled in her bed underneath the flowery blanket. Her eyes are closed. She's half asleep, disturbed by a nightmare.

Is this real? It sure looks real. I want it to be real, but I just don't understand.

"I'm here," I whisper to her. I kneel at her bedside.

"Snuggle me Daddy," she repeats, her eyes still closed. I lift up her blanket and crawl into her little bed with her. She wraps her warm arms around me, buries her head into my chest, and I can smell her little girl smell.

"Did you have a nightmare, honey?" I ask.

"Yes," she says. "I don't want to talk about it."

"Okay," I say. Sometimes she wants to talk about them. When her nightmares are really bad, she won't— this must have been a bad one.

For several minutes I lie there, feeling the moment as if I've never enjoyed such fatherly bliss. I don't question why I'm here. It's too much to think about, and I want to just let this happen. The longer I lie, the more tired I get, like I could sink into an exquisite sleep.

I wonder about Lacy, Kaitlyn's twin sleeping in her room next door. Farther down Angie sleeps in our bed. I'm home. I want to wake them all up and tell them I'm here, but I can't. I have no energy to do it. All I can do is lie here. The longer I stay, the more weary I become. I feel like I'm being squeezed away, my daughter's room becoming a blur.

I have a memory of the living room of my house, morning sun coming in streaks across the floor. I'm dancing with my daughters to a song on TV that they love, each girl clutching one of my legs. When I lift a leg, it lifts Kaitlyn like an amusement park ride, up and down. When I lift the other, Lacy is lifted up, and she giggles. I'm alternating lifting my legs, and I'm slowly spinning in a circle to the music, both girls singing along, never wanting it to stop.

Why couldn't I have been like that all the time? Because I let life get in the way. There was always another crisis to fret about, another drink to carry me to sleep without kissing my wife and children goodnight. I realize my priorities were backwards.

"I missed you Daddy," Kaitlyn says.

"I missed you too, baby," I say. I want to kiss her, but I can't move. I have no more energy. "But I'll always be with you, okay? I'm sorry I wasn't always with you."

"I know, Daddy," she says. Then I hear her sleep breathing. She can sleep now that I'm here.

But I'm leaving Kaitlyn's bedroom, even though I don't want to. I have nothing to fight it, so I'm being carried off to the unknown again. Deena was wrong, I'm supposed to be back in my life. I never should have been taken away. But it doesn't matter what I think, so I'm leaving again.

My senses dull to nothing. The room disappears.

7

OTHERS WHO WILL HELP YOU

I think I'm dreaming. There's a half-empty bottle of whiskey on a table in front of me. I reach for it and pour it into a glass. I'm parched and hollow, so I drink what I poured all in one swig, the booze engulfing my throat and nose with its sweet sting. I exhale to the cool taste of the finest whiskey I've ever had as the alcohol freezes my bloodstream.

I lean back in a chair that creaks. I'm high in the mountains, air brisk but invigorating. I'm just going to sit here and finish this bottle and watch nature age. I look up at the sky and study the tapestry of clouds. They're close and spry, putting on a show just for me. I pour another drink and gulp it down. I have no more ambitions than this.

But the scrap of logic remaining in my head knows that I'm dreaming. Responsibility pulls back the curtain of fantasy. I'm back in the foothills surrounded by mountains where I always was. The table, chair, and whiskey were my own inventions. In reality, I'm lying flat on my back looking up at the clouds. I can't move, not even my eyes. I may as well be a corpse. Maybe I am.

How long have I been like this? I have no idea. I can't explain how I made it to Kaitlyn's bedroom and back, yet I'm pretty sure that happened. It was too authentic to be faked, emphasized by the despair I now feel from leaving there. If I concentrate enough, I can still sense Kaitlyn breathing next to me. But even that must be an illusion; soon the sensation fizzles to nothing.

I try to move, but it's no good. If I didn't know better, I'd say some spiteful gremlin has wrapped me head to toe in duct tape. I feel trapped in my own body, and the harder I try to free myself, the more alarmed I become. I try to yell for help, but my lips and throat won't respond, not even a whisper.

I just want to go back home. I need to be back there with my girls. All of this is like one of Kaitlyn's nightmares, and I just need to sleep it off. But I can't even close my eyes, so all I can do is look up at the clouds and wait for something to happen.

Nothing does. Not right away. It's no easy thing to have patience in the clutches of paralysis. I toggle through the worst obscenities in my mind, shouting each of them in my head with no affect. No one can hear me, so what good is it? When I've run out of meditative profanity, I do the only thing I can: lie and wait.

But something does happen. It sneaks into my

consciousness after I've stopped expecting it. I question its reality at first, but I know it's real when I feel my finger move, the one that had touched Kaitlyn's blade of grass.

I've never been so excited about something so trivial. Soon I'm wiggling my finger as if my life depends on it, the simple movement offering me hope. I'm a finger-wagging maniac. Yet it gets even better. After a healthy dose of finger wiggling, I raise my forearm an inch and let it flop to the grass. I'm as astonished by this as I would be hefting a truck off the ground. I lift my arm again, and then again. I'm as pleased with the arm flopping as I am by the finger wagging. I'm learning how to use my body again, and I'm a fast learner. Soon I'm able to lift my entire arm and let it flop to the ground.

Whatever affliction I have, obviously it's temporary. This conclusion allows me to relax. Maybe time is all that's needed, and time I have. I feel like time is all I have these days.

After a seemingly endless period of urging my body to move, I'm elated when I'm able to lift my trunk so that I'm sitting upright, legs still extended in the grass. This allows me to see my surroundings again. I'm right where I found the glowing blade of grass in the foothills, and I'm still very much alone. The grass is no longer illuminated, and I can't even tell which sprig was Kaitlyn's. I search for it, but it's no good. I have to just let it go. I wonder if this is what the security guard meant by staying away from little lights? If so, I failed at that. In any case, when my recovery is complete, I'll resume my way toward flat ground and try to forget what happened here.

My plans are interrupted by sounds scattering toward me from the left. Thinking it may be Kaitlyn again, I turn my head toward the noise to diagnose what it is. Some sounds are not easily forgotten, and I only need a second more to decipher it. This is not Kaitlyn. The electrical buzzing and the chilling thump-thumps echo among the mountains, announcing that the creature is back.

I gasp. This is not good. I'm in no condition to stand, much less run away. Then there's movement out there, the deranged beast lumbering over the foothills toward me, closing the gap all too quickly. Once again I'm forced to imagine being torn apart by this monster, and all I can do is rub my legs and squint as I try to move. In return I get an inadequate twitch in one leg. I'm screwed.

It gets worse. The pulsating buzz changes. It's louder, and I'm hearing it in stereo. I look to the right, my distress increasing to shock. Charging from that direction is a second creature. Then, as if this is nothing, I hear even more buzzing. A third creature is coming from in between the two. They're competing in a race, and reaching me first is the prize.

"You've got to be kidding me!" I pull and slap my legs as if beating them senseless will revive them in time. It helps a little. Both legs begin to twitch, but this won't be fast enough. I keep at it with nothing else at my disposal, but I'm getting nowhere.

The three creatures converge twenty feet in front of

me. They stop to growl and scream into each other's faces. It's a symphony of buzzing thump-thumps among their primal screeching, and I can't think over the tornado of sound.

I can see now that none is the creature that chased me earlier, but they might be the same species. They're gigantic, well over ten feet tall, with horns jutting from their heads, but each one is also unique. One is tall and skinny, its bony arms hanging at its sides so far they almost touch the ground. Its horns point straight up, embellishing its height. Another beast is more proportioned, and its horns sag to match the perpetual frown on its round face, like a sad pug. If a monster were forced to wear a glum expression permanently, this would be its appearance. Then there's a fat one, a jumbo-sized veteran of torment, far superior to the others in girth. Its belly arcs out like the rump of a hippo, yet its head is tiny, topped with two short, spiky horns.

Jumbo doesn't intend to lose this spat of beasts. It throws a raging fit, pounding its fists into the ground to demonstrate its furor. The tirade works—the other two step back to concede the trophy, which is me.

Rivals tamed, Jumbo looks at me. I see something close to a grin form on Jumbo's lips, fangs protruding like a piranha's. Jumbo is a prodigious murderer with a free pass to bathe in blood, and this moment is what it lives for. It hurtles toward me, and all I can do is close my eyes—I don't want to see this.

A violent boom derails the moment. Hot wind follows,

shoving me back and onto my side. I open my eyes to see a cloud of smoke plume into the air. Something has exploded. Jumbo has been slammed back by the blast, skipping across the hill and flopping onto the grass, flesh smoking. As bad as this looks, it's far from a fatal blow. Jumbo rises, shakes its little head, and snarls. It looks past me with apprehension—there's something behind me, the cause of the explosion.

"Pogo!" comes a female voice from behind me. "The skinny one!"

From behind me, a fourth creature, pale blue and bigger than any of them, charges past me toward the skinny beast. When Blue reaches Skinny, they collide and roll into a tussle that reminds me of two giant apes fighting for territory. But Skinny is no match. Blue grabs Skinny by the legs and begins to slam the creature into the grass as if beating dust out of an old rug. Skinny screams like an infant needing a bottle, and Blue raises Skinny again and again, slamming the poor wretch into the ground. Tired of this, Blue twirls in a circle and heaves Skinny like a discus. Skinny flies down the hill into a heap, quivers in a daze for a moment, then rises and scampers far away from here.

Jumbo regains some swagger and charges me again. A figure steps from behind me and walks out to confront the beast. It's a person: feminine, petite, gray skin wearing black clothing. She's frail compared to the monster she's approaching, but she doesn't balk. In fact, it's Jumbo who's afraid. Jumbo stops and begins to back away. She's holding something, some sort of weapon, and she stops and dangles the object at her side. Her arm that holds the weapon begins to twirl, and suddenly I understand. She has a medieval sling, like she's David and he's Goliath. Does she really intend to take that monster down with such a flimsy thing? But there's something in Jumbo's reaction that tells me I shouldn't underestimate it.

The woman unleashes a flash of blinding light from her sling. An object zips forward as Jumbo's eyes widen, but there's no time to evade the projectile. Another violent explosion whacks the creature high into the air. The lifeless form wobbles midair like a damaged Frisbee, then plummets to the ground with a dusty thud. There Jumbo lies completely still, perhaps finally dead.

The third monster, the glum one, is alone to face the woman and Blue all alone, but Glum wants nothing of it. Blue can sense it, and raises a roar toward Glum that's so disturbing it reminds me of a jet at liftoff. Glum cowers at this dressing down, turns, and sprints into the cover of the foothills.

Their work done, the woman and Blue turn toward me. I don't know how I should feel about this. Were they protecting me, or am I a prize they've just won?

My question is answered when Blue rushes towards me, stops a few feet away, and growls and salivates from the biggest mouth I've ever seen. Blue's horns are so thick and massive that a bull would need a hundred years to grow them. The creature's hateful eyes study me like I'm a succulent steak. Then the beast roars with full force, and I can feel the humid breath that smells like rotten fish, teeth clomping shut three times like a crocodile snapping at a gazelle. I tremble, which seems to excite Blue more.

"Pogo!" the woman shouts. Blue looks back at her and hisses, then lowers his head like he understands that she wants him to lay off. She walks up next to him, and he relaxes a notch more.

For the first, time I see the woman's face, and I'm astonished. She looks young, but her complexion is gray, like a rotting corpse, and her hair is short, straight, and black. Her clothing is a hodgepodge of leather strips and rags tied snugly about her like a mummy, her sling hanging on a belt at her side. But the feature that chills me most is her eyes, completely black, as if each eye is just an onyx marble reflecting the sunlight. I can't help but stare at those eyes, trying to convince myself that I'm seeing things. But no, I'm seeing correctly. She stares back at me with the cold eyes of a cobra, and I have to turn away, so I go back to staring at Blue, the creature known as Pogo.

"Nice Pogo?" I say, holding out my hand, palm up. Pogo snaps at it, and I pull my hand back so that he barely misses biting it off. I fall onto my back, covering my face with my arms, unable to stifle my whimpers.

8

CELESTE

"Oh stop whining," the woman says. "We're not gonna hurt you."

I'm shaking.

"Pogo wants to tear you apart," she says. "All demons do. But he won't touch you, so relax."

"Demons?" I ask, looking at Pogo with newfound horror. He licks his lips with his tongue that's black and coarse, spittle hanging from one side of his mouth.

The woman looks disappointed by how pathetic I am.

"Yes, demons," she says. "They're merciless bastards, but Pogo's reformed. He controls himself, with my help. Usually. Anyway, I'm Celeste. I don't really care what your name is, but tell me anyway."

"Zak," I say. "At least, that was my name. I don't understand any of this. I don't know where I am, I don't know what I'm supposed to do, and these things keep attacking me . . ."

"Just shut up," she says. "You're babbling."

She looks me over like a coroner inspecting a particularly messy cadaver. "Zak. I've always hated that name. Anyway, I need to reenergize you. By the looks of it, you went back."

"Back?" I ask. It's like she's not speaking English.

"To the living. You had no idea what you were doing."

"I heard my daughter's voice, and there was this blade of grass . . ."

"I know how it works," she says. "Didn't mommy and daddy tell you not to touch things you don't understand? You can't go back there. It drains your energy and leaves you like the dump heap you are now."

I try to stand but realize I still can't.

"Just sit still," she says. She reaches for my shoulder with her gray hand, her fingernails as black as her hair. I wonder if she's always looked this way, or if she used to be beautiful.

With Celeste's touch comes a white light. As it enters my body, I can see its glow deep within my skin. The light shoots through me like it's surging through veins and arteries unimpeded, intent on saturating every molecule. Celeste squints through discomfort as her head sways back and forth, but she endures like she's expected this. She bears down, her body beginning to twitch, but she won't give up. Once each speck of me is aglow, she pulls away gasping.

I'm a lightbulb. It's temporary—the light fades, but it's done its work. My body has made a wild transformation. I may as well have been given a hundred espressos. I stand upright as my chest heaves in exhilaration. In contrast, Celeste falls flat. Pogo turns and looks around the foothills. He sniffs to make sure the other demons are gone, and they are, for now.

"Hey, this is amazing!" I say. I'm a teenager waking from a solid ten hours, each cell brimming with vitality. I study my arms and legs like they've just been gifted to me. "How did you do that?"

Celeste labors to her feet and wobbles. She closes her eyes for a meditative reset, chases away her instabilities, then opens her eyes to the sun's glow. She sighs. She looks like she just woke up, but otherwise she's no worse for the wear. When she speaks, her tone is sedated by her condition.

"Welcome to the After," she says.

"The After?"

"That's right."

"After what?"

Celeste exhales. "It's sort of self-explanatory, don't you think?"

"I suppose," I say. She means the afterlife.

"This place is all about energy, but not from eating or drinking. You don't need to do those anymore. Energy comes from absorbing it. Demons want your energy—your soul itself, if they can get it—and they'll stop at nothing to get it from you. They can sense you from miles away, like you're a bleeding fish in the ocean and they're the sharks."

"You have to help me," I say "I have no defense against them."

"I *am* helping you," she growls. "Are you always such a crybaby? I'm amazed you've survived this long here."

"I'm just a college professor. Or I was. I'm sort of between jobs right now. I'm not used to this."

"Unemployed college professor. That fits. Anyway, it doesn't matter who you are or what you did when alive, no one is ever used to being here at first," she says. "When I died . . . well, I was clueless too, but I learned. Use that overpriced brain of yours, or you're worthless here."

"You're dead?"

"Why do you think I look like this?" she says, pointing to herself.

"I thought maybe it was a skin condition."

"Very funny," she says. "After you die, you look like this."

I look at my arms. They're the same pasty white from when I was alive, nothing like Celeste's gray skin.

"That didn't happen to you though," she says. "You still look like a living person. The transformation happens when you enter the After, but it didn't happen to you. You're a Half Dead."

"Half Dead?"

She nods. "You're stuck between here and another place. It's very rare. You must be someone important, although I don't see how."

"How did you do that thing? With the light?"

Celeste smiles for the first time, showing neat teeth

that are as gray as her skin. "It's a little trick of mine. I've learned to absorb energy faster than most. I can also transfer it to people and objects. It's a useful skill."

"What did you do him?" I ask, pointing to Jumbo still lying motionless.

Celeste opens a pouch on her belt and pulls out a handful of glowing rocks. "Energized stones. When one hits something it explodes. Works pretty well on demons. Fatso there didn't stand a chance."

"Thank you," I say. "For helping me, that is."

"It doesn't mean I like you," she says. "I loathe demons, except for Pogo here." She nods to her blue friend.

Pogo speaks for the first time. His speech is labored because there's too much saliva in the way, and his tongue flops involuntarily in his mouth like a tail would do. He tells her something in a language I don't understand, his voice screechy: "Etyeye estni admodsana." Then he speaks in English: "The Half Dead is a weakling."

"He thinks you're weak," Celeste adds, in case I didn't catch the insult.

"Well, my self esteem keeps skyrocketing," I say. I have too many questions to dwell on this. "Why did I go back home and then end up back here?"

"Those you left behind, sometimes even people you don't know, can summon you," Celeste says. "If you're dumb enough to answer their call, you go back. Your body doesn't go, just your soul. And you can only experience it for a short time before your energy gives out. Then your soul is spit back here, inside a defenseless body."

"I have to get back to them," I say.

"What did I just tell you?" she says. "You can't. None of us can, once you're here. Don't you know what it means to die? It's permanent. Or don't they teach that at your snobby colleges?"

I change the subject: "I talked to a woman earlier, up there on the mountaintop. She said I have a task ahead of me."

"Your guardian angel," Celeste says.

"Those exist?"

Celeste nods. "Guardian angels aren't exactly like what you think they are, but close enough. You'll see her again, from time to time. And she's right, you do have a task."

"So what is it?"

"How should I know? From what I've heard about the Half Dead, you need to figure it out."

"I don't suppose you have a map?" I ask.

Celeste laughs and brushes the hair from her face. "Seriously? Um, no. And even if there were maps of the After, they'd fill a billion atlases. Plus, it's different here. There's no such thing as day and night. Sometimes it all goes black."

"And when the light returns you're in an entirely new place," I finish her thought. "Yes, that happened to me."

Celeste nods. "We call it the Shift. It keeps a person

guessing, so it's not like you can pull out a GPS and navigate."

"Then how does anyone know where to go?"

"You don't," she says. "You just wander the After for eternity, avoiding demons. The demons who've been here forever know their way around a little better, but there's nowhere in particular to go. If and when you figure out where it is you need to go, it'll be clear to you. How long that will take, no one knows."

"I always thought dying would be more organized," I say.

"Mortunusu wamediama," Pogo says. "Since he is a Half Dead, they will want him."

"Right," Celeste responds. Then she says to me: "Being Half Dead makes you all the more desirable to demons. You're a rare delicacy."

"Oh, how delightful," I say.

I don't know what to make of my new friends, if they can even be called that. But I know that I want to remain with them. "You have to let me stay with you," I say. "I don't have a chance otherwise."

Pogo shakes his head furiously, slobber falling from his mouth. "Nec hapan infirmwezi admodsana. The Half Dead is too weak, let the demons have him."

Celeste raises her hand and Pogo becomes still and silent. "He has a point," she says. "You're weak. You'll endanger us. No, you can't come with us."

Pogo likes this response. He folds his arms in front of him and seems to relax.

"We're leaving," she says. "We've already done more for you than we should have. Enjoy."

Celeste begins to walk away, Pogo following her. I watch in disbelief.

"No, wait!" I shout to their backs. I can't help it, now I'm just mad. "You saved me, and now you'll just let me die? I'm as good as dead if you leave me here!"

"You're already dead," Celeste calls. Neither of them breaks stride. They really intend to leave me.

"Damn it, listen to me! I'm a good person. You can't just let me die!"

They keep walking. I fall to my knees and start smacking the grass. I'm so frustrated that I don't know what else to do. I let my face slump into the grass and allow it to tickle my skin. It reminds me of Kaitlyn touching my cheeks with her little fingers.

I'm going to just lie here in the grass. Where will I go? What will I do? I don't want to face that, so I remain looking at the grass, seeing every blade as if each one is part of a tiny forest. I remain transfixed, watching the hopelessness of the grass for a good five minutes.

Then I sigh. I have to get up and face reality, if any sort of reality even exists now. I have no choice but to continue on my own, to find my way to nowhere for an eternity. I pull myself to my knees.

"Done with your little pity party?" Celeste asks. Pogo is at her side. They've turned around and approached within feet of me, all without me hearing them.

I nod and stand.

"Good," she says. "I'm sure I'll regret it, but you can come with us until we've taught you how to survive here. But you'll do whatever I tell you, and you'll man up a little. Another fit like that and I'll let Pogo bludgeon you with a log."

"Right," I say. "You won't need to resort to that. Thank you, again."

Celeste and Pogo begin walking, and for some reason I hesitate.

"And try to keep up," Celeste says without turning around. I nod to myself and join them as we descend the foothills.

9

TEACH ME

I stay close to my new companions. It isn't long before we're out of the foothills and onto flat plains. I look back to see the mountain peaks behind us like enormous teeth that narrowly missed a meal, and I'm relieved to be free.

Pogo bounds ahead of us, his gigantic blue muscles propelling him forward with startling efficiency. In seconds he's far away, the wide open plains creating the illusion that the demon is much smaller than he is. But just as quickly his frolicking stops, and he looks up at the sky and sniffs the air. He stands very still and observes the sun, cocking his head sideways, contemplating something in that strange mind of his.

"He's an incredible creature," she says to me. "This is his world, it's all he's ever known. He knows it well, in ways you and I never will."

"I can't believe he's real," I say. "How is it that you're friends with something like that?"

"He tried to kill me when we first met," Celeste says, "so I popped him with my sling a few times. I was about to put him out of his misery when he started talking to me. He begged me for his life. I could see there was something special about him—a good side—so I spared him. We've been together ever since. That was a long time ago. He's still a work in progress, but since he knows what it means to be good, I've taught him how to stay that way. He no longer needs souls. I supply him with energy, like I did for you. The other demons are nothing but soul-craving lunatics, but he's unique. An ally like him comes in handy around here."

"He's still horrifying to me," I say.

"Oh, he's not so bad," Celeste says. She looks at me, and I find it hard to read her through those black eyes. "Just don't piss him off."

I nod. She didn't have to tell me that.

Celeste looks back at Pogo, who remains still and continues to look up.

"Pogo!" she calls. "Is it time?"

Pogo turns, bobs his huge head, and gives a subdued growl. "Temkati," he says. "Time."

"Time for what?" I ask.

Celeste turns to me. "It's just the Shift. See you in a second."

With that, I experience the dimming of the sun again, the entire sky going dark, darker, black, and in moments I can't see anything, surrendering to the helplessness of total darkness.

"Celeste?" I call, trying not to express the panic I feel. "Celeste?"

"Just wait, give it a second," Celeste says. I can hear her as if she hasn't left my side, but I can't see her, no matter how hard I try to focus.

"Here, it's coming," she says.

The light comes flooding back with a rush of wind and moisture, and the hot scent of plants. We're in the middle of a tropical rain forest downpour, water rushing onto us through the trees. Pogo, still in the distance, shakes the water from his face and groans, then continues to trudge along as if nothing has happened.

"I would have preferred a luxurious beach resort," I say, squinting up into the rain. I'm already soaked, and I wipe the water from my face, but it does no good.

"There are beaches in the After," Celeste says. "None of them are nice."

"Why does it do that? The Shift."

"It's how the After works," she says. "We're not on Earth anymore. I can't really tell you why the Shift exists, I don't know the answer myself. Maybe it's a way to torture us, who knows? Just accept it."

"The After," I say. "What a wonderfully vague name for a place. And what's after the After?"

"You ask too many questions," Celeste says. She pushes forward to join Pogo.

We walk through the vines and ferns of the lush

jungle, Pogo clearing a sizable path with his body and arms. After a while, the rain stops. Searing tropical heat pours through the trees, cooking us in a leafy steam bath.

We reach a river with water so green it's like liquid turquoise, and it spills over a small waterfall into a frothy pool before flowing downstream. Pogo runs and jumps into the pool, his body sending water splashing high, waves rippling out to the perimeter of the pool. He surfaces and spits out water, looking pleased to cool off.

This must be rest time, because Celeste sits by the pool on a rock underneath a tree. She's watching our surroundings, always on guard for an attack. I go to sit next to her, then realize she may not like me sitting so close, so I angle toward a spot farther off. My indecisiveness throws off my balance, and I trip on a tree root and fall onto jagged rocks, smashing my arm into a stone.

"Ow, damn it!" I yell. I pull myself up.

Celeste won't even look at me. She just shakes her head. "Very graceful. You just might kill yourself before the demons do."

I look at my arm and see that it's bleeding from a sizable scrape, but it's not too bad, and it doesn't hurt much. I grasp the wound with my hand to stop the bleeding and sit. "No one ever mistook me for an athlete. I guess that's how I got into books, very little dexterity is required for reading," I say.

"Waste of time," Celeste says. "You can have your books."

"Well," I say, feeling the educator inside me stir. I see

those eyes again, her way of warning me not to try to convince her otherwise. "I enjoy books, but some authors do ramble on about nothing. It's all about finding the right ones, or, if not books, some other passion. We all have different tastes."

"A lot of good any of that stuff does here," she says. "You should just forget about books and concentrate on surviving."

I let it go because I can tell Celeste isn't in the mood. Still, there's so much I want to know about her. There has to be a way I can penetrate that barrier she puts up whenever we talk. After several minutes of sitting and watching Pogo, I try again.

"What happened to you in your life? How did you die?" I say. Right when I say it, I regret it. After all, it's a very personal question, but I realize this too late.

"None of your damn business," she says.

"Sorry," I say. "I ask too many questions, you already warned me of that. I'll tell you what happened to me instead. I died in a hospital, unexpectedly."

"Doesn't matter how you died," she says. "The fact is, you're dead, or at least Half Dead. Doesn't matter how I died either, so don't ask again."

I've touched a sore spot, and I know enough to meet it with silence. We watch as Pogo lifts himself from the pool, hops onto shore, and shakes the water from his body, soaking us like a sprinkler.

"Hey, do you mind?" Celeste shouts, brushing the water from her face and hair with her hands. Pogo, realizing what he's done, cowers in shame at first, but then he points to us and begins to laugh. His laugh sounds like a tractor stuck in the mud, and he continues to laugh for a full minute.

"Yeah, yeah, very funny, you moron," Celeste says, and she begins to laugh too. I can't express how pleasing it is to hear them both laugh. It gives me hope that they have emotions other than rage.

Laughter subsiding, Pogo finds a high boulder in the sun and perches on top of it to dry. I can't believe what I'm witnessing, the demon looking like a chiseled gargoyle atop a gothic cathedral. I'm distracted by this enough that I don't realize Celeste is talking to me.

"Hey!" she says.

"Huh?"

"Pay attention. I said I want to show you something."

She's picked up a white stone from the shore, and she's holding it out for me to see.

I don't know what the point of this is. My response is underwhelming: "It's a rock?"

"Brilliant deduction," she says. "No, it's not a rock."

"It's not?"

"Not *just* a rock. It's a container of energy, like all things can be."

She shuts her eyes and closes her fingers around the rock. "You have to open yourself to the energy here. Your food is no longer pizza and burgers, it's the air itself. Once inside you, with practice, energy can be transferred."

As she speaks, light flows to her hand, a brilliant green

and then purple. She opens her hand to show the white rock has transformed into a kaleidoscope of colors, light so bright it illuminates her face and nearly looks hot.

"Amazing," I say. "I can't begin to guess how you did that."

"It's a physical and mental act. Think of the energy as coming from your chest, then squeeze it out of your body with the constrictions of your muscles."

"Sounds abstract."

"It's not, if you think about what you're doing," she says. "Give it a try, heal that cut on your arm."

"How, exactly?"

Celeste seems frustrated. "How is it that you're a teacher? You don't understand anything."

"I'm sorry, I'm used to Melville and Thoreau, not magic."

"There's no magic in those dead white guys. And there's no magic here," she says. "Just, shut up. Close your eyes."

Pogo mutters up on his perch, tongue wagging from his mouth like a black worm. His words are loud enough for me to hear: "Admodsana mortunusu wamediama. The Half Dead is too weak and too dumb to learn." Then he spits down into the pool to release some of his drool.

I try to ignore his heckling and close my eyes.

"Now, be calm, and think about energy entering your body, surrounding your wound, and binding it up," Celeste says. "Try to imagine it happening, and when it does, pull the energy in."

I really try my best to comply, but after a few minutes of this, I don't feel a thing.

"Open your eyes," Celeste says, and I open them. "Anything?"

I show her my arm. The wound is unchanged.

Celeste smirks. "Must be a slow learner."

"Admodsana, he is too weak and stupid," Pogo says again. "Waste of time."

"Well I'm sorry," I say. I can't help feeling perturbed. "I'm just not very good at this. I don't see how it works."

"No, you really don't," Celeste says.

Celeste stands, pulls the sling from her belt, and sets her energized rock into the sling's leather pouch. She turns toward the pool, twirls the sling to build momentum, and unleashes the rock, sending it spinning in a blur across the pool and into the bank on the other side. On impact, the rock erupts into a scattering of stones and spray, a cloud pluming as if by a mortar. Pogo roars and bounces up and down on his boulder like a pyromaniac on the Fourth of July.

"But you better start understanding," Celeste says after the explosion settles. "Energy is everything here. If you don't learn that, you're a goner."

I nod. "I'll practice more," I say.

She comes to me, reaches for my injured arm, and pinches the wound. I grimace from this and try to pull away, but she has me tight. The light spills from her hand again, and I stiffen. When she lets go a minute later, the wound is healed, my arm looking as if no injury ever occurred.

"All right," Celeste says, tucking her sling away. "Let's get moving again."

As we enter the thick jungle again, the rain returns.

10

DEAD

Energy. This is what my existence depends upon now, a nebulous concept that I'm not trained to understand. If I knew all about energy, I would have become so much more than a teacher of literature: a nuclear physicist, an engineer, maybe some genius with NASA. But my mind doesn't work that way. I understand words, not science.

Then I begin to wonder: Is energy in the After even relevant to science as we know it? Are there things here that would baffle even the likes of Einstein and Newton? Maybe I'm not so ill-prepared for this. Anyone would be disoriented here.

"Is there any sort of plan?" I ask, catching up to Celeste and Pogo. Both of them can walk much faster than me.

"Plan? For what?" Celeste asks.

"Well, a plan for where we're going, for one thing. Isn't there some sort of goal?"

"Not so much," Celeste says. "I don't know what sort of pleasure resort you think this is, but there's no schedule of activities."

"Right," I say.

Pogo starts sniffing the air again. He stops to zero in, so we stop, too, and give him distance. His sniffing leads him ahead and into a ravine where vines dangle to the ground from enormous jungle trees.

"Mortunusu," he grunts, looking at the ground. "Something dead is here."

Celeste steps forward, putting her palm back and out toward me, the universal sign for *stay back*. I begin to worry that Pogo has stumbled across something dangerous. I can hear them talk in low voices, but I can't make out what they're saying.

"It's okay," Celeste says a minute later, turning to look at me. "Come here, take a look."

"The dead," Pogo adds. "Mortunusu."

I step toward them, pushing away the vines and watching my footing through the snaking roots of the bizarre trees. There's a musty, herby smell among the curtains of greenery, tainted by a hint of something rank.

Pogo and Celeste watch me come to them, as if uncertain how I'll react to their secret. There's something on the ground next to them, I can see it now. But it's not until I'm right there with them that I see faded blue fabric nestled in the ferns. Clothing. Inside it is a body, badly decomposed, decayed bones protruding from the clothing where arms and legs should be. The body is long, the size of a grown man.

I'm repulsed by such a stark display of death. I've only seen dead people at funerals, dressed in their best and beautified by the undertaker. But this is wild, natural death —no funeral here, just a body rotting where it fell with no one to care for it.

"Well that's awful," I say. "And it's wearing a uniform."

"He was a cop," Celeste says, pointing to a badge that looks ready to detach from the deteriorating uniform. On the opposite side of the badge is a name tag: Sheridan

"There are police officers in the After?" I ask.

"Anyone can make it to the After," Celeste says. "Cops, doctors, politicians, a bum on the street. Teachers." She looks at me when she says *teachers*. I try not to take it personally that she's mentioned teachers after bums. "Doesn't matter who you were, if you were meant to be here, you come, and you arrive with everything you carry, like him."

I reach into my pockets, involuntarily feeling for the things I carry, the items I've brought with me from the living. I realize that the cop still has everything from his uniform: belt, holster, even a hat on his head. He's lying flat, arms sprawled, skeletal jaw hanging open below two empty eye sockets long ago cleared of eyeballs. I see a gun nestled in his skeleton hand, a long-barreled police revolver.

"It looks like he was attacked," I say. "Did the demons get him?"

"Well I doubt he died of old age," Celeste says. "It was demons all right, it's what they do."

"But why is he dead?" I ask. "I mean, to get here you have to die. But he's *really* dead."

"You can die here, too," she says. "Think of it as dying again. I don't know where you go when you die in the After, but right now this poor sap's soul is wherever that is."

"We're in hell," I say, and I say it out loud but I really meant to keep it to myself.

Celeste looks at me. "No we're not," she says.

"How do you know?" I ask. "This must be hell or some form of purgatory."

"Things don't work here like you've been taught back in the living world. Maybe there is a heaven and a hell like some believe, but not here. The After isn't eternal torture or suffering, and it's not paradise either. It's something else. Eternal wandering. A holding pen for some people after they die."

"Well, I guess that's a relief," I say.

"No it's not," Celeste says. "There's nothing good about being here. It may not be hell, but it sure isn't a picnic."

All I can do is nod and look like a dope. She likes to show me that I'm wrong. Maybe she senses this, because she actually says something comforting: "Just don't think about it, okay? It'll make you go bonkers, trust me."

"Bondukai," Pogo says, pointing at the revolver. "A gun."

"That's a gun all right," Celeste says, stepping forward and kneeling by the body. She pulls the gun from the cop's hand, which isn't a challenge. The bones of his hand crumble to shards from the dislodging.

She stands and looks at the gun. It's dirty and looks like it's been here for years, but she cleans it with her palms and fingers, returning some of its gunmetal gray shine. She pops open the cylinder, spins it to inspect if it functions, then plucks the six bullets free one at a time. She studies them in her palm, then squeezes each round to judge the integrity.

"He didn't even get off a shot. The bullets look serviceable. This thing should still work." She reloads it, closes the cylinder, and to my surprise, hands it to me.

"Me?" I say, taking the gun from her. I grasp it with the disgust of holding a rancid banana peel.

"Yeah you. You need all the help you can get. Ever used a gun before?"

I pluck a distant memory from my brain. "You might be surprised, but yes. I had this friend when I was a kid. His dad was quite the adventurer. Sort of a wacko, actually. He used to take us to the gun range and let us shoot with him. I mean, what sort of father does that with little kids? We were six or seven. One time we even got to shoot an Uzi . . ."

"Okay, whatever, good times," Celeste says. She reaches down and unhooks the cop's belt, further desecrating the mangled remains. She searches the storage pouches, finding spare bullets in each. One of the pouches has personal items: a pack of gum, a folded piece of paper, and lip balm, but she tosses these aside. Then she begins to rifle through his pockets.

But I'm intrigued by the piece of paper, so I retrieve it from the ground. I see that it's worn yellow construction paper, looking like something the cop carried in this pouch for years. I unfold it like it's Egyptian papyrus, being careful not to wreck it.

Inside the paper in blue crayon is a child's drawing of a stick figure, whimsical smile on a round head and limbs out of proportion to the body. Below the picture in cryptic penmanship are the words: "I love you Daddy."

"It's a note and drawing from his child," I say.

"Well he doesn't need it anymore, and neither do we," Celeste says, still rummaging.

I've had just about enough of Celeste. Does she have any feelings at all?

"Okay, I know we don't need a piece of paper," I say, surprised at my anger. "But the man is dead, we should show some respect. He had a child, a family. Didn't you have a family?"

"Oh I had a wonderful family," Celeste says, standing again, nothing useful found. "Real top notch, if you like the Munsters. Are you done feeling wholesome? We have things to do."

"No, that's just it!" I say. "We have nothing to do.

Least we can do is have some dignity here. God knows we have nothing else."

"What do you propose we do, sing a song for the guy?"

I look down at the corpse.

"No," I say. I kneel. I tuck the note into the cop's shirt pocket, patting it shut. I feel that this simple act returns some integrity to this grisly scene, and I can almost hear Officer Sheridan thanking me.

"Do you think I had a good funeral?" I ask Celeste, keeping my gaze on Sheridan's corpse.

"Beats me," Celeste says. "Nothing much good about funerals anyway."

"I hope this guy had a good one," I say. I begin to think about how the cop's child must have felt at his funeral. Unimaginable pain, the same pain my own wife and daughters must have felt at mine.

"You have to move on," Celeste says, seeming to understand what I'm feeling. "Stop thinking so much."

I stand and nod, but I definitely don't feel up to moving on.

"Here," Celeste says, wrapping the belt around my waist and buckling the front. There's something resembling tenderness in the way she does it, like applying a bandage to a wound. I remember that I'm still holding the dead cop's gun in my hand. She tugs the revolver away from me and holsters it.

"You look like a real desperado now," she says,

standing back. "And there's plenty of ammo in those pouches."

"He's still weak," says Pogo.

"Sure, he may be weak," Celeste says. "But at least now he's packin."

"Of course, it's been a long time since I've shot a gun," I say, looking down at my new sidearm.

"Not much to it," Celeste says. "I bet it'll all come back to you once demons show up. Just point and shoot, but make it count. Bullets are liable to just irritate demons, so aim for the head and they'll feel it."

"Right," I say.

"Course, you're just as likely to shoot yourself or one of us, so try not to do that."

"Sure."

Pogo resumes his lead through the jungle, Celeste following.

I take one last look at the corpse of Officer Sheridan, now stripped of his belt and sidearm. I think I've made a fair trade for returning his beloved note, but it still feels like thievery.

"I'm sorry," I whisper. Sorry that I took his gun. Sorry that he's dead. Sorry that his child is fatherless. Sorry that I'm dead, too.

11

ANGIE

I recall my wife's perfume like the nostalgia of ocean air. I struggle to remember her perfume's intricacies, like trying to hum a long-forgotten melody. I loved that scent for all Angie meant to me.

Thinking about perfume takes my mind off of the drudgery of our journey. The rain forest is blistered with knolls that we ride up and down like an exhausting seesaw. We're swimming in the humidity hanging in the air, incessant drips from vines pelting us as we cut through the undergrowth. I feel inflicted with chronic sogginess.

I begin to wonder what made me think of perfume. Was it random, or did something trigger it? As if to answer, a familiar spicy-sweet aroma drifts through the tropical breeze, capturing my attention. I stop and sniff like Pogo does when he encounters a puzzling odor. Perfume? It's so faint I wonder if that's really what I'm smelling. More likely it's a tropical flower buried in the soup of shrubbery, and my mind has twisted it into something else.

"Etyeye estni piwavi," Pogo says. "He is also lazy." He's taken notice that I've stopped, and he thinks I'm slacking.

"Something wrong?" Celeste says.

"Do you smell that?" I say.

Pogo begins sniffing the air, inhaling and exhaling with piggish snorts. I don't think he smells anything unusual, because he stops sniffing and cocks his head and looks at me with suspicion.

"Smell what?" Celeste asks.

"I could swear I just smelled my wife's perfume."

"Well, come on," Celeste says. "We have to keep moving."

There she goes again, this drive to move when there's no destination. I'm sick of nowhere to go but the urgency to get there, but I nod and keep on.

A few steps more and the breeze hits me again. The perfume scent is undeniable this time, and accompanying the smell is a disembodied female voice saying my name: "Zak?"

I stop and answer on instinct: "What?"

Celeste and Pogo turn again to study me. "Now what?" Celeste says.

"Did you just say my name?" I ask.

"No one said your name. Now you're hearing things?"

"I swear, someone just said my name."

We stand in the rain forest silence, Pogo and

Celeste looking around for any hint of a voice. No more voices come. "We're the only ones here," Celeste says.

But then, just as Celeste turns to lead us away again, I hear a soft whimper, and I almost miss the sound it's so subtle.

"There," I say, pointing to the direction of the sound. It's coming from a cluster of trees.

"There what?" Celeste says. "I didn't hear anything."

"Someone is crying over there, I heard it." I begin to walk toward the trees.

"Wait!" Celeste says. I'm curious enough to ignore her, and I walk up to the cluster of trees and listen.

"Zak?" comes the voice again. When it does, a leaf on one of the trees lights bright blue, just like Kaitlyn's blade of grass.

"Angie?" I call.

Celeste and Pogo have followed me, and I turn to them. "My wife, she's trying to contact me."

"You can't talk to her," Celeste says. "Didn't you already learn this lesson?"

"But, it's my wife," I say. "I can't just ignore her."

"Yes you can," Celeste says.

"Celeste, please," I say. "I know it's dangerous, I know I'm not supposed to, but it's my wife. I didn't get a chance to say goodbye."

I think about how I could have called Angie when I was dying in the ER. My phone was right there, I should have called her.

"Nec valheri," Pogo says. "He should not say goodbye."

"He's right," Celeste says. "Forget it."

"If you stand guard, and bring my energy back when I return, what harm is there in that?" I ask.

"You're the dumbest person I've ever known," she says. "But we'll never hear the end of it if I don't let you. Go to your wife then, just don't blame me when you find out what a bad idea it is."

"Thank you," I say. I've never said a more heartfelt thank you to anyone.

I watch as the two of them back off to give me distance. Then I turn to the leaf, extend my arm, and touch it with my index finger. Just as with Kaitlyn's sprig of grass, the blue light pours onto my finger and hand, and it spreads over my arm and then my entire body as if a blue flame has engulfed me. Everything goes dark.

When the light returns, I'm in the middle of tombstones garnished with flowers. It's a cemetery. The daylight is waning, nearing dusk.

"Zak." It's Angie. I turn to the direction of her voice. She's sitting next to a tombstone, caressing the grassy grave in front of it. I study her hands and her hair, and circle around her so I can see her face. Her eyes are red and wet, as if she's been sobbing for weeks.

"I'm here," I say.

When she doesn't acknowledge my voice, I understand that it does no good to speak to her. She can't see or hear me. I'm confused, because Kaitlyn was able to hear me. But Kaitlyn had been half asleep and a child, and maybe that makes a difference.

"We miss you so much," she says to the ground, then looks up at the tombstone. I follow her glance and see what she sees: a tombstone with my name on it. *My* tombstone. I can't believe I'm seeing it. It's like I'm realizing, once again, that I'm dead, as if there had ever been a doubt.

She misses me. When alive, she had wanted me out of her life. Dead, she wants me back, or at least the man I once was.

"Angie, I'm here. Can you hear me?"

She can't.

"Kaitlyn said she had a dream about you," she says. "What am I supposed to tell her? I don't know what to tell her. She doesn't want to hear that you're gone."

"That was me!" I shout. "Kaitlyn saw me, in her dream, but I was really there!"

"Why did you do this to us?" Angie says, and she holds her forehead in her palm. "You just gave up on us."

"No Angie, I didn't give up," I say. "People die. I had problems, I was trying to fix them." I realize I'm lying to myself. I wasn't trying to fix anything.

She continues, still not hearing me. "I think it was all just too much for you."

"No, I died in a hospital," I say. "My neck." But even

as I say this, I understand what she means. "I didn't give up. I can be the person I was, I just need time to figure it out."

"I loved you so much," she says. "I was always there for you. I was always willing to help. But nothing could help you. Dying was your only way."

Angie thinks I died because I wanted to die. I realize that she might be right, at least partially.

"I don't know what to do," she continues. "The girls need you. I need you, the old you. I don't know what to do next. I don't want to just move on."

I kneel to grab hold of her shoulders. She's oblivious of my touch. "You have to. You have to raise our girls. I'm sorry, but you have to do it," I say.

Angie raises her head. She stares past me, doesn't see me, but she looks like she senses something.

"Zak?" she says.

"Yes, I'm here," I say. I can't tell if she sees or hears me. She says nothing and just closes her eyes and inhales.

"I can't do it," she says. "I don't know how to do it."

I feel the darkness coming. My time is up. I stand and look around in a panic.

"No, wait! I'm not finished yet." I'm talking to the approaching darkness, to whoever it is running this show.

"Angie, please, you have to move on," I say, feeling the pull away from the living. "Just keep trying honey, I know you can."

My body becomes immobilized, and I collapse as if shot by a sniper. The last thing I see is Angie running her fingers along my tombstone like she's caressing my shoulder.

"Angie!" I manage to shout. I don't think she hears me. I still hear her sobs as my view of her disappears. "You have to go on!"

The anguish is smothering. Celeste was right, I shouldn't have gone back.

12

LEFT BEHIND

I'm falling. Or at least it feels that way, plummeting from a skyscraper toward the crowded streets of a metropolis at rush hour, feeling every second of the plunge as I flail and scream. I don't want to land, but here comes the ground, before I'm ready. I'll splat onto the sidewalk like a melon. Will I feel anything? Yes, everything, at least for a second. The payoff will be all of this will end and my soul can rest for good. Quitting is what I'm best at anyway.

But just before impact, the inertia is blocked, and my fall slows, a mysterious force setting gravity's emergency brake. I lower onto the concrete as gently as a baby being set into a fluffy bassinet. I look up at the towering building from which I fell, and I seem hopelessly small.

But my senses have been duped. I see the skyscraper transform from the symmetry of steel and glass to the natural perfection of a tropical tree. Instead of the reflective windows, I see sunlight bounce off slippery bark. The rain forest has returned, or I have returned to it.

Once again I'm a prisoner to my own immobility, bound in afterworld paralysis. The harder I struggle, the more I remain frozen and helpless. It's claustrophobic, except instead of a tight space, it's my own flesh that traps me.

There's Celeste kneeling next to me. She's thinking *I told you so* but she doesn't say it. She closes her eyes and reaches to me, her hand resting flat on my chest. She inhales like she's a bodybuilder about to lift a piano over her head.

I see the blinding white light before I feel it, like Celeste has ignited a flare on my sternum. The liquid light pours over me, and with each inch of its spread, I feel the energizing power. Inside my body there's a curious chemistry of blood, muscles, and organs commingling with light energy, and I regain all functions.

I stand up while Celeste pulls away and collapses. I hear a grunt from Pogo. He's lurking in the distance, on guard like some ghoulish mobster.

"Are you happy now?" Celeste whispers to me, too weak for anything more.

No. I'm not. I'm infinitely more unhappy.

"She told me . . ."

"Ssh," Celeste interrupts. Her eyes are still closed. She's concentrating on her recovery, and she doesn't want to hear my griping anyway. With her gray skin and raven hair, body twisted and lifeless where she collapsed, she reminds me of a deflated, grungy balloon.

Then there's a transformation, subtle at first, her chest heaving with recuperating breaths, her body puffing out. She turns her head to me and opens her groggy eyes, and she squints at me as if to say: *Why do I even bother with you?*

I reach down with my palm up, an offer to help her to her feet. She considers whether she should accept my help, then snatches my hand with her icy fingers, and together we tug her to her feet.

"I'm sorry for not taking your advice," I say.

She wobbles before regaining her balance.

"You can only say you're sorry so often before it starts to be nauseating," she says. "When are you going to start listening to me?"

"I know, I will now. But my wife, she thinks it was my fault," I say.

"What was your fault?"

"She thinks I died because I gave up."

"Is this such breaking news?"

"Yes. I didn't kill myself."

"Not directly," she says. "Answer a question for me. How did you lose your job?"

I shake my head. "My job? What does that have to do with this?"

"Fired? Laid off?"

"No," I say. "I just had enough, that's all."

"So you quit."

"Resigned. That's different than quitting."

"Not really, you just prefer the fancier word. Why did you resign, Zak?"

I hadn't planned on this impromptu life coaching. "Hmm. Well, I thought I had an ideal job. I loved to teach, I'm passionate about literature."

"But something went wrong," she finishes my thought.

"There's a lot of stress in my line of work."

"No more than any other job."

"I don't know. It just started getting to me. The politics of it all. The students. The pressure to publish. The drive to get tenure."

"So you quit."

"Okay, yes, I quit if you prefer that word. I needed some time away." I feel myself getting defensive.

"And did that help?"

"Yes. Well, at first. But the bills started to pile up. We only had my income. And even away from the college there was so much stress. I drank a lot. Then I got sick."

"Qui doa," Pogo says. "He is a quitter." These two make awful counselors.

"The soul knows when it's had enough," Celeste says. "It's why you're here."

"I don't believe that. I don't want to be here," I say. "I need my family back, and they need me."

"Those are just wasted words. You can't do anything about it."

"I don't believe that either," I say. "You said I'm Half Dead, right? That implies that part of me is alive. There has to be a way I can get back."

Pogo grunts to let me know I've said something dumb.

"There's no way back," Celeste says. "Just forget about it. Come on, let's get moving."

I look at the tree where Angie's leaf still hangs without illumination. I step back toward it, hoping it'll light up again, but she's gone. I don't want to leave her again. I'm like a child waiting by his favorite climbing tree, not wanting to ever leave it. If I can just go back to her and prove to her that I'm willing to try harder, I think she'd be willing to give me another chance. I think I can get things back in order.

"Zak." Celeste has grown impatient, but that's okay, so have I.

"I appreciate all you've done for me," I say. "But I don't care to continue anymore. I just want to stay here."

"Really?" she says. "That's brilliant."

"There's a way back there, to my life, I know there is. Don't you want to get back to your life? Isn't it worth trying?"

"No, it's not," she says. "We both failed back in that place. Even if there was a way to return, it's not worth it. We're both rejects, cast here because we failed."

"I don't see how you could have failed," I say.

"Yeah, well there's a lot you don't know about me, and I'd prefer to keep it that way. Now are you coming? Because my charity is about spent on you."

I don't have an answer for her.

Celeste sighs and tosses her arms in the air. "Fine, I'm done. Good luck, you'll need it," she says, and walks away.

Pogo watches her pass, then he begins to follow her when he sees she's serious about leaving me.

I don't want them to go on without me, but I don't want to leave the tree, either. I can't explain why I don't want to go, but I just don't. Neither of them says anything, other than Celeste muttering something to herself. I watch them disappear into the rain forest, dread of being alone swirling with the anguish of seeing my wife.

It starts raining again.

13

———

THE WAY

Angie's tree is more than just emotional comfort. Its complex canopy stretches thick and wide, a natural awning to shelter me from the elements. I sit with my back resting against its trunk and observe the rain, and I'm dry and almost comfortable.

Seeing Angie at the cemetery has provided a glimpse of the reality I needed. It took me dying for her to see what I mean to her, and for me to see how much I need her. The upshot is I'm ready and willing to do what it takes to win her back, but I'm in the After, so how to do it? I have no answers.

Without Celeste and Pogo around, I can't help but think of demons. It was stupid of me to want to stay here. Now I'm alone again, and the vulnerability gnaws at me. I unholster the revolver, its weight so unfamiliar to my hands, which are more accustomed to the texture of books. I open the cylinder to inspect the bullets neatly packed, then close it again. I wonder if Officer Sheridan ever shot anyone with this gun? I prefer to think that he didn't, that he was a good cop, an Andy Griffith, small-town type who didn't consider violence as part of his work. I rest the gun in my hand across my stomach, the weapon buying a slice of courage, even though I know bullets might do very little against demons.

I close my eyes and listen to the rain, smelling the tropical moisture. I'm wishing it were possible to sleep, the bodily function I miss most. Even after a difficult day, waking up fresh always brought a new perspective and energy when I was alive. Here, in the After, my perspective remains constant: I'm not where I belong, and I'd do anything to get out.

But when I keep my eyes closed long enough, a distant cousin of sleep creeps in, a dream-meditation that stifles all the struggles. Scenes of my past come and go, triumphs and heartbreaks, and in this state of mind I carry a shield of semi-indifference.

It doesn't matter how long I've been sitting here, the monotone of rain hypnotic, Angie's tree holding me up like an old friend, but it must have been a while. I become aware, faintly, that something in my surroundings has changed. I don't even know how I've determined this, but I don't question it. Something is here with me, and it makes me squeeze the revolver's handle. My eyelids quiver over indecision between opening my eyes to reveal something terrifying or remaining closed in denial.

Is it possible for a demon to sneak up to me without

buzzing, without my hearing its giant footfalls? I doubt it, but something is here, in front of me, and I have to do something about it. Ignoring it might be the last poor decision I ever make.

I formulate an action plan that's not very creative, but it's functional: I'll count to three and open my eyes.

One. Two. *I don't think I'll open my eyes.*

Three.

I'm shocked, I've opened my eyes. I raise the gun in front of me, my fright making the barrel wiggle. I hug the trigger with my index finger without firing, ready to shoot, bracing for the possibility of recoil.

But there's nothing there except the wall of rain falling just outside of the tree's awning, the rain forest exactly as I remember it. Still, I know something is out there, or was there.

A flash like a bolt of lightning illuminates my surroundings, temporarily blinding me as I flinch, and I very nearly fire the gun on impulse. I press my back harder into the tree and hold the gun with both hands, waving it to and fro, ready to shoot if something menacing becomes visible.

Before I see her, I hear her voice from the other side of the tree: "Hello Zak."

I leap up and swing the gun toward the sound of the voice. Sight returning, I see a glowing figure: Deena, the woman I met on the mountaintop.

I lower the gun and exhale in relief, happy that I didn't

shoot. If I didn't know better I'd say she appeared from the tree itself, Angie's tree, and just maybe she did.

"Oh, hello again," I say. "I almost shot you. Thought you were a demon."

Deena is unfazed by the possibility. I become reacclimated to her pale face and the swirls of color that drape her body. But now, instead of blue, light green, white, and gray iridescence, the colors are more tropical: emerald, sepia, mint, beige. She's become a chameleon, assuming the rain forest palette.

"You seem to be at a standstill," she gets to the point.

I nod and pat the tree trunk. "Yeah, well, not much point in doing anything else."

She frowns.

"I'm still not sure of the point of all this," I say. "I had a good life, and I keep being reminded of that."

"Did you?"

"Okay, sometimes, yes, I hated my life."

"Sometimes," she repeats.

"Maybe more than sometimes, I don't know. But now that I'm here and I see what I had—truly see it—I want to go back to the way it was."

"Some things can't be reclaimed," she says. It's a depressing statement if I've ever heard one. I'm about to tell her just how I feel about this when she surprises me: "But in your case, there is a way."

"A way to what?"

"To return home."

"You mean, return, right now, as if none of this happened?"

"It's not as simple as that. In fact, to return will be more difficult than anything you've done before. It's infinitely dangerous."

For a millisecond, Deena's body evolves to solid black, as if the sobering words are reflected in her appearance. I'm alarmed at how menacing she looks, like a phantom, but before I can internalize her appearance, her body returns to the color scheme it was, like nothing had happened.

She continues. "You've learned how worthwhile it is to return. Now you can find out if it means enough to you to make it back."

"It means everything to me," I say.

Deena is silent. Maybe she's debating the validity of my statement. Then: "I believe you, Zak."

I rewind my thoughts to what she said about my return being dangerous.

"Why will it be so hard to go back? Mentally challenging? Physically demanding?"

"That's for you to find out," she says.

I'm annoyed at her habit of being vague. "I'd really like to know upfront rather than finding out on my own," I say.

"It's not that I wouldn't tell you," she says. "It's that I don't know. I only know it won't be easy. Returning never is, and each journey back is different. And if you fail, you could wind up elsewhere. There are far worse places to be than the After, and you could end up in one of them. Forever."

Sounds perfect.

"So I'm supposed to just figure out how to do this?" I ask, trying to ignore that ominous proposition.

"Your friends know the way."

"Friends. You mean, Celeste? Pogo? They already told me there isn't a way."

"Ask them again," she smiles.

"Well, that'll be difficult, since I sort of burned that bridge."

Deena shakes her head. "They never left you."

I look around and don't see them. "I saw them leave," I say, pointing to the direction they went.

"Yes, and they had good reason to leave," she says. Her body turns blood red, her entire appearance conveying anger. I think she's upset with me for not going with Celeste and Pogo. But just as before, the transformation is short, and her tropical colors reappear in seconds.

She continues: "They can help you, but you need to allow yourself to be helped. You won't succeed otherwise."

"I understand," I say. "I'll work on that."

"Good," she smiles. "Now, I need to leave you again."

"Wait, can't you stay longer?" I say. "There's more I want to know."

There's another flash of light. When the temporary blindness subsides, I'm alone again.

Only I'm not alone for long. I hear something pushing through the trees in front of me. Something huge. Tree limbs snap like the cracking of bones, heavy footfalls pounding without care for where they step. It's a demon this time, I know it, even though I can't see it yet. It senses me like flies to a rotting carcass.

I raise the gun again, and the barrel shakes like it did before. I have to shoot whatever comes into view. I have to protect myself, but I'm wishing for a rocket launcher instead of this police pistol. I think I've stopped breathing. All of my bodily effort is focused on aiming the gun, my last flimsy line of defense.

When the bulky form emerges from the foliage, I pull the trigger. I'm unprepared for the shock of the recoil. The sound hammers at my ears, the shot goes wild, and so does the gun. It flies from my hand and cartwheels across the ground while I cringe.

The demon roars at me like an old Chevy Caprice Classic without a muffler, but I can barely hear from the gun blast ringing my ears. I'm dismayed when I see the thing is a demon all right, but it's Pogo. He turns to look at the sapling behind him that the bullet has shattered, cocking his head to study the damage. I've missed, but Pogo is still mad. He turns back to me and roars again, louder this time, mouth unhinged, his blaring screech so deafening I wince from the shockwaves.

I remember Celeste's words of wisdom about Pogo: *Just don't piss him off.*

"Oh God," I say, holding my hand out to Pogo, a futile apology forming on my lips. Too late. He bolts toward me, enormous footfalls like a charging rhino.

14

A PLAN

It's like an out of control dump truck is coming right for me, and all I can do is stand there and watch like an idiot, hoping it'll miss but knowing it won't. Pogo's charge is unceasing, he's going to plow through me, break every bone I have, and then break them further.

Somehow I hear Celeste's piercing cry through the mayhem: "Pogo, no!"

Pogo stops right in front of me, his brawny legs tearing up the ground to halt his momentum. He growls into my face with breath so hot it's like facing a bonfire. But instead of mauling me, he picks up a fallen tree, snaps it in two like it's uncooked spaghetti, and begins to stomp it to splinters.

"Mutus!" he yells through his tirade. "Half Dead is so dumb! So dumb! So dumb!"

"Easy!" Celeste says, coming to Pogo's side. She touches his arm with both hands, the picture of tranquility. She understands him, knows how to soften him with nothing more than touch and words. "Accident, Pogo. Okay?"

"Accident," Pogo repeats what she says, stiffening to her words, fighting his desire for payback. "Ajalte. The dumb Half Dead had an accident." He leaves the ravaged limb alone and pants away his rage. A few seconds more and he steps away, turning to look at me with those hateful demon eyes before he goes to sit in the crotch of a tree.

"Nice shooting," Celeste says to me. "You hit that mean old sapling right between the eyes."

"I thought," I begin, but I realize I should just let it pass instead of offering lame excuses.

"Sorry for the scare, Pogo," I call to him. He still looks like he wants to throw me around for an hour or two. Then he shakes his head to clear fog from his brain, and the effect is that he begins to laugh. "Half Dead is dumb, he missed. Desindwa!"

"Yes, he missed," Celeste says, stooping to retrieve the fallen pistol. "Half Dead is still learning. But he's slow."

"Slow," Pogo repeats. "Sssssslow."

"My apologies to you, too," I say to Celeste.

"You don't have to apologize to me for being a lousy shot, I could have guessed it."

"No, not about that," I say. "About everything. Being a burden to the both of you. You have no reason to help me, but still you do, and I'm a moron not to be more appreciative."

When Celeste stares at me and says nothing, it's

impossible to tell what she's thinking. Still, something I've said has made an impact, and I feel better for saying it. Until I realize my words have missed the mark again.

"There you go again with your apologies," she says. "I never liked apologies when I was alive, and I like them less being dead, especially coming from you. So save it."

She shoves the gun at me handle first. I take it and hold it like the foreign machine of murder it is. "Right, I'll . . . save it then."

"Good. Now let's see you shoot that thing again," she says.

"Won't that attract demons?" I ask.

She laughs at me. "You're a demon banquet and the dinner bell is sounding. Nothing we do could attract them more. Plus, you need the practice. You're horrendous. Since you have a knack for maiming trees, try aiming for that one."

She points to a tree that's practically right in front of me.

"It's not very far away," I say.

"Brilliant. Therefore it should be impossible to miss. Show me."

I shrug and raise the gun with both hands, but it just feels heavy and awkward. I pull the trigger with a flinch, and the gun recoils and booms, filling the air with gun smoke. I've missed. The tree is unscathed, but I feel happy just to have not dropped the gun again.

"Desindwa!" Pogo shouts. "You missed."

"Did you drive a car with those eyes?" Celeste says. "You must be blind."

"I have perfect vision," I say.

"Well, I'm pretty sure you missed by a few feet," Celeste says. "You're much worse at this than I thought."

I sigh, my frustration returning. "Maybe you should just have the gun, I'm not cut out for this."

"Never mind," she says, deflecting my defeatism. "Here, hold it like this."

She repositions my hands, right hand holding the handle, left one cupped underneath the right, supporting it like a saucer.

"That's better," she says. "Line up the sights on the tree, and when you have it, ease the trigger back. Let it surprise you."

The gun shoots. I've missed again.

"Keep trying," Celeste says. "Take your time. Aim."

I summon patience this time. I just focus on being still, and I let the trigger surprise me like Celeste directed. The gun booms, bullet slamming squarely into the tree.

"Lucky," Pogo laughs.

"Lucky or not, it's progress," Celeste says. "Now you have a sporting chance of hitting something right in front of you. We'll keep working on this, but later. We have to go."

I remember Deena. "I saw her again," I say.

"Saw who?"

"Deena. She said there's a way for me to get back."

Pogo hops out of his tree and watches to see how Celeste will react.

"Just because there's a way doesn't mean it should be tried," she says.

"Why did you tell me there isn't a way if you knew there is?" I say.

"Because the way is nuts. It's completely crazy."

"I don't care," I say. "I have nothing to lose."

"You have a lot to lose Zak, more than you know."

Pogo begins to bounce up and down like he's agitated.

"How can I not try?" I say. "With your help, isn't it worth trying?"

"With our help," Celeste says. Her expression is distant, something similar to fear. "We've already helped you more than I care to admit."

I turn from her and look at the tree I just shot, the hole punched into its bark still smoking. From somewhere deep inside of me, primal anger, the rage of a desperate survivor, has emerged. The gun is somehow lighter in my hand, and I feel something I don't often feel: courage. I raise the gun with one hand, don't even concentrate, and pull the trigger like a madman. Blam blam! A third pull ends with only a click. The bullets are spent, and the tree is splintered, additional holes sizzled into the bark.

"Bonzuri!" Pogo shouts. He bounds up to the punctured tree to inspect it, then looks back at me in surprise. "Good."

"Definite progress," Celeste says. "Where did that burst of testosterone come from?"

"From me, I guess," I say, staring at the gun. I've surprised myself. But that felt really good.

"You need to let that angry guy outside more," Celeste says. "But let it work for you, not against you."

"I can try."

Celeste takes the gun from me, pops the cylinder, expels the empty casings, and hands the weapon back to me. I remove bullets from a pouch on my belt and begin to reload it.

"Now, about helping you get back home," Celeste says. "It's not that I'm jumping for joy to help, but somehow I still have some charity left. If you stop talking to the living, and if you avoid acting like an infant, we'll try to help you return."

"Really?" I say. I hadn't expected this.

She nods. Pogo looks worried by her decision, but he's silent about it.

"That's great, thank you. But do you know how to get there?"

"No," she says. My confidence deflates for a second. "*He* does."

She points to Pogo, who steps up to us, looks up at the sky, then turns around.

"Viamna," he says. He extends a blue finger to point out the direction. "Way," he says again. "A bad, bad way."

Gun reloaded, I shut the cylinder with a click.

15

RIVER OF DEATH

Pogo has found his stride, scouring a path through the jungle like a farm implement slicing up a hayfield. I think he enjoys ripping the rain forest to shreds, and he never tires or rests. We pick our way through the wreckage behind him.

Visibility in the jungle is a thing to behold, ten feet at best, nothing at all at worst. If something is in here with us, it would be child's play to ambush us, but I have to think Pogo's nose won't allow that. This doesn't mean I trust that with my life. My mind begins to see attackers that aren't there, to hear them slinking through the jungle beneath the sounds of Pogo's ruckus.

Then Pogo falls. More than that, the ground has opened up and swallowed him whole. I hear him grunt, followed by a curious rumble.

I feel myself leap back, nerves forcing me to the defensive. I hunch into a ball and stare toward where he fell.

Celeste bounds forward—she wouldn't think of cowering like me. She makes it to where Pogo has fallen and looks down. She's reaching for something, and I'm confused until I see one of Pogo's hands surface, pulling up on a vine. This is followed by his other hand, then his big blue head. Celeste can do little to help her friend, but he manages to pull himself up. He stands and looks down with bitterness toward where he fell. Celeste pats his arm to calm him.

Sensing that the danger has passed, I walk to them. The mystery of what consumed Pogo is solved when I see through the undergrowth that he nearly fell off a cliff hidden by the vegetation. I look down to see a river gorge a hundred feet below. He must have caught himself on the vine.

"Close one," Celeste says to Pogo. Eyes wide, he looks spooked by the prospect, but fear isn't something he allows for long. He growls down into the gorge, finishing it with a loathsome hiss that echoes down the canyon.

The gorge is fifty feet across, rough cliffs on both sides covered in beards of moss and ferns. Gushing water has cut this gorge over centuries, but the river flowing down its center is relatively tame at the moment. The green water drifts past like someone has dumped buckets of teal paint upstream. The river bottom can't decide whether to be deep or shallow, and the water bubbles onto rocks and slaps shoreline strewn with stones and driftwood. Darker points mark deeper holes, painting the river with spots like the back of a Burmese python.

"It's too damn dense around here," Celeste says. "We should follow along the gorge, keep an eye on it so none of us takes a nosedive down there."

I shrug to show my indifference, but she's talking to Pogo, not me. He answers by angling his course parallel to the edge of the gorge. He's not dwelling on the close call, and continues smashing his way through the rain forest.

I'm beginning to wonder if all demons are as relentless as Pogo. If so, do I really have a chance surviving the After much longer? I'm woefully outmatched. This leads to another realization. I try to sort it out in my mind but can't, so I try Celeste after a while: "I guess all the crazies back in the land of the living who believed in demons were right," I say. "Except the demons are here, in the After, and not with the living."

"Not quite," she says.

"No?"

"Sure, they exist here, but they can visit the living just like you can," she says. "All it takes is some idiot in the living world to allow them through."

"Why would anyone do that?" I ask.

"It's not intentional, unless you're stupid," she says. "Demons take advantage of weakness. If someone calls, on purpose or not, demons answer. If the demon is lucky, it can even attach itself to someone for long periods of time in the living world, feeding off the person's energy."

"Like a possession? *The Exorcist,* and all that?" I ask.

"Exactly," she says. "People who are possessed have a

big old demon sucking off them. No offense to the blue guy ahead of us, but demons are just big soul maggots."

"Pleasant," I say. "How would a person call a demon?"

"You might think you're praying, you might think you're talking to a dead loved one," she says. "You might flat out contact one, like through a seance or a Ouija board. Or you might invite one into your life without even knowing you did it, in times of suffering or stress."

"But if you lead a good life, have spirituality, clean living . . ."

"Sure, it all helps, but no one's safe. Everyone has times of weakness, and we all make mistakes, sometimes really bad ones. If you ever get back to the land of the living, get to know a priest or a shaman, or anyone who knows what demons hate. People have no idea what they're dealing with."

"Oh," I say. I regret asking about all of this. I begin to think about demons stalking my wife and daughters back home. Maybe Celeste senses this. "You can calm down though, there are plenty of things in life to get you. Car crashes, cancer, falling in the shower. All of those are just as likely to happen."

"Falling in the shower seems a tad more pleasant than being possessed," I say. There's no disagreement in her silence.

It's possible that the gorge is endless, a bonafide natural wonder if it existed on Earth. We follow along its edge for hours, listening to the river tumble over rocks, filling the air with tropical mist. Where is it all leading to? Probably nowhere at all.

I hear a waterfall before seeing it, the unceasing roar like radio static. Pogo and Celeste pay no mind to it, but I stop to look. Water spills over rocks and ledges, its course refined so that it resembles a complex machine of twisting, gushing foam. The water surges into a pool fifteen feet below the falls, where it mixes in a stew before continuing its journey downstream.

My gaze downriver catches hold of movement. There's something coming up the shoreline, too far away to tell what it is. It could be wind blowing at some vines instead of something coming this way, but I stare long enough to see it's not the wind. It's alive.

"Celeste," I call. She stops, turns, and looks at me, and I point to where I see the movement. "There's something down there."

She shades the sun from her eyes and peers downriver. Pogo stops from up ahead and realizes we're looking at something. He sniffs in the direction of the movement, picking up a scent. "The dead," he says.

"There's three of them," Celeste says.

"Three of what?" I ask.

"People. Others who've died and been brought here."

As they come closer into view, I see she's right. It's three people, all gray and black like Celeste. They're the dead, the fully dead, unlike my Half Dead self.

"Are they dangerous?" I ask.

"They're just people," she says. "No more dangerous than anyone you see on the street back home."

"Should we talk to them?"

"What would that do?" she says.

I shrug. I can't think of a reason, except to be friendly, which isn't on Celeste's agenda.

The people don't see or hear us because we're up too high. They walk along the rocky riverbank. As they come closer, I see that it's a man, woman, and child. The man is larger than the others and carries a long walking stick. I wonder if this is a family or just strangers banding together. I'd like to think they're a family, lost in life but at least they're together in death.

One of them begins to speak, the one that appears to be a woman, but I can't hear what she's saying. The man speaks next, his voice raising above hers, and I realize that they're arguing about something. The child walks ahead of them, uninterested in their conflict or fleeing from it.

"Lovely couple," Celeste whispers.

"He probably doesn't want to stop for directions," I whisper back. Celeste actually smiles from my joke.

Then the child screams. I flinch as the sound catches me off guard. She shrieks in shrill bursts as she runs back toward the two adults. I'm about to ask Celeste what's wrong with her when the girl's yelps give way to other sounds, the entire gorge coming to life with buzzing and thump-thumping. Demons.

Pogo growls and creeps tighter to the edge of the cliff as he scans the gorge and sniffs the air. Five demons step from the cover of boulders upstream, descend the rocks next to the falls, and rush toward the people. The people turn and run downriver only to be pushed back by more demons coming that way.

"They're trapped!" I say. I draw my gun.

"Are you nuts?" Celeste says, pulling the gun from my grasp.

"We should help," I say.

"That's just idiotic, even for you!" she says. "There's too many, and if you start shooting they'll know we're here!"

Mouth agape, I know she's right. I don't want to watch, but I can't help it.

Out ahead of the assault from the falls is a tiny demon, the smallest, skinniest I've yet seen, but also the fastest. Tiny is still much larger than any of the people. Its agility is boggling, its body a blur as it sweeps over the rocks toward its prey. Tiny reaches the man first. The man swings his stick in the air to keep the demon back, but this may as well be a toothpick waving at a charging grizzly. Tiny evades the blow, grabs the man around the waist, and tosses him into the side of the gorge. The man hits with a smack, his head bouncing off the rock, and he falls without another move.

A second demon charges past Tiny. This one's face is long and narrow, resembling the muzzle of a horse. In fact, the demon is altogether horse-like, with bulging black muscles and hoofed feet. As bizarre as this makes the demon appear, the creature is no less deadly. Horse Face pounces onto the woman, knocking her flat. Then the beast picks her up by the legs and dangles her like a Barbie doll. Just when I think Horse Face may swallow her like a piece of sushi, others swarm him, the woman falling from its grasp. The demons begin to pound each other while Tiny, the opportunist of the pack, sweeps in and steals the prize, sprinting upstream with the woman flung over its shoulder. There Tiny is mobbed by two stragglers closing in, and I lose sight of the woman from the fracas. All I know is she's a goner.

I'm horrified when a bearded demon rushes forward and grabs the little girl, who squawks at being caught. But this is temporary. A towering demon steps forward and howls at the bearded one. As if the large one's size isn't enough, two elephantine tusks protrude from its mouth, and it wags its head so the tusks cut through the air like swords. Outmatched, Beard drops the girl and steps away. The girl tries to run away, but Tusks snatches her up and holds her high. None of them want to challenge Tusks. By the looks of it, the creature is even larger than Pogo, so I hardly blame them. I really feel for that little girl in the clutches of something so ominous.

Tusks holds her in front of its face, and I turn away. I don't want to see the girl eaten. But a strange flicker of light makes me look again, and instead of a sickening feast I see a transformation. The girls shrivels while the demon expands and illuminates. Tusks seems to inhale her life, pulling out her vitality, leaving only her raw, deflated corpse behind. In seconds she's a wilted sack of flesh.

Finished with her, Tusks drops the girl's pathetic body. Her corpse flops onto the rocks like a battered sock puppet.

Another substantial demon emerges. Unlike any of the others, this one has four horns instead of two, and they scatter above its head like disheveled antennae. Four Horns finds the man's still unmoving body, lifts him up, and mimics what Tusks did to the girl. The odd transference comes again, the man deflating and the demon puffing out. Finished, Four Horns drops him, what's left of him, and belts out an energized victory roar.

I don't see the woman. The demons are still battling over what must be her upstream, but I've had enough. I finally turn away, and I wish I had done it sooner.

"Let's go," Celeste says. "They're gone, and we will be too if we hang out here."

"Good God, what the hell did they do to them?" I ask.

"They took their souls," she says. "And I'm not about to end up like that, so snap out of it and come on."

Pogo leads the way again. I take another look at the girl's body. If a human could shed its skin like a snake and leave it in a pile, it might look like that.

Demon bellows fill the gorge. They sound like they want more, like this meal of three was only a morsel. I leave them behind, not wishing to be the fourth, knowing I'll never be able to unsee what I just saw.

16

COLD

W e resume our slogging through the rain forest. When I nearly decide I'm fed up with this stifling place and its slapping leaves, everything vanishes, surrendering to the Shift. I still can't get used to it, but at least the Shift doesn't dawdle. Its odd magic comes and goes with precision, and we're plopped into the shock of our new location.

Snow. Everywhere is snow, so white I feel like I may never be able to process colors again. I couldn't have imagined a place so contrasting to the rain forest, tropical soup shoved aside by barren winter.

A ruthless wind sweeps icy slivers into my face that sting on impact, like hundreds of pinpricks. I can't see through the blizzard's gusts, but I don't think there's much to view anyway. The place is an expanse of boundless white, an empty nothingness.

The only comfort is my Half Dead body is semi-indifferent to the cold. I know this place rivals the arctic, but the cold feels no worse to me than a draft from an air conditioner. Celeste and Pogo are unaffected, like this is any other place to pass through, Pogo carving a path into the deep snow like a cutter ship.

"I feel like we're in the North Pole!" I shout to Celeste through the deafening wind.

"You won't find Santa Claus here!" she shouts back. "And I'm pretty sure we'd be on the naughty list anyway."

By *we*, I think she means herself and Pogo. But I begin to evaluate myself in that way, the way we were taught when we were kids: Am I going to be on the naughty list? Will Santa bring me coal?

I suppose boozing as much as I did would be a huge strike against me for Santa. And quitting my job was irresponsible. But it's not like I robbed a bank or murdered someone with a hatchet. I'm a little pathetic and helpless, but I'm not dangerous. Wouldn't far more ruthless people get top billing on the naughty list?

My point in trying to answer this absurd ethical question relates to my confusion about being tossed into the After. It feels like punishment. Maybe that's why I haven't felt right being here, because I don't feel evil. I've made mistakes, and I need to fix them, but I can't fix them from the After. So why go through all of this?

Sidetracked in thought, I don't notice that Celeste has stopped in front of me, and I almost run into her. She's halted because Pogo has stopped in front of her. I try to look past them, but the lack of visibility makes it impossible.

"Something wrong?" I ask. Celeste turns and shushes me, her index finger over her lips.

Demons? I mouth. She nods. I cringe and look around, remembering there's nothing to see. But do the demons know I'm here? Are they sensing me right now? Even with my friends right in front of me, being stuck in a snowstorm with the prospect of demons in the area feels very lonely.

Pogo looks like the Abominable Snowman, his blue body and hair so thick with snow that he's completely white. The snow gathers higher on his back and head while he stands still to allow his senses to scan ahead. I can't tell for sure, but I wonder if I hear buzzing in the background of the howling wind.

After several minutes of this waiting, Pogo turns and points toward the direction we've come. We begin to double back, and Pogo sets an aggressive pace. Those two are much faster than me. Now and again Celeste turns to urge me forward with a wave of her hand. Are the demons following? I have no way of knowing.

We trudge for at least an hour. The whole time I wonder whether I'll be overcome and mauled by sadistic monsters or if I'll keel over from a heart attack. The effort to keep up pulls at my chest. I'm heaving and puffing like an old steam engine. Almost at my breaking point, I realize that Pogo is slowing down, not from fatigue but maybe because we're safe again. If Pogo had detected demons, and I shouldn't doubt it, maybe we've eluded them for now.

Our retreat takes us into a pass with icy peaks on each side. There are actually trees here, hearty conifers, protected from this ungodly weather by being wedged in the lowlands between the peaks. I'm amazed that anything can live here.

I need to rest, and I'm grateful that Celeste realizes this.

"We're safe, for now," she says. "Let's take a break. And you really need to work on your cardio."

Pogo grunts, either in agreement or to mock me, steam coming from his nostrils and hovering in the air before vanishing like a ghost.

"If I get home, I'll join a gym," I say, sitting with my back propped against a sturdy cedar. I blow into my hands for warmth.

"Is the cold affecting you?" she asks.

"A little," I say. "It's weird, I should be a Popsicle in this place."

"It's been years since I've felt cold," Celeste says. "Felt anything."

Pogo begins to gather firewood by breaking dead branches from the surrounding trees and scooping up the pieces. In minutes he has a substantial pile, which he sets close to me. Celeste digs a hole in the snow with her hands, picks out some smaller pieces of wood, and builds a small teepee for a fire. I'm curious how she intends to light it, but that's answered when she closes her eyes and touches one of the sticks. Her hand glows blue and the stick begins to smolder. A simple flicker of flame follows, which tickles the other pieces into a healthy blaze.

"Interesting way to start a fire," I say. When the flame begins to fade, Pogo bends down and blows on it, his cloud of breath fanning oxygen until the fire recovers, snapping and hissing as the flames leap high. Celeste feeds the fire with larger pieces of wood.

I put my hands toward the fire and feel its warmth, realizing that I'm colder than I thought. "All we need now is marshmallows," I say.

"I'm fresh out," Celeste says. "I can't even remember what one tastes like. Doesn't matter, food is useless now."

"I was a big fan of burgers," I say. "With guacamole, tomato, some mushrooms. Onion rings on the side."

"Half Dead eats no more," Pogo says. "Nec manduku-la." He knows I don't need to eat, so he figures it's unnecessary to think about it. Maybe demons know nothing about fantasies.

"There was nothing like a good pepperoni pizza," Celeste says. At least she knows what it's like to dream.

"Pepperoni, spinach, and onions," I add. Celeste looks at me like I've said something vile. "Or just pepperoni," I say. "Nothing wrong with that."

"Maybe I could call in an order," I continue, tossing a twig into the flames. "Pepperoni for you, with onion and spinach for me, and about six hundred larges for Pogo. Is there delivery in the After?"

"Not unless you're okay with the delivery guy stealing your soul," Celeste says.

The flames devour the dry arctic wood, and the blaze envelops the area with heat.

"So what are we journeying toward exactly?" I ask. "I'm thinking about *The Lion, the Witch, and the Wardrobe*."

"The what and the what?" Celeste asks.

"Well, it's a book. There was a movie. Anyway, some kids go to Narnia, this wintry, magical land, and they get there by going through a passageway through an enchanted wardrobe."

"Corny book plots aside, we do need to find a passageway," she says. "A portal, to be exact."

"And Pogo knows where this is?"

"He says he does."

"How does anyone know their way around here?"

"That way," Pogo says, pointing in the direction we had been heading.

"When you've been in the After as long as he has, it's not so hard," Celeste says. "Think of getting to a location as something like using a big combination lock. To find the way, you have to travel through the right sequence."

"I don't get it," I say.

"Your location before the Shift affects your location after the Shift. Let's say, back in the rain forest, we went in the opposite direction. Maybe instead of this subzero nightmare we would have ended up in a bayou. Pogo knows which direction to travel in order to get to the next place he wants after the Shift. It's no different from memorizing relationships between freeways, except there are millions of them and none of them are marked. But he's old enough that he knows many of the ways. All demons do."

"That way," Pogo repeats. "We'll go there, but the way is a very bad way."

"Why is it bad?" I ask him.

Pogo begins to gesture for us with his arms. "We will walk through hot lands and fire rocks," he says, waving his hand, spittle leaking from his mouth. "Then aqmaj, deep and dark water, and then tall pavernga. We go to the terrible tall cave. A bad, bad way, not a good way."

"He doesn't like where we're going," Celeste says. "None of the demons do. It's only a place for people like you, the Half Dead. Think of somewhere you fear most, and that's what he's feeling."

"I never liked public restrooms," I say.

"Okay, that's an awful example," she says. "How about a public restroom submerged in rancid, alligator-infested water with no exit and fire everywhere?"

"That would be worse," I admit.

"You wanted to do this Zak," she says. "It won't be fun, but it's best not to dwell on what it'll be like."

"If it gets me home, I'd travel right through hell," I say.

"You might not be too far off," she says.

"Go," Pogo says, pointing in the direction he wants. "This way. We have to go now."

"He's right," Celeste says. "Let's get a move on."

Pogo stomps on the fire with his foot, sending embers sizzling into the surrounding snow, snuffing out the bulk of the blaze. Then he kicks heaps of snow onto it, finishing the job. Smokey the Bear would be proud, but forest fires aren't his concern. He's erasing evidence that we've been here.

We leave our spot behind. I'm reluctant, like leaving a warm bed in the early morning. The icy peaks seem to be looking down at us from above, watching us crunch through the snow, waiting for something.

17

ATTACKED

The pass swallows us. Perpetual winter has piled snow deep into the pass's trough, its cocoon shutting out wind and sound. I hear each icy crunch of our steps bounce off the steep slopes surrounding us. The tallest of the peaks juts upward to our left, icicles clinging to it like banners atop a tower.

I watch Pogo push through the snow, comforted that his unflappable brawn leads the way. But then he stops, hunches, and gazes up at the peaks, vapors of breath drifting from his nose and mouth. Celeste and I also stop and look. I feel my innards constrict, entangled in the notion that something's wrong again.

Pogo sniffs the air like a buck in the crosshairs of a hunter. As if in response to his suspicion, we hear a subtle chorus of sound resembling the grating chirp of crickets. As the sound intensifies, it mutates into something more sinister: a growl, then a roar from somewhere high. The perfect acoustics of the pass allows us to pinpoint the source, a large figure standing on top of the highest peak. Then the roar fades to a chorus of buzzing thump-thumps. One by one, more figures step into view on the peaks all around us.

"Oh . . . oh damn," I say. I'm trying to count the demons. I get to eleven before I realize it doesn't matter, we're woefully outnumbered.

Pogo shouts to them in his demon language and steps forward, his flailing arms catching snow and scattering it into clouds. I feel the vibrations of his yell like it might dislodge my spine from my body. But whatever he said has no impact on the demons. Their numbers swell until we're looking at an army of demons surrounding us from above. They shout down in response to Pogo, their medley of taunts dwarfing his.

"What do we do?" I say.

Celeste turns to me: "Time for that angry guy of yours."

"I'm pretty sure a million of my angry guys won't make much of a difference."

She grabs my arm and repositions me between her and Pogo. "Aim and fire when they're close enough. You'll be okay."

I want to believe her, but I definitely don't feel like I'll be okay. Celeste removes her sling and loads it with one of her stones. Pogo begins to bounce in anticipation of a fight. Then we watch as the demons bound down the peaks—hundreds of them—their growls and thump-thumps like barbarian war cries. We may as well be waiting for a nuclear inferno to sweep down and vaporize us.

The demons make quick work of their descent. Three charge ahead of the others, the trio close enough that I hear their panting and grunting. Celeste twirls her sling, leather whistling through the air to build momentum, then unleashes the stone. This is so innocuous to them that they ignore it, but that costs them. The stone bludgeons one in the chest with the force of a bazooka, blowing the demon back into the slope and tossing the other two senseless. The eruption of snow and fire excites Pogo into screaming fits. He yells more insults and points and laughs at the fallen corpses.

"Pogo!" Celeste shouts. When he looks, she points to two more coming from our right. "Less taunting, more fighting!"

Pogo understands, and he runs off to meet them. The closest one to him has a set of long teeth that dominate his face like rickety planks of an old cottage. Teeth chattering in the excitement of battle, the demon races forward to meet Pogo. Anyone else would be intimidated by those teeth, but to Pogo, they're an irresistible target. Pogo clobbers Teeth with a meaty fist to the demon's maw, shattering the teeth to pieces. The demon falls away, whimpering and holding its wrecked mouth.

The second demon is a shrieking, flailing, bag of bones, like the thing hasn't consumed a soul in years. Ribs and cheekbones protrude from its skin, and its entire body shakes with desperate hunger. Bony jumps onto Pogo's back, wraps a skeletal arm around Pogo's neck, and pounds the side of Pogo's head with its other hand. Pogo's eyes roll back from strangulation, while each blow induces a wince. At first I fear he's beaten, but I'm always wrong when I doubt Pogo. He raises an arm and shoves his elbow back, catching the demon in the chest. Bony detaches and flops flat. Pogo lunges and stomps on Bony's head like extinguishing the campfire back at the conifers. This only excites Pogo more, and he jumps on Bony's neck and chest, howling with each earthshaking stomp until the demon is sufficiently crushed.

Teeth is standing again. He's damaged beyond repair, but outrage has taken over. He leaps for Pogo from behind, but Pogo turns to meet him, clawing a gash into Teeth's jaw. Teeth is stupefied that his face has taken another blow, and the hesitation allows Pogo to grab him by the neck and slam him to the ground. There the stomping begins anew, Teeth helpless against Pogo's savagery.

Celeste lets another rock fly, the weapon's ridiculous power again scattering a pack of demons with a resounding blast. She reloads patiently, no shortage of demons bearing down, and picks them apart with another well-timed shot.

I remember to draw my pistol. I wave it toward the charging demons, but it feels inadequate to what Pogo and Celeste can do.

"Are you gonna shoot or just point?" Celeste says, loading another stone. She lets it fly, the explosion pulverizing two more.

I hear a grunt from behind me. I turn to see a demon rushing forward, complex horns flowing from its head like a stag's rack. I aim and fire, but either I miss or the bullet has no effect. Stag continues to rush through the snow with its red eyes affixed on me, and I try to remain calm as I pull the trigger again and again. I know I'm hitting Stag now because the beast jolts as if stung by bees, yet still keeps coming. My final shot hits it in the cheek, and I see blood flow down Stag's neck. The creature claws at the wound and bellows, but still comes.

Pogo intercepts Stag right in front of me. The stench of Stag's hot breath is appalling, its roar so violent that I wince. Pogo grabs Stag's leg with both hands and snaps it like a cracker, the raw pop of bone followed by Stag's miserable howl. Pogo then lifts Stag and tosses the creature into another charging demon, and they collide and drop. Pogo is making this whole attack look silly, at least for the moment.

Celeste is twirling her sling again, but before she can fire, a demon sideswipes her and brings her down, rock flying off target and exploding in nearby snow. The demon maintains hold of her and pins her to the ground like a lion to a baby gazelle.

"Celeste!" I shout, but we're being overrun now. Something hits me from behind and I fall face-first into the snow. I'm temporarily blinded by the snow, but I can hear demons everywhere.

I'm pulled from the snow, huge demon hands clutching my waist from behind. I shake the snow from my face and feel the demon's breath on the back of my neck. In front of me, I see Celeste's limp body being pulverized by two demons. I feel a tormented yell coming up from my throat, but before I can let it out, there's another jostle, and I'm free from the demon's grasp. Pogo has tackled the demon that held me, and now he's tearing the creature apart with the brutality of a wolf mauling a bunny. I almost pity the demon as Pogo eviscerates it, gouges out its eyes, and then stomps the bloody hell out of the thing. A crowd of attackers is circling us, but they're wary of what Pogo can do to them, so they keep their distance.

Job done, Pogo goes for the demons attacking Celeste. They scatter, leaving her crumpled in the snow, but Pogo tackles one and begins beating it senseless.

I don't want to see the violence anymore, so instead I look to Celeste. I'm amazed and pleased when I see her move. But one of the surrounding demons is brave enough to seize the opportunity. He knows Celeste is battered and Pogo is occupied, and he rushes to attack her. Celeste sees him. She stands on battered legs and pulls a rock from her pouch. There's no time to load it into the sling, so instead she heaves it. By the time she does, the demon is much too close, almost on top of her. The demon is blown back, and Celeste is flung in the opposite direction. She lands near me in the snow, crooked and broken.

In the background of the chaos comes an undeniable rumble. Pogo has finished his work and looks for another target when a dozen more demons come upon us and circle. But instead of looking at us, they look upward to the strange sound coming from the peak to our left. I look, too, and can't understand what I'm seeing at first. It's a white wave that paints the side of the mountain with a cloud of cotton, and it's coming fast. Then I understand. It's an avalanche set in motion by Celeste's latest blast.

"Oh good Lord!" I shout.

Pogo looks at me, then Celeste, then the dozens of demons eyeing the oncoming avalanche. He's formed a plan in that tormented noodle of his, but what? He hops to us, lifts Celeste and me as if we weigh nothing, holds us under his arms like two footballs, and sprints away from the impending trajectory of the avalanche. We'll never make it—I can see that the wave is much faster than he is. But he looks determined, our lives literally in his hands, and he passes through the ring of the surrounding demons without them offering a fight.

But I've underestimated Pogo again. He runs like a track star, g-forces pulling my head back as we go. I look back to see some of the demons following us, bounding for the same means of escape. But they've understood too late, and they're slower than Pogo, so we gain a lead.

Ahead I see the heart of Pogo's plan. He's aiming for a ridge perpendicular to the slope that forms a natural trough. If we can make it over the ridge in time, it might shield us from the avalanche. I'm not sure if we can. I can't look. I close my eyes and try to wish all of this away. But I hear the avalanche collapsing fast, drowning out all other sound and thought.

I open my eyes just as Pogo leaps to the protection of the ridge, tumbling over with us to safety. The avalanche flows along the other side, as if we're on the safe side of a natural levee.

There we hunker, ground quaking like the entire mountain is collapsing right next to us. A cloud of powdery snow drifts up, spraying our faces with cold moisture, but we're safe, both Celeste and me in the protection of Pogo's huge arms. The demons behind us have been wiped clean from existence.

I close my eyes again to tolerate nature's rage. Like the end of a bad dream, the noises begin to fade until soon it's silent.

I open my eyes to see Celeste's face, eyes staring at me with cold emptiness.

"Celeste?" I say, reaching to touch her face. She's still and silent. "Celeste?" I say again, placing my palm on the side of her head. Pogo stirs and looks at his friend. He gives her a gentle shake, but her body doesn't respond, eyes still open like she's viewing something vague.

She's gone.

Pogo has rescued us, but it's too late for her. He sets her in the snow like laying a baby into a crib.

"No, Celeste!" I say. "This was my fault. They were after me."

Pogo turns like he wants to tell me something when a demon bounds over the ridge on top of him, spilling me from his grasp. Somehow the attacker has dodged the avalanche, the surprise of it taking Pogo off guard. The attacker reminds me of a wolfman with his shaggy head and protruding snout. He bites Pogo's neck and tears off a hunk of blue skin, then claws Pogo's back wide open. Pogo counters by lifting Wolf and slamming him headfirst into the snowy ground. When I suspect he'll stomp Wolf to demon paste, two more demons leap over the ridge and jump Pogo like thugs in an alley, biting and clawing as they cling to his trunk and limbs.

I still have the gun in my hand, but I remember it's empty. I fumble with my belt to find more bullets. As I do, the bloodiest death match I've yet seen unfolds, all three demons maiming and pounding Pogo. They screech like boars tussling over barnyard slop as I pop the empties from the cylinder and reload the gun. Chambers loaded, I step up to the mayhem. From six feet away, I aim at the head of the demon holding Pogo's back and shoot. The gun lifts with each shot, but I fight to bring it back down, emptying all six shots into the demon's brain. This pries the demon from Pogo, and it claws at its head, not understanding the irritation of bullets. Then the creature continues to scrap as if nothing happened.

As patiently as I can, I reload. This time I take aim at Wolf and pump all six rounds into his head. I'm dismayed by the insignificance of my bullets, but my scant help is all the advantage Pogo needs. Wolf steps aside and looks back at me in agitation. Pogo summons a primal screech, shoves one demon into the snow, drops another with a shattering kick to the shin, and tackles Wolf. This surge invigorates Pogo, allows him to seize the upper hand, and he doles out equal turns mauling each demon. Then, for a few minutes, he stomps and batters and crushes his opponents to death. He explodes to a place he's tried to leave, once again embracing the total demon he is, his sliver of goodness escaping in the winter wind.

Once the three demons are obliterated, Pogo wobbles toward me. Only then can I see how mangled he is, blood dripping down every slope of his flesh, hunks of skin missing. Even worse, he's looking at me like all demons do: like I'm a target.

"Pogo," I say. "It's okay, you've beaten them. Easy, buddy."

He roars at me, the wounded animal he's become forcing his muscles to clench like he's ready to pounce.

"No!" Celeste says as loud as she can muster. She's still alive! Pogo heeds her command and bounds over to her. He inspects her, helpless to do anything else.

"Away," she whispers to him. "Take us away."

Pogo scoops her up with all the care he possesses, then he comes for me. I'm reluctant to let him pick me up in his condition, but I don't have a say in the matter. Luckily for me, he's come to his senses, and he lifts me and trots away with us, looking over his shoulder for more demons. I look, too, and see no more coming, the rest truly engulfed by the avalanche.

Pogo limps up the pass. We teeter with each scuffling step, but he succeeds in getting us far from the avalanche. It's progress, but I can see that our situation is dire. Celeste doesn't speak again, has closed her eyes and not moved, and Pogo might collapse soon.

Pogo knows this, too. He's been looking for something, and in time he spots what he wants along the slope of the pass. He stumbles his way toward it, and once we're closer, I can see it's the mouth of a cave.

Pogo enters the cave and sets me down. I watch as he lays Celeste on the cave floor, her body still not moving. Then he begins stacking boulders in front of the cave entrance. His breathing is labored, and each stone he stacks takes a toll. But one by one, he seals us in, and in minutes it's as black as night. Then I hear him fall with a defeated groan.

I remember my cell phone in my pocket. I pull it out and turn it on. It still has some battery left. I turn on the flashlight app, and it lights up the cave. Pogo lies on the ground from his wounds and exhaustion, his chest heaving with exertion. Celeste is lying prone on the rocky floor, and I go to her. She, too, is breathing, but barely. Somehow she's still clutching her sling, and I remove it from her hand and set it next to her. There's nothing I can do for either of them. I listen to the wind coming through the cracks in the boulders, and hope I won't hear the thump-thump of demons. For now it's just the wind, and we're safe. I sit next to Celeste and run my hand through her hair, touch her battered cheek.

"I know you wanted me to stop saying I'm sorry," I whisper to her. "But I'm so sorry for this."

The only response is the continuous whistling of the wind through the cracks in the boulders.

18

CAVE

I find a lonely routine in the darkness of the cave. To conserve the power in my phone, I only turn on the light every couple of hours and cast it across Pogo and Celeste. I watch their labored breathing and wonder if they'll survive, trying to think of something I can do for them. The best I've done hours ago was remove my holster and prop it under Celeste's head. It's probably the worst pillow she's ever had, but it makes me feel like she's a little more comfortable. The routine continues with me turning off the phone and enduring another couple hours of darkness by thinking about a relaxing place: reading a book on a blanket spread over a grassy meadow or relaxing next to a fireplace over a pint in the pub of a ski lodge. Invariably that trance is broken when the wind whistles through the rocks at the cave entrance, and I wonder if I'm hearing demons. Each time, I rationalize that it's just the wind, and we're safe behind Pogo's impenetrable wall.

To break up the pattern, I steal a moment to turn on my phone and look at photos of my family, pictures I took over the last couple years of my life. Most of them focus on the twins, Kaitlyn and Lacy making funny faces at the camera. There's one of Angie, too, a passive smile on her face as she poses across the dinner table on her birthday. Angie's expression tells me a lot. There's concern there, dissatisfaction with something, and it reminds me of seeing her at my graveside. *What happened?* she seems to be telling me with her eyes. Everything in her expression signals that she's wondering what consumed the man she married.

A notice pops up on my phone saying that I only have five percent of the battery left. What will I do when the power runs out? I'll be blind in the darkness with no way to check on Celeste and Pogo. I turn the phone off again.

What was it Celeste had said about energy in the After? Something about opening yourself to it, letting it in, and once inside you, energy can be transferred. This is as puzzling to me as reading instructions for splitting an atom. I don't know where to begin. But I decide to try. I close my eyes and imagine Celeste guiding me through it like some grizzled sorceress, telling me to breathe and think of a pure white light of energy entering my head from above, flowing into my body like filling an empty vessel. I don't know for how long I imagine this, but I'm giving it an honest to goodness try, concentrating on nothing but energy and its permeation through every cell of my body. I might be imagining things, but after a prolonged effort, I begin to feel something: a revitalization of sorts, a clarity of mind and a surge of energy from my chest, ripples of impulses streaming through my core and into my extremities.

I open my eyes, surprised and exhilarated by the prospect of success. I turn on the phone and see the red power bar indicating that the battery has very little energy left. I have to transfer my newfound energy to it, but how? I stare at it, eyes wide, willing my energy into it. Nothing. Transferring energy seems like a much bigger fish to fry than absorbing it. But I keep at it, doing everything I can think of to power that phone. Still nothing. I'm frustrated when I see the phone go completely dead, the darkness of the cave taking over, the lonely whistling of the wind all my senses can identify.

"Zak," Celeste whispers through the darkness. I reach for her, find her shoulder and grip it.

"I'm here," I say.

"Keep trying," she says. I didn't realize she was watching me.

"Okay," I say. "Are you going to be all right?"

She doesn't answer.

I spend what must be hours more with my phone. It feels futile, and maybe deep down I'm doubting this will even work, but I'm on my own in a dark cave with time to kill, so I persevere. I have to tend to my friends, and I can only manage that with light.

Celeste doesn't speak again during my efforts, and I begin to think her words were just some semiconscious delirium. Even so, I'm encouraged by the sentiment anyway. She thinks I can do it, so why can't I?

Then, while I'm staring into the void of the cave, thinking nothing but sending energy to my phone, the screen flickers on and off. I look down at it in shock. It wasn't my imagination, the phone absolutely lit for a millisecond. I stare at it, watching like a fisherman waiting for a lunker to take the bait, and then it does. The screen lights and stays lit.

"There you go," Celeste whispers. "Nice work, professor."

I don't know what surprises me more, that Celeste is conscious again or that I've succeeded.

"I guess I can be taught," I say. "How long have you been awake?"

"I've been here," she says. "Healing."

I remember the pounding she took. *Healing* feels like a gross understatement. She needs extensive surgery and a hospital, neither of which exist for us anymore.

"I wish I could help somehow," I say. Powering a phone is one thing. I doubt I could heal a person with my meager skills.

"There's nothing you can do," she says. "Anyway, we're okay."

"Neither of you looks okay," I say.

"Looks are deceiving," she says. "Inside we're healing at an incredible rate."

"I was worried you'd die."

"I'm already dead, remember?"

"Right," I say. "Confusing semantics. What I meant was, I was worried you'd die again."

"We'll manage," she says. "Thanks to Pogo. If he hadn't come to the rescue, that avalanche would have been the end."

"I still don't know how you survived that beating."

"It takes a lot to kill a person. To die again, as you put it. Pogo is especially hard to kill, the big oaf. He's the James Bond of demons."

"Are you in much pain?"

"Yes. But not as much as you'd think. Pain is just as dulled as everything else. It's not like pain in the living world."

"I'm pretty sure when I died it was the worst pain I'd ever felt," I say. "I'd always hoped for a much more peaceful death."

"I died in a car accident," Celeste says. I'm stunned that she offers this private detail.

"Was it quick?" I'm worried that she'll snap at me for prying, but I'm sensing she's ready to share.

"Of course not," she says. "It was long and excruciating."

"I'm sorry," I say, then put my hand over my mouth like I've just said a swear word. I keep forgetting that she doesn't like me saying that.

"Me too," she says. "I regret that day of my life above all others."

"Well, it was probably just your time," I say.

"It shouldn't have been. It was my fault."

"People make mistakes driving," I say. "Just drive through Boston sometime."

"No," she sighs. "It was much more than a mistake."

I wait for her to find the words, not wanting to pressure her. She continues: "I was troubled throughout my life. Angry. Impulsive. And I was having a really bad day. Bad days and sports cars don't play well together."

"Did you drive off the road?"

"I was going over a hundred on the freeway just after rush hour. I lost control, jumped the median, slammed head-on into another car. A family of five. We smashed together so tightly that it was like both cars merged into one. I killed them. All of them, and eventually myself. They died instantly, but my death was slow, pinned in that mess. I remember every agonizing second. I think I was made to feel everything for what I did."

"Good God." I have nothing else to offer.

Celeste raises her hand to her face and rests her palm on her forehead. "I can still see those people, all five of them in the oncoming car, like it just now happened. That feeling will always be there, nagging at me, reminding me."

"Sort of your scarlet letter."

Celeste looks at me, confused. She's never heard of the reference. I venture an explanation: "It's from a book. *The Scarlet Letter.* Hester Prynne is a Puritan woman who commits adultery. The village learns of this and forces her to wear an embroidered scarlet letter *A* on her dress, so everyone knows what she did and she can never forget it."

"Doesn't seem like a very harsh punishment," Celeste says.

"It was if you were a Puritan. They weren't fond of being reminded of their sins."

"You and your books," she says. "If only my punishment was to wear a damn letter."

In the silence I begin to think about the idea of forgiveness. If ever there was a person who needed it, it's Celeste.

"You know, I've thought a lot about God since I got here," I say. "I mean, there has to be a God, right?"

"Very unlikely," she says.

"I think there is. What's he doing with us here? In the After?"

Celeste looks like she doesn't know where I'm going with this, and only shrugs.

"Well, in Sunday school I was taught that God forgives us," I say.

"So you've gone from a bookworm to Sunday school teacher in less than a minute," she says. "Sunday school is brainwashing, you know that, right?"

"I don't know," I say. "I do believe God forgives, in time."

"Okay, I'm pretty sure that, if God exists, he wouldn't forgive me," she says.

"What if you're wrong?" I say. "Wouldn't it be better

to think there's a chance he forgives you? That there's a chance even those people in the car forgive you?"

Her troubled stare warns me that I've gone too far again. "Not a chance," she says. "I took everything from those people. Young, hopeful, happy people. I swept them away in a millisecond with my misery. You have no idea what that's like, or what you're talking about, as usual."

She's returned to her old, angry self, spilling into a rant: "No one ever gave me a break, right from when I was born, so I'm not expecting one now. So don't get all Sunday school on me. You're wasting both of our time."

"But . . ."

"Just forget about it, I shouldn't have told you about the accident."

"Okay," I say.

She closes her eyes and goes silent. I watch her, trying to understand her, but I know there's still much about her I don't grasp. I also close my eyes. I try to think of other things: a tropical beach where the waves roll in green-blue and caress my feet with warm foam, Angie at my side, my life as it once was. But the whistling wind in the cave reminds me that I'm still far from home.

19

OUT

It's a game now, a challenge to restore power to my phone like filling a crossword with letters. But I'm far better at crosswords, and I'm still very much a novice at the transference of energy. I keep the phone off most of the time to conserve the battery, pouring all of my concentration into it while it's idle. The battery percentage slowly ticks upwards, my success measured one point at a time.

I find it difficult to concentrate on a single abstract task for hours on end, so I rest between bouts of intense focus. Deep in a daydream during a break, eyes closed, a sound captures my attention, something large rubbing across the rocks. Is it demons outside the cave trying to find a way in? I sit up and listen.

No, this is *inside* the cave, I can tell by how close and clear it sounds. The scuffling is followed by an unsettling howl, an injured animal attempting to shake off its wounds. Pogo.

I turn on my phone and point the light forward, scanning for movement. The beam finds Pogo's eyes, two floating red spheres locked in on me. The eyes squint, bothered by the light but entranced by opportunity. Pogo is hunched, head lowered like a lion stalking. He's partially revived from his wounds, but something is entirely wrong with him. The evil still in his bones has seized control.

I shine the light toward Celeste, but somehow Pogo's howl didn't penetrate her deep healing trance. She lies still, except for her chest slowly rising and falling.

"Hey, Celeste? Something's wrong with Pogo here," I say. She doesn't acknowledge me, her body frozen in convalescence.

I move the light back on Pogo while I remember that my gun and holster are still serving as Celeste's pillow. Pogo moves laterally, eyes still focused on me. I've become his target and he won't relinquish his stare, saliva beginning to drip from his mouth.

"Pogo, it's me," I say, stepping back to the wall of the cave. "Zak. Friend."

There's no negotiating with a demon, and at the moment, Pogo is all demon. He begins to buzz like the others do, the thump-thump of energy transforming his blue body into a glow of yellow and then blood red. He shrieks, provoked by my words, then charges at me, a perfect blend of speed and mass. I dive to the side as he collides with the wall behind me, shaking the entire cave, bringing loose stones and dirt onto his back.

"Pogo, stop!" Celeste has finally stirred, and how couldn't she? It's like a tank has just plowed into a supermarket. Despite her injuries, she stands but she looks like she's ninety and hasn't stood in years. I stumble into the center of the cave, selfishly putting her between me and her malfunctioning beast. Pogo writhes to his feet, rocks and dust scattering from his body. Now he howls at Celeste, his new target.

"Pogo!" she shouts. But he charges, and Celeste just stands there, the epitome of calm, palm out like a traffic cop trying to halt a runaway bus. I hope this act of bravado will amount to something, but I can tell it doesn't have a chance. He rams into her with a sickening smack. I dive away while he drives Celeste across the cave and crushes her into the boulders that seal the cave entrance. The cave shakes again as Pogo and his impromptu battering ram punches a hole through the boulders, spilling in sunlight. They tumble outside into a heap, Pogo's rage exploding in devilish wails as he drags her far out into the snow.

I pull myself up and step to the entrance. I fight for sight through the blinding sun and glistening snow. Once adjusted, I see Pogo on top of Celeste twenty feet out, holding her there like a cat with a mouse, roaring up at the sky as if the sunlight pains him.

I have to do something. I jump out into the snow.

"Pogo, here!" I shout. He turns to look at me, the expression on his face pure evil and rage. He peels himself off Celeste and begins his slouched, lateral pacing, circling closer to me, my Half Dead scent too much for him to ignore.

"Calm, Pogo," I say, holding out my hand. "Friend, remember? Zak? Your best buddy the Half Dead?"

Pogo shakes his head to refuse his rational side. He crouches deeper, building inertia to spring at me and pulverize me into pudding. I have to try to dodge him again, but I don't know if I can. He launches himself at me, and I make my dive, but it won't work this time, I know it.

Then there's an explosion. Pogo launches skyward while I'm tossed to my back. I see Pogo fly over me, his body flailing midflight. He crashes headfirst into the boulders beside the cave entrance, falling flat on his back, as lifeless as the snow underneath his body.

I look the other way to see Celeste on her knees, empty sling in her hand. She's launched one of her rock grenades at Pogo. I stand, stare at her, then back at Pogo in disbelief, backing away from him in fear that he'll rise again.

"Pogo you big dumb blue son of a bitch!" Celeste calls. Then she slumps face first into the snow.

"Celeste!" I run to her. When I reach her side, I'm afraid to touch her, but I have to turn her over or she may suffocate. I take my time moving her, lifting her head from the snow with care and rolling her onto her back. Her eyes are open, and I can see the breath stream from her lips in the cold.

"Celeste?" I say again.

"Pogo gets a little punchy when he's hurt," she whispers.

"A little punchy," I repeat. "Are you okay?"

"Give me a while," she says.

"Will the punchy, um, go away?" I say, looking toward Pogo.

"Decent chance," she says, and passes out.

Well this is just a terrific time. My nervous system is a shambles from the flushing of adrenaline. Like a convict tasting the harsh realities of prison life for the first time, I deduce that I'm still not used to the intensity of the After.

Like a fool, I allow my panic to control me. I'm no longer safe around Pogo, and I run into the cave to retrieve my gun. I reattach the belt to my waist and move outside to watch the wind blow snow in drifts over our de facto camp. I see Pogo quiver on some demonic impulse, and it's enough to send me fleeing from this place. But where? For now I just run across the pass, not looking back, wondering how long I can afford to be on my own again.

I scale a peak on the other side of the pass, my surplus energy making easy work of the ascent at first, but I begin to tire halfway up. (Celeste is right, my cardio needs work.) Just what am I doing anyway? Where can I go? Sit on top of the peak? Then what?

I find a boulder to sit, rest, and observe. The magnificent sunlight is almost warm, but it decides too soon to depart behind a cover of ominous clouds floating down the pass. I watch as a storm front sweeps in, darkening the white landscape in shadows. Snow begins to fall, the pretty kind that flutters, the kind that kids can catch on their tongues. So I try it, catching flakes on my tongue like a child, like my daughters might do, feeling the chilly prickles of snow melt in my mouth and disappear. This begins to calm me, my voice of reason returning.

I'm running away again, like I always do. Like I did with my job and my family, like I do whenever there's something in my way. Down in the pass I can see the specks of Celeste and Pogo being buried by the coat of falling powder, and it begins to feel wrong to leave them there. But I can't help them, can I? And I know they can't help me at the moment.

I fester in indecision, watching the storm have its way. The wind hurls the snow down the pass like it's applying a fresh coat of white paint. If this were a view from a warm winter cottage it would be breathtaking, but instead it's foreboding.

I know I didn't just hear a demon. It was the whistling wind pumping through the pass like an enormous horn announcing the blizzard's arrival. But somewhere out there in the obscurity of white came a noise, and in my current state of mind, all unknown noises are demons. Visibility is now only a matter of feet. I can't even make out the base of the peak I'm on, much less Pogo and Celeste across the way.

I stand and listen, again hearing what must be the instruments of the wind, but the translation in my head is something far more sinister, something that tells me to move.

I begin to hop down the peak, coordination all but lost through the steep slope and rushing snow. It was inevitable that I would fall, but it still surprises me when it happens, my shin catching a rock hidden beneath the powder. I tumble the rest of the way down, and I imagine myself looking like a video of an extreme skier gone wrong. I feel every bounce, fight to recover, and fail in totality, until the slope plops me into the snowy blanket of the pass.

I've defied logic. Motionless on my rump, somehow I'm unhurt from my ludicrous descent. I stand and begin to push through the storm again toward what I hope is where I left Celeste. I should at least try to bring her to the cave and out of this wretched weather.

The Shift has other plans. Darkness smothers my surroundings, disintegrating the falling flakes and powdery landscape from view. I cry out but can't hear myself through the roar of the blizzard I'm leaving behind, and I'm driven to my knees by the confusion.

"Celeste!" I yell. She must be near by now, but can she hear me?

The light returns with a dry heat, like I've been yanked from a freezer and tossed into an oven. I reach down to clutch what had been snow, but as my eyes adjust I see it's sand, hot and smooth, so fine it squeezes through my grasping fingers.

I'm in a desert.

And I'm not alone. Pogo is right in front of me, eyes widening at the delight of my scent and flesh placed on a sandy platter at his feet. He buzzes like a power line. When he growls it jostles my brain against my skull as I fall onto my back, kicking up sand as I try to crab-walk away from him.

He pounces. I'm done for.

20

SHE RETURNS TO ME

Pogo is on top of me, mashing me into the sand with his colossal weight, sparing a second to revel in the kill. But Celeste has appeared from nowhere. I see her hand touch a glowing energy rock to the side of Pogo's head, and he stiffens.

"Pogo, off!" she demands. "Don't make me blow you up again."

He steps away from me, Celeste raising the rock in her hand above her head like a quarterback, ready to heave it at him. But she doesn't have to.

"Pogo, cessavu utu," she says. Her words are calmer, the tone that a horse trainer would use to settle a spooked stallion. I decide that she's telling him to stop acting like a lunatic.

Pogo shakes his head. "Bah! Nec cessavu utu."

"Half Dead is a friend," she says. "Zak. Celeste. Calm." She steps up to him and touches his side, allowing some of her energy to trickle into him. The energy she provides has the effect of a cup of coffee to someone who woke up on the wrong side of the bed: a step toward returning to sanity.

"Calm," he repeats. Like succumbing to hypnosis, his eyes roll back white, and his body quivers with electrical impulses. He squats on his rump.

"Calm," Celeste repeats.

He sways and nods to the inaudible song of normalcy. His pupils return to view the world without the filter of malevolence. The peace in his expression suggests that he's won the struggle, for now.

"Good," Celeste says.

She turns to me. "He's okay now."

"Maybe we should wait and see," I say. "Just to be sure."

"Zak, he's fine, no worries," she says, putting the rock away. She offers me her hand, and I grasp it as she helps me to my feet. She doesn't look completely healed, but better than she was in the cave.

"Right Pogo? You won't hurt Zak now, will you?"

Pogo shakes his head. "Half Dead is a friend. A very weak, but good friend."

He steps up to me, reaches his arm out, and touches my shoulder with his claws. This is his idea of being gentle and friendly, but even that's rough and fearsome.

"Friend," he says again. He turns and looks around, sniffing the air and contemplating something. Then he runs off toward the ridge of a dune, his feet tearing up the smooth desert sand.

"No harm done then," Celeste says, watching him.

"Yeah, except for him pounding the hell out of you earlier and very nearly doing the same to me," I say.

"He didn't know what he was doing," she says.

"Does this happen often?"

"We all lose it sometimes," she says. "You of all people should know this."

"But when I lose it, I don't go ape and try to massacre everyone," I say.

"That's because you're not a demon. They're wired differently. Especially him. When he's injured, he reverts to his old self."

We watch as Pogo ascends the dune, the dusty sand kicking up behind him. When he reaches the top, he stops and looks around.

Celeste shouts over to him: "Do you know where we are?"

He points toward the other side of the dune, then turns to us. "That way!" he shouts.

We join him on top of the dune. In front of us is a commanding view of a humbling stretch of desert, as dead as the arctic world we've just left. Merciless winds have shaped the sand into ripples, pits, and slopes. The intensity of the red is enough to make the sky look dingy, as if even the atmosphere itself is torrid and barren.

"Nice place," I say.

Celeste takes this opportunity to give Pogo more of

her energy. When finished, we allow her to rest a while longer. She's endured a lot of punishment, and if we're to continue through a desert, she needs to recover more.

It's Pogo who decides we're ready a bit later. He bounds down the other side of the dune to begin setting our pace. Celeste sighs. "Well come on, it won't get prettier staring at it."

We have another miserable journey ahead of us, but I'm glad to be on the move again. You don't know what goes through a person's mind being trapped in a cave for days on end. I bask in the openness and free my mind of lingering claustrophobia. Celeste and Pogo aren't in the mood to speak, which suits me for the moment. I feel my body's machine gear up and regulate to the gliding movements across the grains of glistening red, my lungs pumping hot exhaust.

In time, the dunes flatten, like we've reached the bottom of an ocean long since dried up. We can see for miles in front of us, but nothing is out there to see. An hour in, it looks the same behind us, the dunes well out of sight, heat clinging to the ground because it has nowhere else to go. I begin to feel a reverse claustrophobia, like my world is too large and I need something to contain me. It's a fickle thing, the human mind.

"I keep thinking," I say through the slogging, "any moment now, we'll come across a nice wayside saloon, where the beer is ice cold. Kenny Rogers is playing on the jukebox, a bowl of peanuts is on the bar, and a baseball game is on the tube. Maybe there's a pretty barkeep named after a location, like Cheyenne or Sierra."

"A little rednecky, don't you think?" Celeste says. "But minus Kenny Rogers, that actually sounds tolerable."

At first, neither of us notices that Pogo has stopped. We discover this at the same time. He's staring at something off to the left.

"What?" she asks him. He doesn't answer, but he looks agitated. We look where he's looking, but I see nothing out there, even if I let my imagination run wild.

Pogo points. Seconds later, I see something where he's pointing, but I don't know what I'm looking at. There's movement out there, but I can't tell what. It might be a person. A woman? Yes, it's a woman!

"Imbavu," Pogo says.

Whatever that word means, it registers instantly with Celeste. She grabs my arm and drags me forward. "Keep moving."

"What is it?"

"It doesn't matter Zak," she says. "We have to keep going."

But it's too late, I look again. There's something familiar about the person coming toward us, something unmistakable about her walk, her silhouette standing out over the red sand.

"It can't be!" I say, pulling myself free of Celeste's grasp as I watch the figure approach.

"It isn't who you think it is," Celeste says.

I know better. When you spend enough of your life

with a person, you get to know everything about her. You can identify her in a crowd, her imprint so finely embedded in your memory that even a glimpse is enough.

Angie!

I don't know how, but the figure walking up to us is my wife.

Pogo rushes up to Angie, her stride unaffected when he circles her in agitated suspicion.

"Pogo!" I yell, concerned that he'll hurt her. "No Pogo, friend!"

Pogo turns to me and shakes his head, no. *Not friend.*

I don't understand, but I also don't care. Angie is here, as real as when I last left her. I walk toward her, feeling the full impact of her stare. Somehow she's found me, and that's all that matters.

Now I run to her. Pogo growls at me, but it's too late. I've reached her.

"Angie, how?"

But I don't need an explanation. I feel her embrace as if I haven't felt it in years, and she kisses my cheek and neck.

"I missed you," she whispers.

"I missed you, too," I say, squeezing her closer.

Celeste runs up next to us, her sling drawn and loaded.

"Hold on, whoa!" I yell to Celeste, pulling Angie behind me to protect her. "What are you doing?"

"You have to get away from it," Celeste says, sling dangling.

"What's wrong with you two?" I say. "It? This is my wife!"

Pogo shakes his head.

"It's not her," Celeste says.

"Zak, who are they?" Angie says. I turn to see her looking terrified.

"It's okay," I tell her. "These are my friends."

"Oh," she says. "I like them."

I stare at her a second. I won't acknowledge the feeling in the back of my mind, the nearly subliminal perception that something isn't quite as it should be. This is my wife, I can see her, hear her voice that sounds as it always did, even smell her scent that is so uniquely her.

I turn again to see that Celeste and Pogo remain ready for a fight.

"What are you guys so worried about?" I ask.

Before they can respond, I feel my airway being choked. I reach for my neck to dislodge whatever's got a hold of me, but I feel only my own skin, something invisible locking my throat shut. I flail my arms in panic, pointing to my neck to express that something has me. Pogo and Celeste are trying to understand what's wrong with me, their stances tense but helpless to intervene.

I feel a powerful pressure restrain my entire body. Like being in an invisible rocket ship, I feel my stomach lurch as I'm thrust high into the air, straight up, so high I can see the vastness of red surrounding our location. I look down to see Pogo and Celeste watching me from below. There, too, is Angie, except it's no longer Angie. She's transformed into something ugly, a decaying mass wearing a tattered cloak, her skeletal arm pointing up at me. I roll and twist with the wag of her finger, and I realize I've become her gravity-defying puppet, subject to the whims of her magic.

The thing that once was Angie shrieks, the kind of cry that breaks glass and shakes foundations. Pogo answers with a roar of his own, and he leaps for her. But the thing just raises its other hand and Pogo bounces away like he's hit an invisible wall. The Angie creature waves her hand and Pogo cartwheels across the sand like an oversized tumbleweed in a cyclone.

But there's Celeste, taking advantage of a free millisecond to lob a rock at Angie. Before Angie can react, the rock hits her abdomen and detonates, blasting her back.

Released from the thing's invisible grasp, my throat goes free. I can breathe again, but there's a new problem. I'm falling, the invisible rocket gone, my stomach dropping, the sandy ground coming too fast. But Pogo is back on his feet. He lumbers forward and dives, catching me like an outfielder making a Gold Glove snag, and we tumble into the sand.

When we come to a stop, I'm grateful to be unharmed. But I see the Angie creature standing in the distance, and it looks mad and injured. Celeste doesn't allow it the satisfaction of survival. She sends another rock at it, catching its leg, blowing off the limb and upending the creature to a fiery collapse into the sand.

"Pogo!" Celeste shouts, pointing to the fallen creature. "Finish it!"

Pogo releases his grip on me and stands. Seeing I'm unhurt, he walks forward in a crouch toward the creature. Gaining confidence that there will be no resistance, he charges full speed. His anger seems to build with each step, fueled by the humiliation of being repulsed earlier. He pounces onto the thing and begins a two-minute rampage, a horrible mutilation that mixes stomping, clawing, and screeching, the sand flying from the frenzy. This climaxes when Pogo picks up the lifeless creature and rips the body in two at the waist. His exclamation point is plucking off the creature's head and tossing it toward us. The severed head skips across the sand like a lopsided soccer ball and stops a few feet in front of us, the inhuman, dead eyes looking past us.

"That is definitely not my wife," I gasp.

"You mean *was*," Celeste answers.

"Was, right. But what happened to my wife?"

Celeste pats me on the shoulder. "I tried to tell you. That wasn't your wife."

"Then what was it?" I say.

"That thing was sent here for you," Celeste says. "And it almost killed you, because you still won't listen to me. I use very simple language with you. How is it that you're an English professor?"

Pogo isn't done. He's come for the head. He picks it up and studies it like a trophy, then pops it in his hands, the gooey mass falling to the ground. Then he stamps it into the sand.

"Okay, okay," Celeste says, touching Pogo's arm. "Dead, Pogo. Very good, such a thorough job."

Pogo stops, satisfied with his work. I'm once again grateful that Pogo is on my side, but in the way that the World War II Allies were grateful to have Joseph Stalin. I think Pogo will always horrify me. The evil is just too close to the surface for my taste, but I'm still relieved to have his help.

"Now," Celeste turns to me. "If you can make an effort, just once, to do what I tell you, maybe you'll get home."

I take another look at the remains of the Angie creature scattered every which way. "I will, but it was her, I could swear it."

"Let's go," she says. "There could be more of those rancid hose bags lurking around here."

We continue on.

21

SAND

No one speaks again for an hour. We may as well be camels enduring the Sahara in silence, unaware of our destination. The constant transition from mayhem to boredom is taking its toll on me, particularly the mayhem part, but I never was a fan of boredom either. I have to speak eventually to avoid going bonkers.

"So what did you do for fun back home?" I ask Celeste.

She looks at me with perturbation, as if skeptical of the word *fun*. Then I see those black eyes go to a place they don't often go: fond contemplation.

"Anything dangerous," she says.

"Oh?" I say. "That's fun?"

"Let me guess what's fun for you," she says. "Reading a book?"

"Well, sure," I say.

"Not for me," she says. "I was an adrenaline junkie.

Skydiving, mountain climbing, base jumping. You can't get that feeling from books."

"Well, you can actually. Books about Mount Everest, stories from the trenches of World War I . . ."

"Not the same," she says.

"Maybe not quite the same," I say. "But you rarely get injured reading."

She's not buying it.

"I always liked roller coasters," I say. "That's the closest I ever got to adrenaline. Besides being hunted by demons."

"In the absence of anything else, a good roller coaster has its place," she says. "But there's nothing like genuine risk to get the heart going. Skiing the backside of a mountain or surfing a huge wave."

I'm beginning to see how Celeste has been able to thrive in the After.

"This place must be like a constant adrenaline rush for you then," I say.

She shakes her head. "Not the same either. When I was alive, escaping death meant something. You could feel it. In the land of the dead, where feelings are numb, it's just drudgery."

"Would you go back to the living, if you could?" I ask.

"Well I can't," she says.

I've taken it too far again. I can feel her anger pushing up like an ugly weed. I decide to be quiet. In my mind I think about sipping a giant glass of iced tea while reading a book about Mount Everest, hoping chilly thoughts will take my mind off of the heat.

Nature interrupts my daydream with a muted rumble. We hear it long before we learn its source. Something comes up from behind us, sounding like a tank division thundering over the sand.

We turn to face it, but there's nothing to see except the desert. Pogo becomes anxious, his body stiffening in reaction to trouble.

"What?" Celeste questions him.

He looks up at the sky and sniffs. Then he stares at the horizon, focusing on something we can't sense. He points: "Sonantivua. A storm is coming."

"Storm?" I repeat. I look hard to see any evidence of it. There's only a hint of darkness in the direction the sound is coming from.

"Maybe it won't be a bad one," I suggest. I've hexed us with wishful thinking, because in mere minutes a colossal storm comes into view. A red cloud miles wide replaces the horizon like a mountain range creeping across the desert.

"We have to find cover," Celeste says.

"What cover?" I ask. This painfully flat place could not have less cover. We have nowhere to go, and we all know it.

Pogo rears around and sprints away from the storm anyway.

"Where's he going?" I ask.

"We have to move," Celeste says, and runs after him. I

follow them in a jog, stealing a glance back at the storm. It already looks closer, so I increase my speed to keep up with Celeste and Pogo.

The cardio issue returns, and promising to join a gym is no help at the moment. Apparently, Celeste and Pogo could run for hours, but I tire after five minutes. They urge me on from up ahead, and I struggle forward, stealing glances back at the storm that seems to gain a mile a minute.

"There!" Celeste points way ahead of us. Already the wind has begun to churn dust and obscure my vision, but I see what Celeste sees: a boulder in the far distance. We haven't seen boulders in hours, so I wonder if this is a mirage of optimism. But as we get closer, I know it's real.

We close the distance to the boulder, Pogo reaching it first. He disappears behind its bulk, Celeste joining him there. But I'm too far behind. She waves me forward as if a ravenous shark is on my tail. I don't have to look back at the storm to know it's almost upon me. I can feel its pressure closing in, the uproar walloping my ears.

I make it to the boulder right when the storm does. Just when I'm sure I've won, the surge of blowing sand sucks me in, twists me sideways, and lifts me off the ground. I feel something grab my left leg. The sand is pelting my eyes, but I can see that Pogo has caught me. He yanks me down to the protection of the boulder, his arms holding me like I'm his teddy bear.

We huddle into the safety of the boulder. It's so massive that it dwarfs even Pogo. We're wedged into its concave side, the upper lip forming a half-roof. Our only choice is to sit and wait out the storm, encased in its murky darkness, watching it rush past.

The magnitude of the sandstorm boggles my mind. An hour in and it's as strong as when it first hit. But it's unable to keep that pace, and it begins to recede to something closer to monotony, the wind tapering to tolerable gusts, the roar abating enough for us to hear one another speak.

Celeste sifts her hand through her hair to scatter the granules nestled in her roots and scalp. "I'll be picking out this junk for months," she says.

I look out at the screeching storm and begin to think about my imposter wife that Pogo dismantled.

"Do you really think there are more of those things out there? Like the one that looked like Angie?"

"I doubt it," Celeste says. "And even so, they couldn't get through this."

"It's just a hard thing to get out of my head," I say. "A spouse monster trying to kill me."

"I keep telling you, it wasn't her."

"Yes, I know that," I say. "But just before the thing tried to kill me, there was an expression I've seen from Angie before. A sort of contempt. I remember . . ."

I realize I've stumbled across a memory I've kept well hidden.

"You remember what?" Celeste asks.

"Angie looked at me that way before," I say. I realize I'm close to a confession. It seems like a bad idea to divulge it. Celeste says nothing, giving me freedom to keep silent if I choose.

"I think I know why I'm here," I say. "In the After."

"You're here because you died," she says. "It's not hard to figure out."

"There's more," I say.

Celeste folds her arms in front of her to anticipate a long explanation. I give her a short one.

"I tried to kill myself."

Pogo grumbles to digest this idea. Celeste has no reaction.

"How?" she asks.

I'm hesitant to provide the details, but I'm too far into it now. "A while ago, even before I quit my job, I went into my garage, closed it up, and turned on the car ignition."

"That's pretty dumb, Zak."

"I know. I may have gone through with it had Angie not found me there," I say. "I remember that she looked at me like that fake Angie did. A mix of anger and disappointment. It was the perfect cap to a long list of my failings."

The wind diminishes a notch more. I watch the peacefulness of the subsiding chaos, similar to a neutral ending of a traumatic film.

"Well what did you expect from her? She caught you trying to kill yourself," Celeste says. "I would've clocked you one. I've done stupid-ass things in my life, but I never tried suicide."

"What's really detestable is my own father committed

suicide when I was young," I say. "My family was never the same after that. But there I was years later, ready to do the same thing to my own wife and kids."

"Like father, like son," Celeste says.

"Is it why I'm here?" I ask. "Because of my suicide attempt?"

"Who knows? Probably. Doesn't change anything. I'm not your psychiatrist, but you have to learn to get over yourself."

"Kind of a problem for me," I say. "I hang on to things."

"Well stop," she says. "If you would have succeeded in offing yourself, would that have been better?"

I shake my head.

"Then consider yourself lucky. Your wife found you and stopped you because she cares about you. She still should have socked you right in the beak for being so dense."

Celeste stands and stretches. "We can get going in a while. This rock sure saved our butts." She pats the rock wall as if to thank it for being there.

"You never did tell me what that Angie thing was," I say. "You said someone sent it. Who could do that?"

Pogo stands up. "It was Cause," he says.

"What?" Celeste asks him.

"Cause nuntuma misumbe," he says. "Cause custezim. This was a warning to us."

"Oh," Celeste says, looking at me. "Pogo thinks it's someone named Cause who sent her."

"I'm not familiar with that name," I say.

"Me neither. Pogo says he's the one guarding the portal that you need to use to get home. Cause knows we're coming, so I guess sending the imposter was a warning. Or maybe he was trying to test our strength."

This sinks in. "But if he can send someone who looks like my wife, what else can he do?"

"I don't know," she says. "Whatever he's got, we can handle it though."

"Right," I say. "Okay. Are you sure?"

"Reasonably sure."

Pogo steps out into the desert, now restored nearly to what it had been before the storm, the sand smoothed like an enormous Zen garden. We can still hear the storm rumbling away, but its abdomen is devouring land miles beyond us.

"This way," Pogo says once he's got his bearings again. "Cause is this way."

22

HOTTER

Sky swept of clouds by the sandstorm, our bodies roast with renewed intensity from unimpeded sun. The flat land has become dotted with giant stones like the one that sheltered us from the storm, and we pass in and out of their shade. I feel like we're in a grand museum hall and the rocks are sculptures. There's one that looks like a bear standing on its hindquarters, and another like a giant human head that scowls as we pass.

"Pogo," I call. He looks over his shoulder at me, horns reflecting the sunlight, expression irritated that I would have the audacity to speak to him. "Thank you for catching me back there," I say. He just shakes his head and faces forward again.

"He isn't much for the warm fuzzies," Celeste says. "I'm not even sure he knows what *thank you* means. His language doesn't have a translation."

"Oh," I say.

"Half Dead is slow," we hear him mutter. "I had to catch him. He is too weak."

Watching Celeste walk in front of me, I try to imagine what her career was when she was alive. When all you do is meander through one abysmal landscape after another, there's time for thinking about such things. I've narrowed it down to professional skydiver, mountain climbing guide, and circus lion tamer. I'm curious enough to ask.

"So what did you do for a living back home?"

Celeste looks at me. "You sure are nosy. Why do you want to know that?"

"Well, I told you my job."

"Unfortunately, yes, you did," she says.

"I imagine yours was more exciting than college professor."

"Accountant," she says.

"You were an accountant?"

"Yeah, is that surprising to you?"

"A little," I say. Disappointing is more like it, but I try not to express it. Her response tells me I don't hide the letdown: "I know it's nothing flashy. I always had a knack for numbers, and it paid the bills."

"Did you like it?" I ask.

"No, but I think anyone who claims to like a job is lying, or not using the right word. More like *tolerable*. That's a good word for a job. It was tolerable to work with numbers all day instead of people. I always understood numbers. People, not so much."

I'm in no position to argue the semantics of job satisfaction. By her measure, I suppose my teaching job was intolerable, yet there were parts I enjoyed.

"I liked working with my students," I say. "Some had no business being in college, but most were likable enough. It's why I got into teaching, to help people learn. I might have tried to remember that more often, I guess."

"If I could have made a living in a shack in Antarctica, I would have. Nothing good ever came to me from people."

I could spend a lifetime walking a desert trying to figure out what Celeste has against people. I doubt she'll tell me why, if she even knows.

"What about relationships?" I venture. "Sort of difficult by yourself."

"You mean romantic ones? Tried that, it never worked out," she says. "They rarely do, just look at the divorce rate."

"Lots of marriages succeed," I say.

"Like yours?" she says. I don't know whether to rebuke that or agree with it. She doesn't give me a chance: "Can we just change the subject? This is creeping me out."

Pogo stops and looks at the sky. I've seen this reaction often enough to know that he senses the Shift is coming. I feel something too, an anticipation that only my soul understands. The desert goes black, and for the first time I endure it with calm patience, experience reminding me that the transition is safe.

We ride out the Shift until it spills us into a land altogether different but of equivalent desolation. Instead of the red desert, we've arrived in a world of charred black-ness. Hot sulfur seeps from vast slabs of volcanic rock, some glowing with crimson heat. I've never seen a lava flow in person, but I recognize one when standing in the middle of it. Off to the right is the volcano itself, its summit recently opened like the bursting of a boil. Lava trickles from the wound into a salmon-red river that empties past us. This is the benign aftermath of the volcano's eruption, the land still steaming from the blast, trees sizzling limbless, trunks cemented into cooling lava rock.

We have nothing to say to each other about this new world, all of us preoccupied with the awe and potential danger of it all. We begin walking away from the volcano, our instincts intent on putting distance between it and us.

Yet we can't escape the overpowering stench. Steam spews from cracks and holes in the rocks and hangs with us, tainting every breath with noxious gas.

"Is it safe to be breathing this?" I ask.

"Doubtful, but unless you want to hold your breath, it'll have to do," Celeste says.

But the hot rotten-egg stink begins to have a physical effect on me. It singes my nose and scalds my throat and lungs. The potent aroma attacks my brain, mimicking an unsettling drunkenness, a disorientation that blocks out my senses. I'm spinning, or is it my mind? I lose my breath.

"Are you okay?" I hear Celeste say, but I can't see her. My world has shut off. My eyes and mouth feel soldered shut, and even my ears begin to plug like I'm being submerged in motor-oil.

A new voice fills my ears. It's not Celeste or Pogo.

"Zak," comes the grating whisper, almost taunting, somehow familiar.

My sight returns, but I can't make sense of what I see. It's a scattering of visual fragments. Something has unlocked snippets of my life and is projecting them in a three-dimensional collage. The action in the images congeals like the mixing of oil paint. I see memories, things I never wished to see again, my failures: resigning away my professorship, drinking myself to sleep each night, arguing with Angie, me inside the car in the garage with the engine idling.

"What do you want?" I ask. "Celeste, there's someone here!"

"Zak," it says again.

"Who are you?"

"Never go back," it says.

I hear it laugh at me, the cackle of a lunatic.

I feel my entire body go numb, legs giving out from under me. I fall flat on my back.

"Zak," I hear my name again. This time it's Celeste. She's at my side, tapping my cheek to coax back consciousness. My true vision comes back to me, and I see her face looking worried, her incessant tapping on my cheeks beginning to irritate me.

"What?" I ask.

"You fell," she says.

"I fell? Where is he?" I ask.

"Who?"

"I heard a voice."

Pogo comes into my view. He looks down at me and sniffs, then steps back. "Cause," he says.

Celeste looks at him. "Cause? He was here?"

Pogo nods.

"How could he be here?" I ask, pulling myself up to a sitting position. Neither of them responds, but I know the answer. Cause can be anywhere.

Pogo takes another step back. From beneath him comes a crack like the snapping of a sheet of ice. Pogo looks down. The lava rock under his feet gives way like the releasing of a dunk tank platform, and Pogo drops out of sight, a swarm of lava gas sweeping him away.

"Pogo!" Celeste screams. She rushes to the edge of the hole that just swallowed him, fighting the scorching heat to peer down. I jump to her side, heat toasting my face like I'm standing at the door of a gigantic oven.

We hear Pogo's defiant roar before we see him. When the gas clears, we spot him three feet down clutching an outcropping of rock with one hand, his other arm hanging uselessly to his side, smoking and splattered with hardening lava. Below him is an underground river of lava churning up bubbles of toxic gas.

"Climb up!" Celeste shouts, helpless to do anything else. Pogo struggles with the suggestion, pulling his body up half a foot before sagging down again. He's too enormous to pull himself up with his one good arm, and he begins to howl from his wounds and the heat broiling his underside.

I have a rare moment of impromptu genius. I remove my belt and secure the buckle tight to create a makeshift lasso. Celeste understands. She takes the belt from me, drops to her stomach, and inches over the edge, arm lowering the belt toward one of Pogo's horns. But Pogo begins thrashing around as if being electrocuted, his body bubbling and cooking in front of us. I worry that his fits will crumble the outcropping.

"Hold still!" Celeste scolds, which is easy for her to say. But Pogo stiffens when he sees the lasso. He inches his head up so his left horn bull's-eyes the loop, and Celeste tugs like setting the hook on a marlin. The belt slides tight.

"Grab my waist!" Celeste screams.

I grab hold of her, feeling the muscles of her slender frame tighten.

"Pull!" she shouts, and I lean back and yank at her waist. We're in a tug-o'-war of life, and our opponents are bulk and gravity.

"Harder!" she shouts. "Pogo, pull up!"

This isn't going to work. I don't want to see Pogo die, but we can't budge him. We may as well be trying to fish a Volkswagen out of a sewer.

But I also refuse to accept this. I search myself for more strength and summon it, pushing off the lava rocks like I'm the anchor of this team. Pogo meets this surge with a yowl, freeing up a burst of his own survival energy, and we begin to inch backward.

"He's coming!" Celeste calls. "Keep pulling! Pogo, climb!"

Over Celeste's shoulder I see Pogo's smoking head protrude above the hole. He plunges the claws of his good hand into the slab in front of us, and with a screech of torment he lifts his upper torso onto the ledge where he teeters.

I rush forward, grab his free horn, and yank. The horn is so hot that it sizzles my hand, but for Pogo's sake I won't let go, and I bite my lip to fight the pain. Celeste pulls the lasso like wrangling a steer, all three of us working against gravity's last assault. Our efforts inch him forward until the teetering stops. Pogo lifts himself the final distance and collapses, his body free from the hole's fury. Celeste and I fall with him, inhaling the putrid air, both of us staring at Pogo's charred body. He groans while his body smokes and sputters like a half-roasted pig, muscles twitching with trauma.

"Hang on, I'm here," Celeste says to him. She pulls herself up, reaches out to him, closes her eyes, and begins flushing him with reviving energy. I watch while the scent of roasted demon, an odor I never knew existed, sabotages my sinuses, like decaying skunk on a griddle.

I realize that the hole could widen at any moment from Pogo's weight, sending all three of us into the lava below. But it's pointless to say it out loud. Pogo's life is at risk and needs attention now. Instead I issue a silent prayer for the rock to hold, just a bit longer, for the sake of my friends and all they've done for me.

Celeste's healing powers never cease to amaze me. Minutes later, and Pogo is already feeling some relief. He's stopped his twitching, but he still looks a fright.

"We have to move, it's unstable here," she says. "Pogo, can you walk?"

Pogo lifts his head and pulls himself to unsteady feet. He takes a couple steps, groaning but capable of more. He nods.

"There," Celeste says, pointing to a gradual rise to our left. She wants the safety of higher ground. We walk to it, both of us helping Pogo as best we can, but it feels like two dinghies trying to assist a battered oil tanker.

We make it up the hill, and Pogo sits to rest. Celeste continues the healing while Pogo moans.

We hear a crash from where we just left. We look down the hill to see that the ground next to the hole has imploded and fallen, a hissing sound indicating that the lava river has consumed the falling rock below. I don't think many of my prayers have been answered before, but that one certainly was. I sigh away my relief, appreciating the safety of the hill that feels like a sturdy island in a tropical storm.

For the next hour, I take turns watching the healing and making sure the hole doesn't widen, pausing to gawk at my blistered hand that's minor compared to Pogo's wounds. But the hole is finished growing, whereas the healing progresses well. Pogo's wounds begin to close and normalize. Feeling much better, he speaks, taking both of us off guard.

"Thank." He looks over at the hole still smoking at a safe distance. Then he removes my belt still dangling from his horn. "Thank," he repeats, handing me the belt.

"You're welcome," I say, taking the belt and reattaching it to my waist. Then I find myself teasing him: "Pogo fell, Half Dead had to catch."

"Catch," he repeats, not understanding my humor at first. Then he gets it, and somewhere in his misery he finds the energy for a guttural laugh. I join him, my own laugh feeling like a welcomed release. Celeste opens her eyes long enough to admire the moment with a relieved smile.

"All right, sit still now," Celeste tells Pogo when the laughter begins to wane. "You're still a charbroiled burger, so let's make you closer to medium rare and get out of here."

She closes her eyes and continues her work.

23

GUARDIANS

"Better?" Celeste asks.

Pogo stands and surveys his arm. His blue skin has prevailed over its charred and festering former state. Spots of puffy pink hint that some healing is yet to come, but a miraculous recovery has taken place. Clumps of lava rock, cooled and hardened now, still cling to his skin like scabs. He whisks them off with one swipe from his free hand, rocks clattering to the ground.

"Better," he says.

We give Celeste time to regain her energy, then we resume our crossing of the volcanic rock that makes us labor for every step. It will be years before the elements smooth over this place, creating soil and reviving plant growth. But the farther away we get from the volcano, the less the ground smokes and the cleaner the air becomes. Pogo seems especially happy to be out of danger, but he still takes regular glances back the way we've come to gauge our progress.

Celeste, walking a few feet in front of me, says something, but I can't make it out.

"What did you say?" I ask.

Celeste and Pogo stop, turn, and look at me.

"No one said anything," Celeste says.

"Well someone said something. You didn't hear it?"

"It's nothing," Celeste says.

I try to swallow away the concern in my gut that's telling me Cause is back. If it's him, ignoring him like any schoolyard bully is all I can think to do. We continue on.

A few seconds later I hear something again. It's a high-pitched voice, this time from behind us.

"Wait, there it is again!" I say, stopping to look behind me.

Celeste and Pogo stop again. They must have heard it this time because they don't say anything to refute it. We wait and listen.

"Cuddle," it says. It's a soft, girlish voice.

"Lacy?"

I turn to look at Celeste. Her expression is dubious.

"Daddy?" Lacy says. With the sound of her voice, a solitary rock, nearly spherical, erupts in a brilliant blue light. It's not Cause after all, it's my daughter trying to communicate.

"Lacy!" I shout, and rush toward the rock. I kneel next to it, reaching out a finger to touch it.

"Zak, don't!" Celeste yells.

My hand hovers over the rock while I consider touching it. Lacy's voice reminds me of her exceptional talent for speech. Much more talkative than her sister, Lacy craves being heard. Some day the girl will have her own talk show or be a celebrated orator. I always found it hard to keep up with her words, and I'd even ignore her when I just didn't have the patience or energy. I realize now that hearing her speak should have been a simple pleasure to enjoy, never to be squandered. This is why it's easy for me to justify moving my hand closer, even though part of me wonders if it's another of Cause's tricks. It doesn't matter, because before I can touch it, I feel the pressure of Pogo's arms yank me up and away.

"Hey!" I shout.

"Mabayus! Bad Half Dead!" Pogo says like an impatient babysitter.

"Daddy!" Lacy whimpers.

"We've been over this," Celeste says, looking up at me in Pogo's arms. "Nothing good comes from interacting with the living."

I understand this, I really do, but Lacy's voice is too much: "Where are you Daddy? Don't leave!" she calls.

"I'm right here sweetie, I've never left!" I say.

"We're leaving," Celeste says. She turns and walks away, Pogo following her with me still in his arms. I don't know why I think I can get away from his clutches, but I try anyway. His arms may as well be steel cables, and the more I struggle the tighter his grip becomes. I feel like he may crush me flat.

My rational mind understands that leaving is best, but my paternal side knows I'm abandoning my child. Yet my distress is useless inside Pogo's hold, and after struggling without gain for several minutes, I go limp and quiet. We walk for what must be hours, Lacy's rock so far behind I'd never find it again anyway.

Celeste stops and studies the dejection on my face. "All right, put him down," she tells Pogo. He obeys. I stand on my own again, staring at the ground.

"That was for your own good," she says to me.

"Was it?"

"Come on, we have to keep going."

I stand there fuming. "Was it for my daughter's own good to be ignored?"

"Let it go. She's back in the living, safe and sound."

"Not sound. She needed me!"

"She'll get over it," Celeste says. "She's not the only kid who's been left alone to figure things out. It's how life works."

"I just wanted to talk to her, to tell her I'm coming back for her," I say.

"You don't need to confuse the kid. Just move on, pay attention to getting back, and stop messing with the living."

"She's my daughter! How could you just keep me from her?"

"Forget about her!" Celeste shouts. "Do you have a hole in your head?"

"I can't just forget," I say. "This is my family you're talking about."

"Do you need me to have him carry you again, or are you going to walk voluntarily?"

I groan. I feel my facial muscles go tight, animated by rage. "I appreciate that you're trying to help, but just who put you two in charge of my life?"

"If you have to know, Deena did," Celeste says.

I'm about to continue my rant when Celeste's words register. "What?"

"Do you really think we're helping your sorry ass because we want to? Do we look like good Samaritans? I could find better things to do, even in this hellhole."

"Why would Deena do that? I don't understand."

"No, you wouldn't," she says, turning to walk away.

"Celeste, what do you mean?" I say, grabbing her shoulder to stop her. "What does Deena have to do with this?"

Celeste mulls over her response. I sense that her words pain her: "Deena assigned us to you."

"Assigned you? You've talked to her?"

"In life and death, others are there to help," she says. "Most of the time, people don't even know they're there. Deena is the main one for you. But she can assign others. Usually these others are souls that need to prove they can help."

"You and Pogo," I say.

"Yeah," she says. "So you're stuck with us, and we're stuck with you."

"Why didn't you tell me this before?" I ask.

"Slipped my mind," she says. Those black eyes tell me otherwise, and then she admits as much: "It's not something I'm exactly proud of. Serving you just reminds me of the mistakes I've made. You're part of my punishment. Pogo's too."

"The Half Dead is punishment," Pogo grunts.

"Pogo knows where the portal is because Deena told him," Celeste continues. "He only needed to be told roughly where it is, and he knows how to get there. But Deena made it happen."

This makes sense, but I'm still trying to process that Celeste and Pogo have been assigned to me. "I don't really want to be anyone's punishment," I say. "I'll talk to Deena about it, next time I see her."

"Don't bother," Celeste says. "It isn't something to negotiate."

"Why? I can tell her I wouldn't feel right about it," I say.

"No one cares how you feel about it!" she snaps. "No one cares how anyone feels about it."

I retreat from the admonishment by staring at the volcanic ground some more. I wish that Deena were here to sort all of this out.

Celeste inhales and exhales her frustration, and a fresh breath seems to calm her. "Underneath all of that misery and helplessness, you're a good person, Zak," she says.

"Thanks, I think."

"You have a conscience," she continues. "I never

listened to mine when I was alive, and that's how I got here. But right now, tell your conscience to screw off about this. You didn't ask for any of this, so stop feeling bad about it. That won't help you get home."

"I thought you were trying to help me because you wanted to," I say.

"Well, the point is we *are* helping you," she says. "Deena assigned us so we could feel what it means to care. Maybe in some demented way we're even enjoying it. Is that fair enough?"

"I suppose so," I say.

"Then let's get going," she says. "That daughter of yours needs you back. They all do."

We continue our course over the lava rock, acting the part of prehistoric creatures traversing a land newly birthed.

24

INTO THE DEEP

I realize now that it doesn't matter how far away we get from the volcano. Lava rock dominates the land because this place is nothing but volcanoes. We pass by new ones, some dormant, others looking ready to burst at any moment, some just smoldering like abandoned bonfires. Our objective is to stay as far from any of them as we can.

Pogo is still agitated, and I can't blame him. Each of his steps is like walking over a rickety bridge that could give way without warning. But something else is bothering him. He looks up at the sky far too often, anticipating an event that won't come.

Celeste picks up on this, too. When he stops to give his full attention to the sky, she questions him. "The Shift?"

It feels too early for the Shift, and Pogo confirms this by shaking his head, no.

"Then what's got you so worked up?" she asks.

"Dendayo aqmaj," Pogo says. "The water is next."

"What water?" she asks.

"Big and bad water."

"What does that mean?" I ask Celeste.

"You heard him. Use your imagination, our next location has water, and he doesn't like it."

"I have to be honest," I say. "Water doesn't sound so bad after being in a sweltering desert and now this place."

We spend hours more walking much slower than usual, Pogo bogged by restlessness. I try to predict just what sort of water is coming. Maybe another lake? A swamp? A beach? An atypical confidence follows this speculation, like I believe we can handle whatever the Shift brings next. So when Pogo stiffens, signaling that the Shift is upon us at last, I'm ready for it, very nearly welcoming its arrival.

But as we exit the volcanic world and wade through the Shift's darkness, my overconfidence leaves me unguarded. When the Shift dumps us into the next world, instead of the return of light, I'm enveloped in a freezing, watery void. I know I'm underwater because I inhale a gulp that's salty and cold, my throat and lungs rejecting liquid with desperate heaves. My eyes sting from the salinity, but I keep them open to find the dim light of the surface.

I burst above water with a cough and gasp, but the reprieve is quickly erased. A massive whitecap smashes into me without warning, tumbling me upside down and back into the darkness. My frantic kicks and paddles are useless against the water's power, and I have no idea where to find the surface. Instead of struggling, I go limp and let the water carry me, concentrating on holding my breath. But the more you focus on such a thing, the more you crave to breathe again, and desperation forces me to paddle. It's dumb luck when my struggling actually gets me back to the surface. When I break through, I'm surprised that I've done it, and I alternate between breaths and hacks.

Momentarily recovered, I tread water and try to look around. Swells rise all around me. I'm a decent swimmer, but I can barely keep my head above water in this wild sea. The sky is purple with clouds hanging low from a whipping storm. Rain sweeps down in angular columns that bend in the gusts. Pogo was right, this is bad.

Celeste and Pogo should be here, but I can't see them anywhere. I worry that the sea has already swallowed them. I spin in every direction to find them, but only the ocean surrounds me. With each crest I pull my trunk high above water for a better look, but they're nowhere.

"Celeste!" I shout, but I can't hear my own voice over the squall, so how can they?

Instead of a response, I see a massive swell form in front of me. It's so huge that it sucks in the surrounding water, pulling me like it has me by a rope. I'm unable to get on top of it, and I inhale a breath as the swell pulls me under. I feel like I've been run over by a cruise ship, and my body is again forced into underwater gymnastics.

My breath won't last, and it feels like the swell has enough power to keep me under for hours. My squirming against the flood just increases my exertion and the need for air, and I panic for oxygen. I'm going to be lost here forever, flushed so deep into the sea that even the sharks won't find me. But I'm awestruck when the wave's energy shifts in my favor, pulling me to the surface like I'm some ancient buoy. I burst above water and flounder to stay afloat, sputtering to regain my breath, wiping my eyes free of salt.

The passing swell has left the sea flat for the moment, and I'm surrounded by bubbling white. Without waves blocking my view of the horizon, I see Celeste and Pogo bobbing in the far distance. Maybe the rogue wave has churned them up from the deep.

"Celeste!" I shout. She hears me because she waves her arms. I swim in their direction, but I'm fighting a force infinitely stronger. We're being pulled apart by currents that would paralyze an ocean liner. I can't reach them. Just to seal the deal, the sea builds up again, swells screening Pogo and Celeste from view. I scream their names, but I know it's a waste. They're gone.

I grow tired of kicking and crawling over the waves. My eyes burn from the salt, my throat and nose are raw from the wash of seawater. So when I spot the object that might lessen my suffering, I clear my eyes with pruned fingers to make sure I'm seeing correctly. Yes, floating fifteen feet from me is a log spiked with nubs that were once its branches. The driftwood is raw and ugly from its watery journey, but to me it's a beautiful treasure. I rush for it with the vigor of Tarzan, and with a final reach I grab one of its spokes and refuse to let the sea strip me from it. My other hand reaches around the trunk, and I grip it just as tightly. Whitecaps wallop me, but I will myself not to let go.

This is my pastime for more hours than I care to know. The sea catches the log wave after wave, and I hang on as the log bucks with the ocean. Between waves I search for Celeste and Pogo, but I'm forced to admit they're still not close.

I'm reminded of sea tales from literature where terrors of the ocean are vivid: Melville's *Moby Dick*, Hemingway's *The Old Man and the Sea*, and an obscure favorite of mine, Crane's "The Open Boat." Celeste considers me an idiot for thinking a piece of writing can mimic reality, and now I see that she has a solid point. Hammered on a log for hours in angry seas makes reading about it in a comfortable chair seem immeasurably tame.

I hear the shore before I see it. At least I think it's the shore. Rhythmic rumbles sound like more eruptions from the storm at first, but I recognize that it's monster waves attacking a hidden shoreline. My eyes confirm it when the shoreline comes into view while I'm riding the crest of a swell.

I think of "The Open Boat" again, four men stranded in a dinghy for days after their ship sinks off the Florida coast. Approaching land at last, they decide to bring the dinghy ashore through gigantic waves pounding the beach. I strain to remember who lives and dies at the end of the story, until I realize that this isn't the best thing to think about. Go away, Stephen Crane and your realism! I'm heading shoreward whether I want it to or not, and I'm about to reenact Crane's story, my dinghy only a shabby log.

The storm has had its way with the sea for too long, and I feel the kinetic energy coming to a furious climax, the land refusing to budge. I drift right in between this struggle. I feel the sea heave high, and on top of the wave I have a perfect view of the oncoming beach, much closer now than before. Like a rat being washed through a sewer, the current drags the driftwood in, and I feel its pull, see and hear the crashing of water in front of me like I'm plummeting over Niagara Falls.

I cling to the trunk until the ocean has had enough of that. As the water crashes, the log jolts, freeing my grip, and I'm tossed again into turbulent darkness. I brace for impact with the sand, but it never comes. The wave has flushed so many tons of water onto the shore that it cushions my fall. I surface into a flood of foam and ride the water's thrust up the shore. My legs find the bottom, and I bounce across the sand like a broken airplane skipping off the runway. As the strength of the wave dwindles, I commit to the idea of standing, and against only fleeting shoves from water, my feet dig in. Waist deep, I urge myself forward, walking up the beach until I'm well out of danger.

I sit in the sand and pant. I watch more waves crumble to shore, the most monstrous waves I've ever seen, and I don't understand how I've survived. But here I am, alone on shore, safe again. I keep hoping the surf will throw Celeste and Pogo onshore, but the only thing alive here is the sea.

I stand and begin to scream their names. It's not that I really expect them to hear me, it's a reaction to what this latest debacle means to me. I may have survived the ocean, but without Celeste and Pogo, I can't get home.

"Celeste!" I shout out at the sea. "Pogo!" I may as well be screaming into a deafening jet engine. "God damn this place!"

I should be exhausted, but my anger throws me into a jog down the beach. I stop at intervals to spy on the waves, looking for anything resembling my friends. I continue to shout and curse until my throats hurts, and what good does it do? It can't erase what I'm feeling. My way home is gone, but there's something else that's just as bad: loss. I think of what those two have done for me. If it's true that they were assigned to help me, I feel betrayed that they would be taken. Worse, I'm sickened at the thought that they're gone. They're my friends. A jagged friendship, but I've grown used to their presence, like somehow they've sprouted into new parts of me: one part that's a demon and the other part a lost soul.

I plop onto the sand like a child who no longer wants

to be at the beach. The rain spits down like dry heaves, the storm beginning to die. I pound the smooth grains of sand as if they're living things that I want dead, then I pick up handfuls and whip sand at the sea.

Pogo and Celeste are absolutely gone, I know it. I curl into the sand, clutching it in handfuls, close my eyes, and begin to weep for my loss.

25
<hr>

BEACHED

I've resumed daydreaming in order to blot out this place. The sand is my bed, and I may just lie here forever to rot, eyes closed to hide anything resembling the After.

But in time I feel something warm on my back. I imagine that I've been stretched on a quilt with my back to a soothing fireplace. I embrace the comforting warmth without moving or questioning its source. An hour of this and the chill is purged from my body, but still I lounge in the heat.

I know I can't just stay here forever, even though I have nothing else to do now. The idea to move along occurs to me, but I don't want to face it. In the end, the curiosity of the heat makes me open my eyes. I see the sand in front of my face. The lustrous particles twinkle, reflecting a blossoming sunlight, the source of the warmth.

I pull myself to my feet and see a much-changed land-scape. The waves still pound the shore, but with an impact that's closer to routine. The sun penetrates subsiding clouds, and the violent gusts have been replaced with pleasant sea breezes.

The sea reminds me a little of the lake that began my journey into the After. But that had clearly been a lake, enormous but calm, and this is some ocean far more wild and dangerous. Both could be just two of thousands of such bodies of water in the After, for all I know.

I appreciate that I've survived, I really do. I wish I were more thankful for it, but I'm just not feeling it. Instead I watch the waves that have snatched my friends away. Were Celeste and Pogo whisked to some other armpit of the After, or did they drown? Or are they still out there, exhausted, losing hope that land will ever come?

I begin to walk along the beach, returning to the spot where I came ashore. When I see something in the sand, I feel a smile escape the grasp of my futility. I walk up to it and stare down. It's the tree trunk half-buried in the sand, parallel to the shoreline. I'm certain it's the one that brought me to shore. I recognize the spoke that I clung to.

"You made it," I say to the trunk.

I sit down on it and face the ocean, running my hand across the log's weathered surface and patting the moist wood. Some time ago this had been a tree, tall and alive, unaware of the possibility of death. Then something had pulled it up and away, a flood or a storm, shattering its life and shaping it into this decrepit log for me to use as a raft and now a bench. I realize that we have a lot in common. I was a tree once, before I was plucked from my roots and tossed into a journey I didn't want, turned into a dead facsimile of what I once was: a piece of human driftwood.

I'm happy to sit for hours on the log and watch the waves abuse the shoreline. This is the same view people would pay thousands to enjoy on a vacation, and I pretend that's all this is: an obnoxious, eternal vacation. I'll stay here as long as it takes to realize that Celeste and Pogo truly won't be coming up out of the water.

I find myself mumbling words from "A City in the Sea," by Edgar Allan Poe. It's another one of my obscure favorites, long since committed to memory so I could recite it to my students. Was I allowed to memorize it just for this moment? "Lo! Death has reared himself a throne / In a strange city lying alone / Far down within the dim West, / Where the good and the bad and the worst and the best / Have gone to their eternal rest."

A whisper continues the poem from behind me: "There shrines and palaces and towers . . . / resemble nothing that is ours."

I jump to my feet and turn to see Deena standing there, her pure white form so out of place on the beach, as if a majestic birch has sprouted from the sand.

"Hello again, Zak," she smiles. Her echoey voice arrests all of my attention, a sort of divine hypnosis.

I smile back. "I thought I was the only one who knew that poem," I say. "Nothing enthralled my students more than talking about Poe and the macabre."

She won't answer me, but continues to smile. She seems to search the sea behind me, then looks into my eyes with that impeccable flush of white anchored by the intense blue of her irises.

"You are distraught," she says.

I shrug. "Things have taken a turn," I say. "Can you blame me?"

"No," she says, stepping to the log. She sits and pats a spot on the log next to her, the gesture for me to join her there. I sit again, and we say nothing for a long while, the waves saying the words for us.

"You're almost there," she says.

"But I don't even know where *there* is," I say. "Without Pogo, I have no idea where I'm going."

"Have faith in your friends. They aren't finished helping you," she says. "More importantly, have faith in yourself. This is all up to you."

"Wait, they're alive?" I say, standing from my excitement.

"What do you feel?" she asks. "Do you believe they're alive?"

"I don't know," I say, failing to hide my frustration. "Maybe they are."

"Maybe they are," she repeats. I don't know if she's repeating my words or agreeing with me.

I study the surf for signs of Celeste and Pogo, but it's no surprise when all I see is the predictable tumble of waves onto sand.

Deena stands with me. "Come on," she says. "You

should see this." She walks away from the log toward the tree line behind us.

I follow her across the sand and into the woods, keeping my distance behind her, feeling the cold shade from the treetops. In this forest, only the strongest have survived the bombardment of salty winds, each trunk like a pillar of unwavering granite. Undergrowth has no claim here, and its absence makes our passing effortless. The land slopes up, hinting that the ground had once been mountainous, reduced over millennia to a tolerable incline.

Deena walks in silence ahead of me, as if her feet aren't even touching the ground and the forest is unaware of her presence. I'm not sure I want to go where she's leading me, but I have to trust her. The colors flash from her skin, scattering a lavish palette of light across the mossy bark of trees. I look past her and see that the forest ends up ahead.

We exit the trees and arrive at the ledge of a cliff. It surprises me that a cliff would be so close to the seashore without bordering it, and in the opposite direction of the shoreline. What lies beyond it is even more astounding. Out there is a vast openness, fog just below the edge of the cliff so thick it resembles a white ocean. The fog extends out past our line of sight, jagged peaks protruding through it along the horizon like islands jutting from a sea of milk. I know I've never seen anything like this on Earth or in my dreams.

There's more. In the center of it all, a natural structure equal parts impressive and fearsome dominates the view. It seems to hover in the clouds in its browns, blacks, and grays, a dead place, flat on the sides, but rising sharply into a mountain, converging into a towering spire. I want to cower from it, retreat even, return to the beach and the comfort of the log. Why did Deena bring me here?

"That's where you need to go," Deena says, pointing to the spire.

"No it's not," I say, but I'm in denial. She looks at me. It makes me realize that I don't really have a choice in this. If I want to get home, that godforsaken spire is the way.

"That's really the way?"

"I told you you're almost there," she says.

"So what, I just hail a cab and go out there?" I ask. "It seems a little inaccessible."

"There's always a way," she says. God help me, but sometimes I just want to shake this lady. Why does she always need to speak in mysteries? I'm about to ask her what the hell she's talking about when she turns and looks back the way we came.

"Did you hear that?" she asks. I turn with her. I didn't hear anything. I step that way and listen.

"I didn't hear . . ." I cut myself short when I sense something has changed, a turn of events my brain has sensed but is unable to comprehend. I turn toward Deena, but she's gone.

"Deena?"

I huff, feeling my temper begin to fill the void of abandonment.

"Deena!" I shout. "Where did you go now?"

I clench my teeth, rational words twisted into a frustrated hiss. I throw my hands up into the air and stand in silence. It's a pathetic tantrum, but it's all I can manage.

Then there really is a sound. It's like Deena had heard it before it happened. It's coming from down at the beach, nearly inaudible, as natural as the sea breeze itself. I listen closer. When I hear it again, there's no doubt what it is.

"Zak!" Celeste calls.

"Celeste!" I shout. Then I go running through the woods like I'm about to miss my train. "Celeste!" I shout louder, sprinting down the hill, dodging the trees like a shifty halfback. I break through the tree line and feel the weight of the beach sand under my feet. I stop to look. Celeste and Pogo walk the shoreline dripping wet, Celeste calling for me as if she's almost given up hope.

I run to them, calling their names, screaming like a madman in my excitement and desperation for them to see me. They notice me and stop to wait for me to arrive.

I rush to embrace Celeste, feeling her cold, wet body in my arms. She hugs me back, or is she pushing me away? I can't tell, but I don't care.

"Are you all right?" I say, holding her out in front of me to look at her.

She looks out at the sea in disgust, rattled by its power. "I'm fine. To think I used to like the ocean."

"Too far, it was too far," Pogo says, shaking his head. "Nimbali sange."

"He didn't mean to take us so far out to sea after the

Shift," Celeste says. "That storm didn't help anything, either. Plus, Pogo swims like a rock, but we managed."

"I thought you were gone," I said.

"Yeah, well, it takes more than a hurricane to kill us I guess," she says. "Nice beach you have here. Sure beats bobbing around out there."

I remember the spire. "I saw Deena again," I say.

"Oh?"

"Yeah," I say. "Come on, I have something to show you."

But Pogo has already caught on. He's looking toward the woods, staring beyond the trees, recognizing this place from a distant memory. We can't help but watch him look with an apprehension we don't expect.

Pogo points to where Deena had just taken me.

"Cause," he whispers. "We are here."

26

RIDE

We stand near the edge of the cliff. The uneasy feeling returns when I see the spire. It evokes the same emotion that might come from staring at Castle Dracula in the gloom of the Carpathians.

"Is that it?" Celeste points to the spire, as if there's any doubt.

"Yes," Pogo answers. "Cause."

Celeste steps right to the edge of the cliff and looks down. The fog layer obstructs her view below, so she kneels and peers over for a better look. I join her there, the rocky ledge burrowing into my knees. We watch the fog flow like icy sheets along a river. The fog thins, and for a millisecond, we catch a glimpse through. We see tiny dots of dead landscape far below, like from the window of an airplane. Then the fog covers it up, as if it realizes it showed us something it shouldn't have.

"We'll have to find a way down," she says.

Celeste looks at me, her jaw tightening in anticipation of a protest from me, but I don't have one. I know she's right. The only way over to the spire appears to be down.

"We'll have to walk the edge and inspect every part," she says. "There has to be a way down that's manageable."

Pogo begins hopping around. He shakes his head in an emphatic no.

"No?" Celeste asks him. "What do you mean no? I don't see any other . . ."

"No!" he groans, and his head-shaking continues. He hops in place, like words aren't enough so his body has taken over.

"Pogo, relax," Celeste says. "Why not? Is there another way?"

He stops. He nods, slowly at first, then furiously, nodding up and down with all certainty.

"Well how then, genius?" Celeste shouts. "Tell us how!"

Pogo stops nodding. He searches the sky with his serpent eyes, and we follow his field of view to see nothing we haven't already seen. Maybe he sees nothing either, but he's absolutely looking for something. Out there is something he's seen before, but can't see now.

"Hey," Celeste says. She stands and touches Pogo's arm to knock him from his trance. "What do you see?"

Pogo points to the sky. "We will fly."

"Fly?" she repeats.

"We will fly there," he nods. "Voluka."

"Okay, I'm lost," I say, returning to my feet. "Unless we can somehow sprout wings, flying seems iffy."

"I'm not sure what he means either," Celeste says. She gets in front of Pogo's view to attract his full attention. "Fly, Pogo?"

He becomes disturbed again, nodding and hopping around, looking up at the sky, his movements amping up. It looks like he's a prizefighter before a fight, summoning strength to conquer an enemy. He stomps, he flails his arms, and he grunts and moans.

Celeste brushes me back, signaling that Pogo needs his space, and I'm not about to argue. We retreat and watch from a safe distance, and it's a good thing. He transitions into a demonic rampage. He's become the unbridled monster we've seen before, leaping up and down, causing the ledge to shake, spilling rocks over the cliff. Then he begins tossing loose boulders over the side while he roars into the abyss.

Satisfied after minutes of this, Pogo stops and looks at the sky. There's still nothing up there but clouds, and there's an eerie anticipation as we watch for whatever is coming. Nothing does.

Pogo turns, runs past us to the tree line, and steps to the tallest tree, its trunk twice as wide as his own abdomen. He leaps for the tree's lowest limb, and the branch bows when he catches it, but it's solid enough to support him. He flips himself up to a stand on the branch, then jumps for the next limb, swinging up and up like an orangutan. We watch him climb to the top, so high in the air he's only a dot.

"Guess he needed a better look?" I suggest.

"Maybe," Celeste says, staring up at her friend. If she knows what he's up to, she's not saying.

We hear Pogo's roar descend upon the land like a foghorn. Even when his call stops, we hear the echoes racing away. He's silent for a time, then he does it again, the rumbling roar as powerful as before.

"He's calling for something," Celeste says.

"Calling who?" I ask. I almost don't want to know the answer, and Celeste doesn't reply anyway. We wait and listen to his calls, long roars followed by silence.

Celeste walks to Pogo's tree and finds a seat on a boulder next to it. "Looks like this could take a while," she calls to me.

I walk to her, find a fallen limb near her, and sit.

"If he's calling an airline, I don't need a window seat," I say.

I get Celeste to smile from that one. "Let me guess, you're afraid of flying?" she asks.

"On an airplane? No, I'm okay with that. I just have a feeling he's not calling a seven forty-seven."

"Probably not," she says. "But Pogo will get us there. Trust him. Bigger question is what we'll find out there." She points to the spire.

"What do you think's out there?" I ask.

"The gate for you to get home. Simple as that."

"Forgive me for being blunt, but I'm finding nothing simple about the After," I say.

"Nothing is," she says. "Even when you were alive, was it simple?"

"I suppose not."

"We may not be of much help to you over there. I don't know exactly what sort of psychotic horror show awaits. You're going to have to trust yourself, have faith that you can get through it."

I inhale and breathe out. "I know," I say.

"You do?"

"I guess I do," I say. "I was never very good at that, trusting myself, having faith. I could trust myself to read books, and to teach freshmen about literature, but not much else. It doesn't seem like such a difficult thing, to believe that everything will work out. But it is for me."

"Everyone has some trouble with it," Celeste says. "I did."

"You did?"

I think of what I know about Celeste. In life, she was impulsive, angry, an adrenaline junkie, on her own agenda. I deduce that there's faith and confidence in that sort of existence, but a shallow form. Maybe she's learning the limitations of that.

"Sure," she says. "It's part of being human."

"I wish I'd been the kind of person who could go skydiving or climb a mountain without fear, and enjoy it, like you did," I say.

"It's not for everyone," she says. "But sometimes you need to take scary risks. Just, jump."

We both stare out at the spire.

"I suppose so," I say. "But I'd be lying if I said my eyes will be open when I jump."

Pogo's roars have become repetitious, so when we hear something new in the background of his howls, both of us key on the mystery sound. It takes milliseconds to solve it. We both stand, recognizing in unison that it's a buzz of a demon coming our way. But from where? It seems all around us at first, then our brains pinpoint a direction: out there, above the abyss, the sky. A demon is coming from the sky?

"Oh my God," Celeste says, looking up. "Now I get it."

"Get what?" I ask. She doesn't respond because the answer is about to plunge from the clouds. When it happens, she points. I see an airplane. No, a bird, enormous wings gliding and then flapping. It's alive and enormous, even familiar. But not exactly a bird. When I realize the buzzing is coming from the flying creature, I form a crude understanding.

"A flying demon?" I ask. "Demons can fly?"

"Some of them," Celeste says. "I've seen them before. Pogo must know they live out here."

"Celeste, we're not going to ride that thing."

"That's exactly what we're going to do," she says, looking up at Pogo. We hear him roar again, one final bellow to call out his position. He's lured in the flying demon on purpose. Is he nuts?

I step back, my vision focused on the sky. Are we this desperate? I realize that we are, but I want no part of it. The flying demon will devour me before giving us a ride. I step back farther. I want to run away and dive into the ocean and hope the thing can't swim.

"Zak, it's okay," Celeste says.

"But, it's coming right at us," I say, pointing out to it. "It's coming for us. It's coming for me."

There's really no disputing this. Celeste knows I'm like a big prime rib to these things, juicy and irresistible.

She looks up at Pogo again. "Pogo has a plan, just wait."

I keep stepping backward. My brain wants to believe her, but my soul won't. My instinct to flee is too strong. I have to retreat and find cover in the trees, and there's nothing that can tell me otherwise.

"Zak!" she yells when she sees me turn and run. "I said a wait!"

I ignore her. I hear the buzzing thump-thumps of the approaching winged demon, and I stop, turn, and look at it. I see it's mottled with gray and black, wings spread in a gliding descent, unwaveringly targeting me.

There's some solace among the trees, like I'm enveloped by wooden warriors, and I'm a mouse hiding from a falcon. I hear Celeste calling me, imploring for me to stay put. It doesn't matter, I've shut down, my feet planted into the ground like I'm a sapling. The oppression of doom has transformed me into statuary.

But Pogo really does have a plan. The patient hunter, he's rigged me as bait and waits for the perfect moment. When the flying demon soars past the edge of the cliff, Pogo leaps. His dive is astonishing, like an absurd circus act. The hollow eyes of the flying demon fail to notice the trap while homing in on me alone. The buzzing thump-thumps shatter my ears, and I wince. I see Celeste leap behind the protection of boulders, realizing her position is about to become perilous.

Pogo has timed his jump with precision. He lands on the flying demon's back, driving the beast into the ground, tearing an angry trench as they ride the inertia. I jump behind a tree for protection against shrapnel showering into the woods. The ground bucks as I watch a path of destruction cut right past me, carving up the land like two malfunctioning backhoes.

But the trees decide to put an end to the commotion. The demon's wings smash through the timber, shattering trees and sending them flying, but each blow also slows the pace. Soon the two demons only inch forward until the winged demon's head rams a hefty trunk, and with that the upheaval gives way to a dusty silence.

The winged demon squawks, only now realizing the effects of Pogo's trap. Its wings flap against Pogo's grip, but Pogo has only begun. He grabs the demon's head and slams it into the tree again and again, shelling bark from the tree and orange blood from the demon's nostrils. Then comes the stomping, the winged beast no match for Pogo's blows falling on its head and back like anvils. I begin to wonder if anything will be left of the demon to ride.

When Pogo's work is done, he pulls the demon up by the neck and holds it up as if posing a ventriloquist's dummy. As a final assertion of authority, Pogo roars into the demon's face for a full ten seconds, then tosses the creature away. Thoroughly defeated, the winged demon cowers from Pogo. I almost feel sorry for it standing on shaking legs, wings looking wilted, blood streaming from its wounds. Nonetheless, Pogo has secured our ride.

Celeste steps through the debris to join us. She looks at the winged demon, shaking her head. "Now that was a beat-down," she says. She turns to me. "Ready to ride?"

"Not particularly," I say.

27

SPIRE

I try to guess what Cause will be like. In the After, that could be anything. He could be the Grim Reaper or the guy who bags my groceries. I sift through the villain archetypes to find one that fits. Maybe an intellectual who hides psychosis beneath an expensive suit. Or flamboyant and vain, with no attempt to conceal his evil. Even a monster, oozing and foul but you can't help but stare.

I retreat from my own mind, since I'm stumbling toward a truth I'd rather not uncover. I block my thoughts by watching Pogo, who has returned to his usual self. He sits on his rump twisting vines together into a rope, looking like a demented Cub Scout in pursuit of a merit badge. Finished, he takes his rope and wraps it twice around the winged demon's abdomen. I think we're meant to hang onto the rope while we ride. Pogo ties the rope off and tests the strength by giving it a few tugs. The winged demon jostles from the yanks, but the rope holds.

"We will fly," Pogo tells us.

"Are you sure we can ride this thing?" Celeste asks Pogo. I'm glad she does, because it's all I can think about. I mean, we're really going to do this?

Pogo responds with an adamant nod. He reassures us like a used car salesman showing a jalopy, swatting the winged demon's head.

"He flies strong," he says, pointing out to the spire. "Voluka."

The winged demon responds with a squawk, lowering its head in misery. The creature is like any well-broken stallion, and Pogo seems satisfied.

Celeste turns to me. "All right, saddle up then."

I look at the winged demon, its back as high as an elephant's. "How, I can't . . ."

Pogo sees that the demon is too tall for me. He pounds on the demon's back, forcing the creature onto its stomach, its wings tucked to its sides like a hen on the nest. That's a little better. I step forward, reach out my hand, and feel the contours of the demon's leathery side. I grab hold of Pogo's rope and try to pull myself up, but I wiggle and hang from the beast without really getting anywhere. Pogo corrects this by lifting me up with one hand and plopping me onto the demon's back, and I sit there wondering what happened. Celeste pulls herself up and sits behind me, and the demon takes our weight as if we're not even there. I grip the rope to get used to the minimal safety it provides.

Pogo hops on front, grabbing the demon's horns that

curve out, resembling those of an ox. He slams the demon's head forward with a push on its horns and shouts: "Initanza!" The winged demon gets the message. It stands, extends its wings, and begins flapping. The dust sifts beneath the wings as the demon's body clenches for flight. With Pogo weighing it down, I wonder if the beast has the power to carry us. We lift up a few feet, bob, and then glide from the cliff in full flight, quelling my doubt.

We're flying, but only if you dare to call it that. Mechanized flight is efficient and controlled, but riding the back of a demon is bucking, swaying bedlam. My hands are locked to the rope until they whiten with strain. With each rise and fall my body floats like a windsock, but my death grip won't budge. Like a fool, I've trusted a rickety amusement park ride, but it's too late; all I can do is hang on.

Just when my hands begin to cramp, Pogo tames the ascent with a forward tug on the demon's horns. We level. I dig deeper into the demon's side with my heels and legs, the scent of the beast's oily flesh rushing into my nose.

The demon's wings stiffen into a glide. We hang in the air like a kite riding the turbulence. For a time I enjoy this magical silence, even forget where we're going and why. I'm experiencing the impossible, riding the back of a demon in a place I never knew existed. I look behind me to see Celeste grinning, the awe of flight not wasted on her.

I turn my focus to the spire ahead. I thought it looked enormous from the distance, but up closer it's gargantuan. It's thousands of feet high, and an entire city could fit inside it. I'm struck by the lack of color and life in front of me, the spire gray and black, the land surrounding it thorny, brown, and beige, like something dead has held it hostage for centuries. There's something else, a nag in my chest I can't ignore. I sense a sort of turmoil, a duel between apprehension and opportunity, the owner of those emotions watching and waiting.

We feel a jolt from an angry headwind. I watch Pogo fight with the demon's horns to maintain control, the creature's wings making an instinctive adjustment to retain course. The demon howls in frustration at Pogo's meddling.

"Initanza!" Pogo shouts again, pointing to the flatter ground around the spire. He shoves the demon's head groundward, ordering the demon to land. We drop and veer sideways, my stomach flipping inside me, but the winged demon is a wizard of flight, and it regains control. I hunker in tighter and watch the oncoming land with teeth clenched.

We angle toward a meadow, narrow and tiny, too small for us. The winged demon knows this, and it pulls away, but Pogo steers it back on course with another wrench of its horns. Pogo doesn't care how pleasant our landing will be, he wants it done. The demon screeches into submission, ducks its head toward the meadow, and fixes its wings for landing.

As we nose down, it becomes obvious that the winged demon just wants to end the madness. He's going full speed like there's nothing more to lose. He's submitting to a kamikaze, and we're all going to splatter across the meadow. Now we're the ones who've been duped.

I don't like this anymore. We're a sputtering jetliner approaching a gusty O'Hare runway, and there's a terrorist in the cockpit. What could go wrong?

Celeste must know that I'm rattled. "Hang on!" she shouts from behind me, like I have any other option. It only confirms that landing here is an awful idea. I embrace the demon's back like a giant leech digging into its host.

Seconds from impact, the demon's wings twist up, catching the headwind like sails of a schooner. The demon yanks its head back and extends its legs forward, wings slapping back the air and agitating the foliage below. We've come in too fast for such a tiny landing strip. The beast's right wing clips a dead oak, snipping the tree in two with a crack, knocking us off course. We careen left into another tree, left wing bashing it to tinder. This knocks the demon onto its stomach, and we mow through the trees and weeds before reaching a clumsy stop.

The winged demon is ravaged by the crash, but his energy reserve has kicked in, and he thrashes about. Celeste jumps off and I follow, falling hard onto the ground. Pogo rides longer just for the thrill of it, but the writhing intensifies. Pogo swats the beast's neck and leaps away.

Through the clouds of dust hanging in the clearing like mustard gas, I see the winged demon take flight again. It screeches, elated to be free of its passengers. We watch it circle high into the air, bellow one last farewell, and disappear into the clouds, leaving us in absolute silence.

Unhurt, we gather ourselves and look around. Our surroundings defy explanation. Like I noticed from the air, everything is dead, from the bone-dry grass to the scraggly trees stripped of leaves. This place once teemed with life, but something unseen has swept it all away, leaving nothing but skeletons and absolute silence.

Above everything is the spire itself, shaped like a natural version of the Empire State Building, but a thousand times its size. The spire extends down into a wider foundation of sheer rock, a natural pedestal that anchors the spire in place. I have to look straight up to see the spire's summit, and it's almost higher than my eyes can see.

The ground begins to shake. Fixed on the spire, my first thought is it's a rockslide from the spire itself, but the shaking isn't coming from there, it's coming from where we stand. An earthquake?

Between us and the spire is a formidable tangle of decayed trees. They've come to life with the shaking, as if each limb is a tentacle of a monster. Then I understand that the trees aren't moving from the ground shaking, it's the other way around—the moving trees are causing the ground the shake.

I step back, not wanting to know why trees would move on their own. Pogo roars at the trees and stomps the ground, ready to fight something. From deep within the woods, we hear a concert of woody cracks and pops, the entire forest moving as one.

"Celeste, what's going on?" I yell. I can barely hear myself above the clatter. Celeste just shakes her head—she has no idea.

The forest provides an answer. The trees part in the same way that a security gate might open, clearing a footpath in front of us. Then everything stops, returning to the silence of before. We're meant to enter, but there's no way I'm going in there.

I flinch when I hear a voice. It's squeaky, the uttering of a child, but loud and coming from everywhere: "Hello, Zak."

"He is Cause," Pogo whispers.

"What?" I ask. "Cause is a child?"

"Do you want to play?" Cause speaks again. I don't know where to look, I can't pinpoint where the voice is coming from.

Pogo doesn't want to play. His idea of play is crushing and maiming: "Cause!" he shouts, and roars toward the spire. He jumps up and down and growls away any suggestion of play.

"Quiet!" shouts Cause. Pogo's body goes rigid, not because he's complying but because something has got a hold of him. His body twitches as he loses an inner struggle, then he stiffens again. He falls to the ground, the impact of his body stirring up dust.

"Pogo!" Celeste calls. She steps to his aid before the same affliction gets her. She begins to quiver like getting a jolt from a car battery, then relaxes and turns to me. She's lost the struggle already, but instead of keeling over, she speaks. When she talks it's the voice of Cause.

"Zak," it says. "Do you want to play?"

I definitely do *not* want to play. This was a horrible idea to come here, the worst idea ever. I want to call the winged demon back and ride it far, far away from here. Screw all of this!

But those aren't options anymore. I try to get a grip. "That . . . depends," I say, trying to figure out who I'm dealing with.

"You'll play with me," Cause says through Celeste's mouth. "You have to. Come in. Follow the path."

Celeste's eyes close and she collapses next to Pogo. Cause is finished with her, for the moment.

I go to her, kneel by her, and touch her shoulder. Her eyes flutter open, and she looks disgusted.

"This Cause is a *major* tool bag," she says.

I help her to her feet. Pogo is standing again too, bewildered and perturbed.

"We have to get out of here," I say.

"And then what?" Celeste says. "Do you want to get home or not?"

"I want to get home, but . . ."

"There's no other way," she says. "Obviously Cause can do anything he wants to us, this is his place. But we can't give up now."

She's right. Of course she's right. I can see my family

in my mind, waiting for my return as if I've only been on a short business trip.

I sigh and look up at the spire, then over to the path leading straight to Cause's lair.

"All right," I say, nodding. I feel like my nodding is in place of screaming. "Sure buddy, we can play. Let's play!"

We head for the path.

28

INSIDE

I berate myself for always thinking the worst. As we walk the path toward the spire, I assume the role of the death row inmate headed toward the execution chamber. Pogo and Celeste are the priest and the lone prison guard trailing behind me.

Stop it! I'm not going to die. Anyway, I'm already Half Dead, so what's really to lose? Somehow that brings a sliver of comfort to me, that I've already lost everything. Odds are slim that I can get it all back, but it's the carrot that dangles in front of me. Call it faith.

Words would be wasted on this final stage of our journey, so no one tries. The trees stifle the light and the air is stale with an eternal autumn. This reminds me that I miss the fall, the turning of the leaves, the chill in the air, the labor pains of winter. It's a metaphor for missing my family, their growth measured by the changing of the seasons. My life is becoming estranged, the beginning of a great forgetting.

The path ends at an entrance cut into the base of the spire. The opening is three times my height, chiseled out precisely, dark, like the mouth of a mine stripped of its fortune and abandoned.

I guess we're meant to go inside, but it doesn't mean I want to. I want someone else to go first, but when I look back at Celeste and Pogo, I sense that something about them has profoundly changed. Timid is not a word I would have used to describe them before, but it is now. Being transformed into a puppet by an all-powerful being will do that to anyone. No, this is my show now. My friends will be of little help here, as Celeste had guessed.

I step into the cave and sniff the air of sulfur and minerals. I realize I'm blind to whatever may be lurking inside, the darkness spilling a chill into my face. I pull my phone from my pocket. This phone has been through a lot, including being submerged in seawater. Always a klutz, I had bought a durable phone case when I got the phone—drop proof, waterproof, the works. I turn on my phone and it responds, and I'm grateful for the foresight of an expensive case, although I never envisioned needing my phone for the rigors of the afterlife. I turn on the light app to see in the cave. I expect to see something ferocious coming at me from down the tunnel, but when I light the area I see only a straight passage stretching farther than the light can penetrate.

"It goes way in," I call back to Pogo and Celeste. They

say nothing. I inhale a deep breath, turn, and stroll deeper inside.

A few dozen steps in, I hear Celeste and Pogo following me into the cave. I stop, turn, and see that Celeste has one of her energy rocks in her hand, the stone casting a green light, painting their faces a vibrant lime. They may be coming, but they're also keeping their distance. I don't know what to make of this except it's unsettling that I've become the brave one.

We leave the entrance far behind us. Our steps echo through the tunnel that's precise and immaculate. If a massive laser were to sear a rectangular cut through the side of a mountain, its path might look like this. It's not a passage cut by the imperfection of human hands or nature, but maybe the result of Cause willing it to be.

We venture far enough that the light disappears behind us like the sun plunging below the horizon. Our artificial lights take over, but we don't need them long. I see a dim light up ahead. It reminds me of the first signs of sunrise, a glow barely perceptible, the early light of a world waking to turmoil. I could crawl faster than what my pace evolves into, but it's fine with me. I'm in no hurry to see what's at the end of the tunnel. Certainly it's Cause, and I'm not sure I'm ready to meet him up close. I need time to reassure myself that this really is the only way.

The light in front of us becomes bright enough that I turn off my phone and return it to my pocket. As I do, I brush up against the butt of my pistol. I caress it, hoping some of its courage will rub off on me, knowing that it's silly to think a gun can do anything here. I'm still glad I have it, that it might be of some use to me yet, if nothing else a steel good luck charm.

The passage ends. When I step into the full light, nothing I find is what I expected to see. I've entered a natural wonder like no other in existence. In front of me is the interior of the spire, hollowed out and spilling in sunlight from outside through crevices spanning its height. The effect is a cathedral dome, but it would dwarf any church. Its width is larger yet, a geological coliseum spanning thousands of yards. An entanglement of stalagmites, boulders, and giant oaks covers the flat plain in front of me, impenetrable as the Amazon. It looks to be an entire world left hidden to all but Cause.

Celeste joins me on my right, Pogo on my left. We stand and wait for something that never happens, leaving us bewildered about what to do but stand there and look around.

"Did we forget to ring the doorbell?" Celeste asks.

"He knows we're here," I say. I wonder if we're being observed to assess the most satisfying way to annihilate us. He's really taking his time at it.

Then a gust disturbs the trees, a curious occurrence in a space screened from the wind. I surmise that a breeze has gushed in from the same crevices that let in sunlight, but it's the way that the air surrounds and tickles us that makes me skeptical, like the breeze is the residue of something alive.

I hear a familiar sound to my left, a noise I thought

would be unlikely to occur inside the spire. It begins softly, as if the intro to a brooding fugue, then it's bombastic, deafening, coming from right next to me. It's Pogo. He's buzzing like the demons that have stalked me in the After, accompanied by the thump-thumps like a heartbeat, the electric bloodlust of a demon on the prowl.

"Pogo, stop!" Celeste says, stepping between him and me, touching his arm to bring him back under control. It's too late, Cause has him again. It's a simple juxtaposition of energy—burying the good, equipping the bad. Pogo inhales and stands tall. He lifts Celeste and tosses her back down the tunnel. I hear a clatter as she cartwheels into the darkness and out of sight. I look up and see Pogo's sick, serpent eyes.

"Come on Pogo," I say, stepping back. "Cause is using you, fight through it."

My words almost don't exist beneath the blare of his demon sounds, and Pogo is not paying attention anyway. He's gone, replaced by his ugly demon alter ego. I continue to step back, drawing my gun and pointing it toward his head with both hands. He stops, which buys me time to distance myself by a few more steps. I'm happy my gun has this effect on him until I realize his hesitation was only to summon the stockpile of anger he carries deep inside. A roar bursts from his drooling mouth as he vaults forward a step, both arms raised, fists clenched.

I shoot him. God help me, but I blast him again and again. Good shots, deadly shots to his eye, forehead, and neck. I'm stunned by the callousness of my gunplay, the willingness to obliterate a friend at the first sign of trouble. The shots would have slaughtered a human, yet they hardly affect him. With my gun empty, he bellows at me, and I see his legs go tight, springs of inertia preparing to launch. He pounces.

Celeste rushes from the cave and hurls a stone with a crack of her sling, the rock bursting forward and clipping Pogo's legs from under him. The explosion blows me to my back and sends Pogo tumbling to my right. He falls hard head first and unmoving.

"Zak!" Celeste yells, coming to me. "Get up, you have to go! Run!"

I stand on rickety legs. "Go where?" I ask, my ears ringing.

"In there," she points to the forest. "As far from us as you can get. I can feel him. Cause is everywhere. He's . . ."

Celeste stiffens, and I know Cause has her again. I allow my jaw to drop, half at the urge to speak, half to scream. Instead I close my mouth and run. I head for the wilderness of stones and trees that's the heart of Cause's spire world, my only chance to escape my friends.

I hear from behind me the whipping of Celeste's sling, the horrible sound of her preparing to bombard me. It's happened that fast, good to evil in one breath. Without any protest, Celeste wants me dead.

I hear the snap of the sling, signaling the release of the rock. Her aim is always lethal—I've seen this firsthand—but I've also grown accustom to the snapping sound. I react, darting sideways to dodge her aim. The rock zings past me and connects with an oak, the tree of a hundred years exploding to a mangled heap. I look away, the shockwave nearly spilling me down again, but I maintain my balance and stumble to the left. I sprint through obstacles, bouncing from tree trunks to rocks until I find cover behind a boulder the size of a cargo van. I hunker behind it, sucking in air to catch my breath.

I raise the gun, open the cylinder, and eject the spent shells to the ground. My quivering hand pulls bullets from my belt to feed the empty chambers. I wonder if Officer Sheridan ever went through this with this gun, hoping he could reload before the perpetrator found him. My reloading is far from cop-like. It's more like an oafish giant trying to string thread through the head of a tiny needle. It's clumsy, and I'm taking way too long, my shaking like the onset of hypothermia.

Somehow I've loaded three rounds when I hear a twig snap from the other side of the boulder. Celeste is here, she's right upon me, and I'm not ready for her. I slap the cylinder shut anyway, raise the gun, and step around the boulder. She's there all right, sling at the ready with another stone, but she's surprised that I would be on the offensive, her assumption that I'd prefer to hide. That's usually a good bet, but I've surprised even myself. I aim at her head and pull the trigger, eyes closed. The hammer snaps forward with only a click against one of the empty chambers.

I open my eyes to see Celeste smiling. It's not a friendly

smile, it's the smile of bloodthirsty victory. I pull the trigger again, but once more it just clicks.

"You have to load it first, Zak," she mocks.

I pull the trigger again, and this time the gun responds with a crack. I wasn't anticipating it going off, and I flinch. The bullet glances off her cheek, cutting a red line of blood across her face to her ear.

"Hey!" she shouts, reaching for her wound. "You shot me!"

I plug her again. The bullet slaps her forehead, and she stumbles back, onyx eyes in a daze from the devastating blast. She crumples.

"Celeste!" I shout, and I kneel at her side. I've killed her for sure. How could it be possible that I'd murder my own friend?

But she's not dead. I have to remember that Celeste is not easily killed. The hole in her head is horrific, but the breaths are still coming from her open mouth, her chest still rising and falling, her eyes still seeing.

"I told you to run, you idiot," she whispers, the wound momentarily restoring her to the old Celeste. "That means keep running."

"I'm sorry," I say.

"I know," she smiles. "You're always sorry."

Celeste closes her eyes. She's beginning to heal herself.

"All right," I say. "Heal yourself, you'll be okay. You have to be okay. I can't live with killing you."

I'm interrupted by a roar in the distance. Pogo. He's

slowly picking up the pieces back where Celeste's rock dropped him.

"Stop talking," she says, reopening her eyes. "Listen to me for a change. I said run. Pogo's going to come for you."

I stand and look down at her, nodding like an imbecile. I take deep breaths like a sprinter before a race, eyeing the terrain away from here. Then I holster the gun and jog away. Soon I'm sprinting as fast as I've ever run in my life.

29

PLAY

It really is all me now. I choose the direction, I control my next move, I face the consequences of my decisions. This is the disconcerting reality. I'm directing a frigate through wild seas, and I have no business being anything but a cabin boy, plus the crew is gone.

I envision a throne high atop the spire's dome where Cause sits and senses everything. If that exists, I must look like a frantic gopher scuttling through acres of stony undergrowth. If I could will my body to transform, it would evolve from a gopher to a wolf, a beast on the hunt for its own preservation, wild with survival adrenaline. But there's nothing that noble about me.

At least my time in the After has improved my fitness; running for my life is more effective than any health club. There's a bizarre corollary there: When alive, I was running *from* my life; when dead, I'm running *for* my life.

But I'm sick of running. No matter where I end up after all this, there will be no more running.

But for now, it's a run, call it a sprint for the finish line. I dart past obstructions, trip over a tree root, careen into a boulder, shove myself away and onward, dodging tree trunks the size of Grecian pillars, stepping strategically through natural gaps.

I can't keep up the pace. Fear has propelled me here, but breathlessness has shoved fright aside, my legs slowing to ease the burden. I stop, bend over, and prop my hands on my thighs. I wish my mouth could consume air faster. I close my eyes and let the smarter parts of my body make things right again. The body always does the job, recovers in ways we don't comprehend. With a dozen more strained breaths, my breathing slows. I straighten up and try to relax my breaths even more.

I look behind me for signs of someone in pursuit, ready to react at the single flutter of a leaf, but the area I've passed through is a motionless hush. I dare to hold there, to allow my heart and lungs another minute of recovery, my better judgment complaining that I'm being foolish not to move on.

I flinch when I hear Pogo growl. Is he far off? I think so, but I can't tell. The sound bounces through the erratic acoustics of the land, and I can't pinpoint it. I hear his buzzing all around me like a swarm of killer bees I can't see, and that's plenty to urge me on. There's still some distance between us, but I have to keep it that way.

More running. The next stretch of my race is rockier ground. Trees give way to a muddle of boulders, and I become lost in them. But the deeper I go, the more protected I feel, like inside the walls of a castle. I stop and listen. All I hear is my own breath.

I deduce it's safe to walk rather than run. Each turn down a different passage of boulders makes me more confident of this. If Pogo is behind me, he's just as lost as I am. Once again I allow my lungs to replenish the oxygen and calm my system.

This maze of boulders fills me with a bittersweet memory. There's a place near my home called Purgatory Chasm. Believed to be formed by a great glacial melt, it's a natural path carved into granite. Today, the boulders and slopes attract visitors by the thousand to hike and climb. I took my family there once, and for a time it was a great decision. We climbed rocks for hours, the girls enjoying the challenge and wonder of stone. But then Lacy fell on her face, opening a crescent gash in her forehead, forcing a frantic trip to the ER. I blamed myself for the accident, knowing that the outing had been my idea, and we never returned.

There's a problem there. We should have gone back. When you fall, you have to get up and try it again. That should have been the lesson, not to run away. Beyond that, we should have gone more places, tried more things, been a family for as long as we could, but it was me who prevented it, preferring to shut down rather than to live.

I try to distract myself from my failures by running my hands along the boulders as I walk. I start imagining how this facsimile of Purgatory Chasm got here. Maybe instead of a glacial flow, it was formed by the hands of Cause himself, every ounce as powerful as nature. He was bored with his flat landscape one day, and with the clap of his hands he opened the ground for the rocks to escape, then ran his fingers through the piles in artistic paths like a child playing in sand.

In sync with that thought is the sensation that I'm being watched. There may actually be more to it than just a feeling. I assume Cause can see me stepping over his boulders and snaking through his caverns. But I sense that he also sees *inside* me, he knows what I think and feel. He understands my failures and memories as well as I do.

Up ahead the boulders thin out. I stop and wonder if I should double back, because I don't want to lose the protection of this maze. But I hear Pogo's buzzing distantly behind me, urging me forward.

I reach a natural amphitheater of rock surrounding a pool of water that's so blue it looks artificial. Around the pool is a shoreline of scraggly trees reflecting shadows across the water. It's enticing, like I should go down by the water and lounge away my troubles on a flat rock. I walk toward the pond, knowing this is no time for amusement, my goal only to find a way past.

But the peculiar wind returns, almost as if I've triggered it. I stop and witness the stranglehold the gust has on this place. The wind grabs hold of the treetops, then circles the amphitheater like chariots carrying Roman gladiators. I take a step back when the wind comes and swirls around me, the pressure of its presence popping my ears. The gust lifts debris into a cyclone, which spins forth and exhales a roar of suction. Five feet from me, the cyclone dissipates, but before it dies, it births a solitary human figure. He stands in the haze of sediment sprinkling back to the ground.

It's a child. A boy.

"Hello Zak," he says. "I've waited *so* long for you. Can you play now?"

Cause.

I'm pretty good with kids, even comfortable around them, but my confidence drains along with the blood from my face. I look at the simple child, no more than seven, summery in his bare feet, shorts, and t-shirt, his hair gnarled and dirty. What horrible thing is hiding inside this illusion?

"Zak, can you play?" Cause says. I can't think of how to answer that, so I don't. He frowns, and a look of frustration takes over, the childish dejection of an outcast.

"Why aren't you talking, Zak?" he says, stepping right up to me.

I look down at him, but in a way I feel like I'm looking up.

"I'm not sure I know what you mean by *play*," I say.

"Play," he says, shrugging. "We can throw rocks in the pond."

"Throw rocks?"

"Or swim, or play hide and seek. Haven't you ever played before?"

"Yes, it's just been a while. You just want me to play?"

"Sure, it's fun."

"Okay," I say.

Cause smiles. "Let's throw rocks in the pond, come on!" He turns and runs toward the pond, glancing over his shoulder to make sure I'm following, beckoning me to come when I only stand there. He wants to throw rocks. I can throw rocks. Sure, let's just throw rocks. I follow him.

Cause has already reached the shore. He picks up a stone, winds up, and hurls it into the center of the pond. It splashes into the tranquil water, sending shockwaves in every direction. He picks up another and tosses it just as far.

"Nice throw," I say, reaching his side. "Do you play baseball?"

"Nah," he says. "I just like throwing stuff. You try one."

I look down at the assortment of pastel pebbles on shore, round and smooth like a pile of Easter eggs. I'm trying not to think about the surreal nature of this encounter with an all-powerful child, and instead reach down and pick up a rock, a brilliant red one. I toss it far into the pond, farther than Cause threw his.

"Not bad," he says, cocking his head to study the impact. Then he picks up another stone and throws it in. Leisurely, nearly pleasantly, we pick up more stones and toss them into the pond, one at a time. We throw them as if time doesn't exist, the occasional compliment to one another after our tosses, an endless supply of stones feeding our play in what seems like a game that won't end. I become used to this game, even relaxed by it, this simple pleasure of youth. But I can't forget my greater objective.

"I have a question," I say after a while, when I think the timing is right. I turn to him and he turns to me. "Is it okay to ask questions?" I ask him.

"Not really," Cause says. "But okay. What's your question?"

"I was wondering why you're here, all alone?"

Cause squints and thinks about this. "I'm not alone," he says. "You're here."

I smile. "Yes, that's true. But before I came, were you all alone here? A young boy living by yourself?"

"Yes," he says. "Are you going to tell on me?"

I laugh. "No, no. I wouldn't tell, I was just wondering."

"Okay," he says. "Hey, do you want to see a trick?"

"A trick?"

"Yeah, it's a trick. Do you want to see?"

I don't think I do.

Cause shows me anyway. He stretches both hands out toward the pond, palms up. Then he makes the motion of a mime lifting an invisible, heavy object with both hands. But he's no mime. The pond begins to stir like tea swooshing in a gigantic teacup. Cause raises his arms high into the air, and as he does, the pond lifts up. It hovers there in front of us, just the water, thousands of gallons floating midair like a blob of blue Jell-O.

"Do you like this trick?" he asks, turning his head to look at me. You'd think holding up such a weight would cause a strain in his voice, but he speaks as if nothing has changed.

I nod, disbelief stealing my words.

"I like lifting the pond. But do you know what's even better?" he asks.

"I can't imagine," I respond.

"Dropping it."

His arms fall to his sides. The water free-falls, pushing saturated air into my face. The torrent slams into its muddy bed, sending a wave of water into our feet. I watch water wash along the shoreline, then recede back into a boiling blackness, no longer an innocent blue.

Cause laughs and jumps on the watery ground, clapping his hands. "Did you like that Zak?" he asks.

I nod.

"Should I do it again?" he asks.

Instead of answering I look toward the other side of the amphitheater. I notice a chasm there, chiseled straight so I can see its full length. The chasm leads to the other side of the spire's interior, and at the end of the path is a cave entrance. It looks identical to the cave I had passed through to enter this place. It's an exit. No, it's more than that, like a place I've always known: the way home.

"You can't leave," Cause says. He knows my plan as if

I've just said it aloud. I look at the child, his expression gone serious, even flirting with anger.

"I'd like to stay," I say. "It's just, I have a family to return to. Two daughters nearly your age, and a wife."

"Oh them," he says. "I know about them." His face sours, and I'm uncomfortable with the significance of that. He knows my family, and he dislikes them.

"Don't you have a family?" I ask.

He shakes his head. "No. And you don't need your family. I can be your family. We can live here, and you can be my big brother, or maybe my uncle. Uncle Zak."

It's a strange thing to try to think, knowing that your thoughts aren't hidden. You can't really do it. Even my most distant inklings are clear to Cause. There are thoughts that I can't suppress, packaged in my mind with the clarity of a newspaper article: I have to get away from Cause, and I have to get to that cave. Inside I'll find the portal home.

"I have other things to show you," Cause says, clinging to the idea that I'll stay with him. "Amazing things. You won't want to leave once you see them, I promise."

I open my mouth to protest, but Cause has raised his arms again. He reaches high above his head, then lowers his limbs to his sides like doing an exercise. When he does, everything disappears. It's as if he's closed the drapes to his world.

The next thing I see is an illuminated blue and white globe over a backdrop of black. I've seen this before in photos, but pictures never looked quite like this. I'm seeing Earth from outer space.

When my awareness catches up, I see there's much more to it. I look down and see a rocky, sandy expanse. It's a powdery gray wasteland, cold and dark, devoid of life.

Cause is beside me, smiling in response to my flabbergasted expression. I don't how it's possible, but Cause has taken us to the moon.

30

AMAZING PLACES

I'm no rocket scientist, but even I know humans can't survive on the moon without a spacesuit, and I'm not wearing one. I'm going to suffocate, freeze stiff, and float into deep space forever. I gasp, afraid to breathe.

"Do you like outer space?" Cause asks me. He's confident, unaware of any danger. I'm sure I look just the opposite, like I'm about to be devoured by a bear. But I look down at myself, and I see that my body is intact. I breathe, and the air is perfectly normal. Either this is one doozy of an illusion, or Cause has defied nature by plopping us on the moon in total safety.

"We're on the moon?" I ask, not yet believing it.

"Yeah, isn't it neat? Earth looks pretty silly out here, doesn't it? Like a little ball."

"It's amazing," I say. Illusion or not, I'm dazzled by this once-in-a-lifetime experience. How many people can say they've been on the moon?

"I can take us anyplace," he says, turning toward me. "There's no need for you to be anywhere else but with me."

I think of the possibilities. Europe, the Caribbean, Japan. Maybe another time period entirely, prehistoric times or the Renaissance. Another planet even, Mars, or other worlds with life that we didn't know existed.

"I can show you more, if you don't believe me," Cause says.

With another raising of his arms, he erases our surroundings. In place of the moon and space, more familiar impressions begin to appear. A marble walkway extends so far in front of us that we can't see its end, light reflecting off the intricate shapes of the tile work. Oak tables and red velvet chairs line the walkway, illuminated by the glow of green bankers lamps. The beginnings of a vaulted ceiling form hundreds of feet above. I smell the unmistakable odor of old books.

On both sides of the walkway emerge hundreds of oak bookshelves like a time-lapse view of sprouting plants extending high into the air. The shelves meet a ceiling and stop, then begin anew on another level, climbing ever higher and repeating the process, story after story until the shelves extend a full ten levels on both sides of the walkway. The finishing touch is the main ceiling ten stories above. A patchwork of murals begins to form in between oak inlays, as if an invisible hand is drawing them in supersonic speed. When the work is complete, I smile, recognizing what the murals represent: the whale from

Moby Dick, Chaucer's pilgrims from *The Canterbury Tales*, Scout, Jem, and Atticus from *To Kill a Mockingbird*. My mouth hangs open as I pick out more images, each one massaging my literary memory.

"Amazing," I say, turning in a circle to take it all in. "It's a library."

"Not just any library," Cause says. "My library. I made it. It has every book ever written. You could read all of them. I like Dr. Seuss. Do you like Dr. Seuss?"

I can't help myself. I ignore the child and walk to a shelf. It's the S's, the familiar names beckoning to be read: Shakespeare, Shelley, Stein. I run my fingers along the spines of russet, olive, and ash, the older ones among them fancifully embossed from when society really relished the printed word. Steinbeck, Stoker, Stowe. Characters mingle in my head from Lady Macbeth to Victor Frankenstein to Lennie Small. My hand reaches toward Swift, removing a copy of *Gulliver's Travels*. I leaf through the pages I've read before, the satirical adventures of Lemuel Gulliver and Lilliput and Blefuscu.

"Remarkable book," I say, turning to Cause and holding up the book for him. He shrugs like he knows it, or he doesn't care. I shelve the book and look in awe at the bounty all around me, more books than I've ever seen in one place.

"Amazing," I say again, continuing my walk through the S's. I'm about to reach for a book with an intricate gilt binding when I see the library begin to disappear. I turn to see that Cause has raised his arms again, intent on showing me more.

"No, wait!" I shout, holding up my hand to get him to stop. I want to see more, to see everything. I try to reach for another book, but the books and the shelves disappear. The entire library is then rubbed away. Maybe it was Cause's plan for me to see just enough to be hooked, like any good novel's first chapter.

The magnificent library is replaced with something altogether different. The first thing to appear is a tranquil lake, its surface blue with reflections from the sky and a murky green from the trees onshore. More of the environment takes shape. Mountains rise and surround the lake, giving the impression of a giant crater.

I'm sitting at a table on the balcony of a rustic European lodge overlooking the lake, part of a quiet village tucked into the hillside. From within the village, I hear a church bell chime six times, and by the light of day I judge it's evening. Spread on the table in front of me is an appealing bounty: sausages, slices of freshly baked bread, a basket of fruit, sliced tomatoes, brie, crackers, colorful canapés.

"Wine?" comes a woman's voice.

I turn to see a woman sitting at the table beside me. She holds a bottle of Riesling, intent on pouring into the wine glass in front of me. She has a European look to her: blonde hair, fair skin, sharp features. I'm shocked that such a beautiful woman would be sitting next to me offering me wine, so I don't know how to answer her. She pours even though I don't respond.

"Have you ever seen anything so beautiful?" she asks when finished pouring. She speaks with an accent, German or Austrian. I don't know whether her comment is referring to herself or our surroundings, or both. "The view," she clarifies when I look confused. "It's wonderful, is it not?"

"Yes," I say. I look around the balcony. We're alone, Cause is gone.

"Here," the woman says, selecting a canapé for me, holding it up like some sort of prize. It's smoked fish atop a cucumber slice garnished with a sprig of dill. She brings it to my mouth and waits for me to open. "These are delicious. Try." I open my mouth. She smiles and pops it in. I chew, the smoky, fishy taste mingling with the dill. I don't recall the last time I've eaten, and the taste is superb.

"Do you like it?" she asks, smiling. I nod and continue to chew, then wash it down with a sip of the Riesling, alcohol instantly hitting my bloodstream. I don't know where Cause has brought me, and I don't know who this woman is, but all of it intrigues me, like being placed in some dreamy painting of Europe.

"Where are we?" I ask her.

"That doesn't matter, Zak," she says. The woman knows my name. "Do you enjoy it here?"

"Yes," I say.

"Then that's all that's important." She feeds me another canapé.

As I chew and then sip more wine, I wonder where Cause is. I look at the woman who watches me while she smiles pleasantly. I want to ask her questions: what's her name, where is she from, what does she like to do? Then I remember my wife. I may be Half Dead, but I'm still married. This thought distracts me from her, and in that process I make a connection. There's something familiar about this woman.

"Cause?" I say to her. She doesn't respond, but keeps watching me while smiling. But I've figured it out, the woman's silence only confirms it. Cause has changed his form into a beautiful European woman. She's as much illusion as everything here, just like the library and the moon. I don't know how he can make everything seem so real, but it's all phony.

"You can do anything, take me anywhere," I say to her, knowing that I'm speaking to Cause. "But none of it's real. It seems real, but because I know it's not, it will never be genuine."

"It's real, Zak," she says. "This place, me."

I stand. "No, none of that's true," I say. "I can't live in a lie. I need to go home again. That's all that's real, and it's all I want."

The woman's smile shifts to disappointment. Along with this change in her expression, our surroundings begin to fade like a painting slowly overrun with thinner. Then the woman shrinks and transforms into something vastly different: the boyish form of Cause. The lake, mountains, and balcony give way to the relative familiarity inside

Cause's spire. We've returned back to his pond amphitheater.

Cause looks at the ground. "It's real if you let it be real," he says. "Whatever you want, wherever you want to be, I can create it. You'll learn to see how real it can be."

"But I can't," I say. "I'm really sorry. I have to go home now."

"Don't leave me," he says, stepping toward me, looking at me with desperation. "You can't leave me, I won't let you go."

"I know you want me to stay," I say. "But I really have to go. I'm needed back home. I want to go back."

"That's stupid," Cause snaps. "No, you'll stay. I won't let you leave." He folds his little arms in front of him in defiance.

I begin a slow walk away from him toward the chasm. It surprises me that my only plan is to just walk away, that my return home depends on this pathetic escape attempt. Cause will stop me without even exerting himself.

"Where are you going?" he screeches. "Stop walking!" I keep on walking, a tickle at the back of my neck hinting that there will be a penalty for ignoring him.

I feel the strange wind again, Cause's breeze. I can see it travel around me through the rattling of the trees. It goes ahead of me, then doubles back into the cyclone Cause uses for travel. Again it spits out Cause and dissipates, the boy hunching to block my path.

"You are *not* a good listener!" he shouts.

I stop. I look at that little face, and for the first time I see outright anger there. Even more, something has seeped into my consciousness, a sixth-sense reconnaissance. I actually feel what he feels: helplessness, loneliness, despondency. I hear what he thinks, and one thought dominates all others: *I can't keep him here.*

I begin again. My steps are calm, deliberate, one stride at a time. I look down rather than enduring Cause's stare. I walk up to him, still not looking, and pass him by, because he can't stop me. I know his secret.

In my peripherals I see Cause raise his arm. I lurch to a stop, dismayed that my body no longer works. I feel an invasion inside me, a virus of energy that's taken over. I'm unable to move my body.

"Zak," Cause says. "You don't want to leave. You don't want to go back home. You didn't want to be there."

I recall Celeste's lessons about energy in the After. Does that apply here, in Cause's world? Is this place even still the After?

I concentrate on my body, imagining it as a power source, like the battery in my phone. I close my eyes and search inside myself. In time, I see it, the red of Cause's power smothering the pale blue energy of my own. With my thoughts, I reach for the red, hold onto it as it writhes like an earthworm, and lift it up so that the blue can breathe again. Then I fling the red away from me. Far, far away.

I move. I look at Cause, and he gasps. I suspect that no one has ever defied him before.

I continue to walk. I feel Cause trying to infiltrate with

his energy, but I won't let him in. Now that I know what it feels like, I lock him out.

I hear a great disturbance behind me, and although I want to turn and see what Cause is doing, I know I have to ignore it. Just because he can't stop me doesn't mean he won't try. I sense that he has one more trick, and the calamity of wind, thunder, and light behind me is his final play, his one last hope. I only have to ignore it.

When the commotion behind me stops, it gives way to a voice calling a single word, perhaps the only word that would give me pause in my moment of truth:

"Daddy!"

I freeze. The voice is unmistakable. I know it's only a deception, but I'm unable to ignore it.

Kaitlyn.

I turn around. What I see suffocates me with emotion. My mouth sags open, but confusion holds my voice hostage. Instead of Cause, standing in front of me is my family: Angie, Lacy, and Kaitlyn.

31

THE FAMILY

I know they aren't real. This is another illusion, crueler this time, appealing to my deepest emotions. My family is here, just as real as that day at Purgatory Chasm, and it's impossible for me to ignore them.

"Daddy!" Lacy and Kaitlyn scream as they run to me. When they reach me, they embrace every part of my body that their little hands can clutch. I almost fall backwards from the force, holding them tight, taking in the essence of young cleanliness, hearing their little breaths.

Angie joins us. Her tears are real, loss swept away by reunion, momentary forgiveness for all I've done. I feel my own tears seep as Angie fastens herself to our family embrace, kissing me the way she always did, her taste just like I remember.

I hear their words in a chorus of emotion. They tell me they missed me, and they make me promise that we'll never be apart again. Just like that, I'm home again. Or my home has come to me.

But wait. This is all wrong.

I pull away. I'm about to tell them they aren't real, to order Cause to stop his charades, when Angie speaks:

"There was a fire."

"A fire?" I ask.

"While we were sleeping, the house caught fire," she says. "We couldn't get out."

"But then . . ." I begin to ask. Why should I ask it, when I already know the answer? My family has died in a house fire, so here they are, with me in the After. Or so Cause wants me to believe.

Truth in doubt, I step away from my family, wanting to distance myself from the tangle of emotion. I want to flee, but I already said there's not going to be any more running. I need to stand pat.

"No," I say, shaking my head. "This isn't real." I look up at the spire dome, knowing Cause is watching from somewhere. "Cause, what are you trying to do?"

"What's the matter?" Angie asks me. "Who are you talking to?"

"Cause!" I yell, ignoring this thing pretending to be my wife. I remember the fake Angie that Cause had sent to get me in the desert. That's all she is, another counterfeit spouse. I continue my rant: "You better answer me! What are you trying to pull?"

"Zak, if this is another one of your breakdowns, I swear . . ." Angie says.

The wind sweeps around us, and it seems to swallow Angie's breath midsentence.

I hear Cause's disembodied voice again: "Is this not what you wanted? Your family is here with you. There's nothing to return to now."

"This is *not* my family!" I shout.

"Daddy?" Kaitlyn says. "Yes we are."

"I'm sorry Zak, but this is your family," Cause says. "I brought them here. I started that fire in your house. I know it was a little mean, but I wanted to play with you, and I realized you wouldn't want to stay with me as long as your family is alive. They didn't suffer long."

"I think you're lying," I say, but my words have no conviction. Inside I'm fearing the sliver of possibility that Cause is being truthful.

"Lying is not nice," Cause says. "I don't like lying."

"Well, your plan didn't work," I say. "I'm still going home. I'm not staying here with you and my fake family."

"That's stupid," Cause says. "You have nothing back there. I plucked your family up and put them here. I did it for you, to make you comfortable here. You have no reason to go back to that terrible place that you hated anyway."

"Why is Daddy acting funny, Mommy?" Lacy asks Angie. "Is he mad at us?"

"I'm not mad at you honey," I tell Lacy.

But I am mad. My nervous energy has transformed into fury. It's possessive, fatherly anger, directed at Cause for using my family as leverage. It's also frustration and confusion. If I go back and my family has truly died, what then? If I stay here and this is all Cause's trick, then I've lost, too. I'm trapped.

"I swear to God, if you've actually hurt my family!" I yell.

"You'll do what?" Cause calls. "Don't be angry. We're friends. Now that your family is here, we can all be friends. There's nothing else you can do. What's done is done."

I feel the need to kick something, the human reflex to lash out when distressed. I'm beaten, and I know it. I recall spending all day trying to fix the washing machine and failing, and when finally giving up, beating it with a hammer. My anger now is like that moment, misery reduced to blind destruction.

The only thing nearby is a stone the size of a softball, jagged, alone on the ground next to me. I kick it, big toe taking the brunt with a smack. The rock tumbles end over end, and the satisfaction of seeing it fly grants me a moment of catharsis. Then the pain travels up my leg and sends a shot to my spine, toppling me to the ground.

"Ow, son of a bitch!" I scream, holding my foot in my hand.

"Daddy just swore, Mommy," Kaitlyn says.

I look up and notice a momentary change. If I had blinked I would have missed it. In a nanosecond, the sunlight from the cracks in the spire goes dim. Everything in Cause's world is a shadow, like none of it ever existed.

Then the light returns, like a hiccup to the power grid. My senses are too slow to process fully what I see next, but with the return of light there's movement. If I trust what I see, I'd say the entire place has been stretched like Silly Putty. The pond, the chasm, the amphitheater, even my family, are all twisted out of place, and then they jerk back to normalcy.

I'm bewildered. I don't know what just happened, but the anomaly seemed to correspond to my kicking of the rock. Why would kicking a rock make everything go buggy? Or was it a coincidence, some natural phenomenon of this place, that just happened to occur now? I rub my foot, the pain subsiding.

"Are you okay Daddy?" Lacy asks.

I ignore her and stand. My rarely used instinct of scientific inquiry has taken over. I walk to the rock I just kicked, pick it up, and examine it. There's nothing unusual about it, just a hunk of marbled granite. I place it on the ground, my family watching me like I'm a pathetic comedy act. I'm not sure whether I really want to do this, but I decide that I have to kick it again. I clench my teeth, extend back my leg, and kick. The rock skips away, bouncing across the uneven ground like a football.

The pain returns, my poor toe once again mangled, an anguished hiss spilling from my lips. Sure enough, the anomaly returns, darkness erasing light in an instant. As before, the light is restored just as quickly, revealing the odd distortion. But now my family has changed to something vastly more dreadful. They're deranged, bloodthirsty corpses intent on devouring me, temporarily unmasked, corrupt manifestations posing as loved ones. Then they return to my normal family again, all three looking at me like I'm bonkers.

"Stop that!" comes Cause's voice.

"Why?" I ask.

"It hurts," he says. "It hurts you."

I've studied semantics far too long to miss Cause's hasty admission. *It hurts.* Have I hurt him? Of course kicking the rock hurts me, but he said *it hurts* first.

The evidence has been laid out before me like I'm a Senate committee hearing the indisputable facts of treason. Nothing here is real, except Cause, his only honesty his intention to keep me here. What's more, somehow my own pain is his, a symbiotic relationship that I can't fathom.

I walk away again. This is what I should have done when Cause first conjured my family: kept walking and not turned back. My escape is just ahead, and I have to leave now while the path is clear.

But from behind me comes an eruption. There are flashes of light and rumbles, the return of Cause's desperate magic. I reach the mouth of the cave, the first few feet illuminated, the rest pure blackness. I stop, pull out my phone and switch on the light.

The chaos behind me has transitioned into something else. New sounds sneak out slowly at first, then consume me. I should learn to always expect the unexpected with Cause. I hear the buzzing of a demon, followed by a roar that's entirely too close.

I have to look. I have to see what's happening behind

me now. I turn to see my imposter family where I left them, but something is happening to them. Pieces of them are falling off, each one crumbling from the head down. Then their bodies completely unravel, like trees incinerated by an atomic bomb, all three disintegrating into piles of ash.

In the wake of my crumbling family is Pogo, the bad Pogo, the pure demon. He charges for me, closing fast, intent on revenge, summoned to prevent my escape. By his side is Celeste, equally brainwashed, rock sling winding up as she runs. Unable to convince me to stay, Cause has ordered my friends to destroy me.

I don't know why I think I have the time to look up at the spire dome, but I look anyway. I take in the light of this place, as if inhaling a deep breath before diving underwater. Then I turn and run into the cave, the light of my phone guiding my way.

32

THE YELLOW DOOR

I jog through the tunnel, the ray of light from my phone bouncing in front of me like the shaky beam of a motorcycle headlight. I leave the sunlight of the spire dome for good. I hear the sounds of Pogo thundering through the entrance behind me, my head start already dwindling, Celeste most certainly right behind him. I don't bother to check how far behind he is. I know it's not far enough.

Unlike the straight tunnel entering the spire dome, this one twists, rises, and falls. My dash through it feels like the erratic run of a bobsledder, a game of whether my reaction time is as fast as the abrupt changes in the tunnel's course. It's a game I begin to lose, as I smack into the walls and scrape and bruise myself. I hear Pogo doing the same from behind me, his commotion outperforming mine with seismic crashes followed by furious hollering.

The passage dips to a pitch far too close to vertical.

Gravity takes control of my legs, forcing them to move faster than they want. I'm out of control, a mining car plunging into the After's belly without a brake. I seem to float, more falling than running, arms thrashing to maintain order but failing. Just when I think I'll plunge into a bungling cartwheel, the passage levels out. My knees and hamstrings labor against the momentum, my feet digging into the rocky floor with labored slaps. I spill into a junction and lurch to a stop.

Surrounding me are entrances to six more passageways at odd angles, as if I've reached a jumbled subway crossing. Any one of them could lead to a dead end or get me lost forever. I wish I could take the time to consider which way to take, but Pogo is coming. Besides, they all look the same, so what's to deliberate?

I choose one. I rush through the entrance and resume my breakneck pace through its schizophrenic path, doing my best to keep quiet to hide my location from Pogo. I even try to block my thoughts, in case Cause is reading them in order to direct Pogo where to go. He'll find me eventually, but why make it easier?

More junctions follow. I might spend an eternity scurrying through these tunnels while never passing through the same one. Each junction leads to more tunnels, more choices, none more promising than the next. My decisions are instantaneous and random, and with each turn I feel infinitely more lost. But the benefit is this also confuses Pogo. I hear his sounds taper off behind me, then disappear entirely.

When I'm satisfied that I've given Pogo the slip, I slow. I'm sure that I'm bleeding from brushing against the tunnel walls, but I don't inspect my wounds. I just breathe and try to think. Where is this portal? I don't even know what it looks like. Only Cause knows where it is. I want to see into his thoughts, to pluck out from his mind a map leading right to it. I have nothing so powerful inside me as that, but I do feel something. I sense that I'm close. Very close. Too close for Cause's comfort.

On cue, I hear Cause's disembodied voice. The words barrel down the tunnel, the echo more ominous than he sounds in the open: "I only wanted to play," he says. "Don't go, Zak. Why would you just leave me here, all alone?"

We have nothing more to discuss. Anyway, it's harder to keep Cause out of my thoughts when I'm speaking to him, so I keep silent and put all of my energy into closing him off.

"Why won't you talk?" he asks. "I don't like to be ignored. It's not nice."

I can feel his anger. It's a tangible thing, like I'd be able to touch it if the intensity was a fraction stronger. I hear him snort, a warning that his wrath is coming. The cave feels hot from it, alive with the heat of his furious breath.

The passage begins to quake, my body along with it. It's an earthquake of sorts, a Cause-quake. He wants to bring the cave down onto me. I've gone too far, and his only recourse is to be done with me like discarding a defective trinket.

As the shaking intensifies, a scream engulfs the tunnel. It's the wail of a psychopath disguised as a child, an infantile tantrum but with the potency of adult rage.

I plug my ears and fall to my knees. I drop my phone, and it topples unharmed, but the light is smothered when the phone lands facedown. I sink into the fetal position and tremble. The scream tries to squirt through my hands and exterminate my brain, so I pack my hands tighter to my ears, grit my teeth, and will the noise away. I do more than that. I demand it to cease: "Stop it!" I yell, or at least I think I do, but I can't hear myself.

I'm surprised when the scream stops like the finale of a maniacal opera. Did I stop it? Maybe, but Cause is not done with me. The tunnel still quakes, and the shaking becomes something else. I unplug my ears, grab my phone, stand, and shine the light on the walls. The tunnel is still swaying, but the movement is more of a convulsion, a living reflex rather than a geological event.

If I were a particle of food inside the human intestine, this is how it might look. The walls of the tunnel have become slick and spongy, a palpitating tube of living tissue. I seesaw with the tremors, extending my arms to balance like a tightrope walker. The tunnel is in distress, trying to disgorge something rotten. I'm lifted and slammed to the ceiling, sinking into its fleshiness, then rebound back to the floor that's equally yielding, like a trampoline of beef liver.

Before I can recover, more shockwaves come. The tunnel is serving as Cause's giant whip. It goes vertical, and I bounce from wall to wall, the object of its whims. I clutch my phone, my life preserver in an angry sea, and I manage to tuck my legs to my chest to endure the jostling. I may as well be a goldfish mistaken for dead and flushed away.

The tunnel levels out again, but I continue to bounce. For whatever reason I remember my trip in the ambulance, the event that began this vile journey. I had nothing then but to pray to God to get me through it, which I realize now is much more than nothing. Praying worked, in a way. Technically I died, but I lived on in this place, the dreaded After. God gets half credit then, and full credit if I make it back home.

I begin shouting his name, God, like he's an old friend who has forsaken me, screaming it so loud it hurts my throat. I say it a hundred times. For good measure, I think it in my mind while I say it: *Please God please God please God!*

Then I think of Deena. Where is she? Does she know what I'm going through, but she's helpless to assist? If she's supposed to help, what good is it if she's powerless? I have to try, I have to ask for her help, too. I shout for her: "Deena! Where are you? Get me out of here! Deena!"

At first there's nothing. I land on my head, flop down on my back, and cartwheel off the opposite wall. Then everything begins to slow. I sense that the energy in the tunnel has changed. The movement is settling, like the residual ripples on a waterbed. My tumbles stop, then all movement ceases. I take a breath and exhale in relief. The tissue of the tunnel returns to its old self, from flesh to sheer granite. The cave is restored.

I fight the dizziness. I stand still and wait, allowing myself to recover and prepare for the next onslaught. That's just what this will continue to be, onslaught after onslaught until I submit, because I don't trust that Cause has left me alone so easily. But I don't want to give up, and I don't want to go back the way I've come, so I may as well go forward.

My phone light reveals the way. Ahead is a straight path that ascends, a breeze blowing a hint that something new awaits. I walk, watching the light peel back the passage that's enlarging. My tentative steps bring me to an opening. It's another junction, much larger than the others, dozens of passageways splintering off.

I stop and listen for signs that Pogo is hiding in one of the adjacent tunnels. This is nonsense, though, since Pogo is as silent as a Howitzer in his current state. Still, I unholster my gun. Then I remember that the gun isn't fully loaded. I take the time to open the cylinder and load it by the light of my phone. Finished, I creep forward.

I see something on the other side of the chamber. I almost miss it, but when my eyes adjust to this place, I'm certain about what I see: a rectangular glow of yellow, roughly the size of a door. That's the key word here, *door*. It's absolutely a door!

I walk toward it. My steps echo up to the cavernous ceiling, but I don't care about the noise. This is no time to sneak. If that's the portal, I'm almost home. My family awaits, the real ones and not things conjured in Cause's workshop of nightmares.

As I get closer, I see that the door is old and weathered, but also familiar. I squint to focus on it. Where have I seen it before? It takes only a second more to call up the memory. This is the same door that I had entered when the procedure failed in the operating room. It's the door that took me here! That being the case, is it also the door that will take me back?

The door is the color of a vibrant lemon. I've never liked yellow, but for now it's my favorite color: the color of the sun, of daffodils, of finches and cheese. The closer I get to it, the brighter it becomes, like it knows I need to use it, like it's ready to bring me back.

I'm running again, but it's okay. This doesn't count as running from my problems, it counts as running back to them, to own them, to live through them and defeat them. I'm smiling as I run. How can I not? I'm going to run right through that yellow door, burst on past and not look back. Easy as yellow banana cream pie.

I collide with the door, or does it collide with me? It wallops me hard, like it has reached up and kicked me with an invisible leg, forbidding me to pass. I fly back and land hard, my head slamming to the ground.

The door doesn't want me to open it. I should have known. I pull myself up, the back of my head throbbing. In a daze, all of my surroundings stretch like a black hole is sucking it all away, my own pain once again having an effect on the environment. Yet just as quickly, everything in the chamber returns to normal. All except for the yellow door. It opens, just for an instant, welcoming in light: ethereal light, the light of life. Then the door slams shut, like the cursed entrance to a pharaoh's tomb.

"Zak?" I hear Cause call me. It's not the disembodied voice, it's the one of a simple child calling from behind me.

I turn and shine my light. The beam catches Cause twenty feet away, his form so tiny in the middle of the chamber, but he terrifies me nonetheless.

"Please don't go," he says. "All I wanted was to play."

"Yes, I know," I say. "And we have played, haven't we? We threw rocks. You showed me the trick, and you took me to amazing places. Thank you for showing it all to me."

"I can show you *so* much more," he says, stepping closer. "I can show you everything, and then you'll see just how fun it is. Stay. You have to stay."

"I can't," I say.

Cause is coming for me. His little boy face is deranged, outraged, fed up.

I aim the gun at him. What will my gun do to him? Nothing.

"Stay away," I say.

"You won't shoot me," he says.

He's wrong. I shoot the little bugger. The blast may as well be dynamite, its boom bouncing off the walls, smoke spitting from the barrel. The bullet should split his head in two, nothing short of reckless murder. Instead the bullet stops and floats inches from Cause's forehead. He cocks his head to study it, then plucks the bullet from the air and holds it in his hand. He tosses it to me, bullet clanking next to my feet.

I pull the trigger again. The blast rings my ears, the smoke again fills the air, and once more the bullet stops and floats. I shoot twice more, but this is getting nowhere. Three bullets now float in the air, held in Cause's hidden grasp. He allows them to fall to the ground.

"Do it again, this is fun!" Cause says. I lower the gun. I don't think anything about this is fun. I look back at the portal, and it's as golden, solid, and closed as ever.

I'm desperate now. What will Cause do? What can he do? What can I do? I feel the weight of failure at this moment of truth. Unless . . .

I keep a thought well hidden in my mind. If Cause were to know about it, he would try to stop me. I have to keep the secret buried in my deepest thoughts, and just act without thinking. But do I have the guts to go through with it? I don't want to speculate on that, either. I point the gun down at my foot. I suffer at the peril of it. This is much more than ripping a bandage from my skin or removing a sliver with a tweezers. This is desperate, fearsome, self-mutilation.

"Zak?" Cause says. He's sensing something. I have to open the door, and open it now, not a millisecond more to wait or I'm finished.

I pull the trigger. The bullet thunders through my foot before Cause can stop it. I crumple, gun falling from my right hand, phone falling from my left while I yell in pain. Through the muted light of the phone, I see Cause fall, too. Like me, he grips his foot, trying to plug the firehose of blood spraying from the wound. He cries like the child he is.

"You shot us!" he screams. "Why would you do that? Why would you shoot us?"

Us. Cause is me, and I'm him. It's really that simple. Why wasn't it clear to me before? Was seeing myself as a child so foreign? He is the *cause* of all of this.

"Zak!" I hear someone call. Celeste emerges from one of the tunnels, Pogo at her side. They're running for me, my friends, in control of themselves while Cause suffers.

I look at the portal. It's open, but barely, like some unseen wind is trying to blow it open, and some invisible hand is trying to keep it shut. Cause is trying to keep it closed, trying desperately. I hear him grunt through his pain, and the door slams shut with a thud.

"Stay away!" Cause shouts, waving his hand toward Celeste and Pogo. They stop, leery of what he intends to do. But he's too weak, there's nothing more he can do but fight to keep the portal closed.

"Celeste," I say, grabbing the gun and pulling myself to my feet, standing on my good leg. "I know what I have to do."

"You do?" she says, stepping toward me.

"Half Dead has found the way," Pogo says. "The good way."

"Yes," I say. "I think."

Celeste stops and stares at me. She's uncertain, doubting that I really know, but realizing that she has to trust me.

I flip the gun around and press the barrel to my chest like it's a crude hypodermic needle. My heart beats furiously against the steel. It knows what's coming. This is a shot I know even I can't miss, a shot that I fear to take, but I know I have to. Celeste once told me that I have an angry man inside of me, hidden from the world, rarely coming out to fight. But it's there, more passion than anger, the desire to live.

I pull the trigger. The last bullet in the gun explodes into my chest, shattering my heart. Cause is powerless to stop it. I flop to the ground, the trauma to my heart sapping my life. I can't breathe. I should feel a pain like no other, but there's nothing there, just an emptiness in my body, a complete shutdown.

Pogo and Celeste rush to me, struggling to understand what I've done. I try to smile at them, but I'm certain it looks like intense suffering. I turn my head to see Cause lying on his back, a wound bubbling from his chest. I look the other way and see the portal flapping open, like a tornado is threatening to remove it at the hinges. Then I see the ceiling of the chamber blurring, the entire place beginning to shake like it's about to implode.

"The portal," I whisper.

Celeste and Pogo understand now. They lift me up and fight through our collapsing surroundings. Cause's world is crumbling apart with tumbling stones and flurries of swirling wind. My friends drag me toward the portal like battling through a typhoon. Three steps more. Two steps more. One step more.

Together we burst through the yellow door partially ajar. I still remember the light, the way it looked when I first saw it, the vibrant light of life warming my face, brighter than I've ever seen. The portal door, the chamber, the spire, Cause, and all of his world crumble behind us with the inconsolable sob of a child, gone forever.

33

DEAD IS A TRICKY WORD

Pogo lifts me. I'm on my back in his outstretched arms, my head facing forward. But where is forward? What is forward? Everywhere is light, so bright there's nothing to discern. It feels like swaying in a hammock beneath an extraordinary sun, one unlike the sun I know, with a superior power to soothe and heal.

The light is more than light. If light could have the density of water, it would be this. It flows around us, politely moving aside as we step through it, tickling us like the warmth of tiny tongues. Submerged deep within this soup of illumination, all sound is insulated, all scents are absent.

I discover something all the more odd and troubling. I clutch my chest and realize I'm still not breathing. Alarmed, I wait for the need to breathe, but it never comes. There should be pain, my foot and chest pierced with bullets, but there's an odd detachment to my flesh, like it doesn't exist. I'm just floating in Pogo's arms, no desire for anything. I'm aware, but am I alive?

"Celeste?" I call. My voice is bizarre, a screechy whisper, the stifled uttering of a ghost. "Pogo?"

I hear nothing from them. I turn to look at Pogo, and even though I know he's holding me, I can't see him through the impenetrable light. If I'm honest, I can't really feel him holding me anymore. I may as well be floating alone in this odd, watery light.

I should be inconsolable by so many things I don't understand, but I'm not. The light is far too comforting. I indulge, let go, and allow it to wrap me up and carry me forward. I'm so sleepy. How long has it been since I've slept? Since before entering the After, a duration I have no way of parsing. I don't fight my weariness. I allow sleep to come. Real sleep, the sleep of a living human being.

This is a dark room. I wake lying in a bed, knowing it's not my bedroom, like stirring from an overnight at my in-laws. I see only the suggestion of a room and the shadows of objects within it.

The intensity of my sleep has left me clueless. What do I know? Almost nothing. I'm somewhere strange. It might be somewhere I've been before, but I can't place it. I could be on a business trip, and this is my hotel room, but I remember that I don't take business trips. Is it a vacation? No, I don't take vacations, either. Did I go on a bender and I'm waking in someone's house with a hangover? That's plausible. I definitely feel hung over.

But these are only hasty guesses. My first reasonable assessment of the situation seeps in from memories of the After. I'm surprised how far I've repressed that place already. I see my recent past like it was long forgotten. My death, crossing the lake, evading demons, meeting my friends: Celeste and Pogo, and Deena. Escaping through the yellow door.

I breathe. It's an impeded breath, something pinching inside my throat. I become aware of a great weight beginning at my shoulder and stretching over my collarbone to my neck. It's the kind of ache that isn't telling the whole story. When I reach for my shoulder, the ache turns angry, the sensation of a hot skillet pressed on my skin.

I groan, but it comes out as a gurgle from the strange obstruction in my throat. I think of Cause. Does he have hold of my throat? Is he clinging to me, not wanting to let go?

I remain still. Moving means pain, but worse, it makes noise. If I haven't yet left Cause's world, I have to remain silent or he'll hear me. I let my eyes search the room for clues of my whereabouts. Is it another chamber of Cause's caves? No, I went through the yellow door, the portal, my escape. Someone needs to assure me that I've escaped, but no one does.

I see lights. Tiny lights, red ones and orange ones, some of them blinking. Some might be numbers, but my vision is blurred. I've slept for so long that my eyes are refusing to focus. I blink them to clear away the sleep, but this blurs them even worse.

I feel the urge to cough. The thing in my throat is itchy. Cause's tiny fingers might be around my neck, squeezing my airway shut, one last grasp to smother me. I cough. It does no good, the thing is still in my throat, and coughing only causes more pain in my shoulder, like from a gunshot.

This makes me remember the gun. I used it to shoot myself. Twice. How did I even manage to do that? I don't want to think about it. I wonder if my shoulder wound is from shooting myself. It feels like it. But no, I shot myself in the chest and the foot, not my shoulder. Then I remember my surgery gone wrong, the pain in my shoulder that birthed a trip in an ambulance. Then there was the hospital, the last place I was alive.

A hospital. I'm in a hospital! A dark, solitary hospital room.

A door opens in front of me. The light from the hallway is blinding, and I squint against it. I see a person standing there, the opener of the door, and the light and my sleepy eyes prevent me from identifying who it is. Is it Cause? Has he found me? Did he hear me cough, and now he's found where I am?

It's not Cause. It's an adult, a female. I can make out hospital scrubs and a stethoscope. Maybe she's a nurse. Cause is gone, I have to believe that now.

"Zak?" she calls to me.

I sputter something that I intend as *what* but it comes out more like *wuff.*

"You're awake," she says, coming to my side.

I really want to talk, but the thing in my throat isn't helping. I have to ask the nurse if I'm alive. But that's stupid, isn't it? Of course I'm alive. I'm alive!

More grunts and gurgles from me.

"You still have your breathing tube in," she says. "I can take that out."

Breathing tube? I remember the small army of medical staff huddled in the operating room to insert that tube. I had been so certain that it hadn't worked, that I was too knotted up, that it had killed me in the process. Didn't it happen that way?

The nurse puts on rubber gloves. Then she grabs the end of the tube that I now realize is sticking out of my mouth. "Okay, 3, 2, 1."

She pulls. I feel something enormous being pulled from my throat. She's retrieving the boa constrictor that had crawled into my mouth, slithered down my throat, and suffocated me, and she's yanking it out foot by foot. I don't want to look at the tube, so I shut my eyes. But she's done, I can feel the tube is out, just like that. I cough from the gag reflex, lick my lips, and swallow. Cause's hands are no longer around my neck. I open my eyes to see the nurse pitching the tube into a receptacle. Only a piece of plastic.

"How are you feeling?" she asks.

"Really out of it," I say. "And sore."

"I brought you pain medication. Would you like it?"

"Yes," I say.

She pulls a syringe from her pocket, finds my IV line, and unloads medication into my vein.

"Am I . . ." I begin to ask the question while the nurse finishes.

"Are you what?" she asks. My eyes are beginning to work better now. I look at the nurse and can see part of her face in the semidarkness.

"Am I alive?" I ask. The drugs hit my system, and at first I regret agreeing to medication. Narcotics roll through my body, sink into my abdomen, and threaten to unsettle my stomach before filling me with the strange weight of numbness.

The nurse laughs. "You're alive," she says. "You gave us a scare though, trying to get that tube in. We almost lost you."

"Lost me," I say.

"You'll be fine now though," she says. "Just have to rest up, and you'll be back to normal soon."

"Normal," I repeat, my thoughts quickly sinking into confusion from the drugs.

"Do I know you?" I ask her. She looks familiar.

"I've been around," she says.

Something about the nurse's presence has abruptly changed. She's thinking about something, plotting what to do, all the while staring at me. My mind jumps to the worrisome conclusion that I've been deceived. Is she really a nurse? Or is it Cause posing as her? He could pull it off, nothing is above him.

She goes to the door and closes it. She stands in the darkness and watches me. I'm on full alert, my condition leaving me vulnerable.

"Do you have any other questions?" she asks. She steps closer, and I see her face lit from the hospital equipment lights. When I see her face again, my fear recedes, anchored by familiarity. She's not Cause. Not by a long shot.

"You're from the ER," I tell her. "You're the nurse who wheeled me to the operating room."

"That's right," she says. I'm happy that I finally remember where I've seen her.

I'm spinning in a wild carnival of painkillers. This place is all roller coasters and Ferris wheels, a house of mirrors in full distortion. I inhale to tame it, but I'm too far in. I seem to sink a hundred feet into the bed. Just what kind of medication did the nurse give me? A powerful one, a narcotic of the gods.

"Thank you for helping me," I say. I wonder if I sound as doped as I feel. "You were very reassuring."

She's silent. She's wondering something, waiting for me to put together pieces in my mind. I'm slow.

"But there's more to it than that," I say.

"Yes," she says. "There is."

I remember when I first saw Deena. A person doesn't forget that, her shroud of white and the iridescence of her skin, the divine offspring of a rainbow. I'm surprised it took me so long to make the connection.

"Deena," I whisper.

She nods. Deena was with me from the beginning, posing as a nurse in the ER, as my guide in the After, now back here in the living.

I lurch up from this discovery, causing another jolt of pain that penetrates my armor of painkillers. I squawk and grab my shoulder.

Deena steps to me. She places her hand on my chest and eases me back down to the bed. There's light on her face, no longer the reflection of hospital equipment lights, but the amazing swirls of light from her own skin. There's a tangible comfort in her touch, a calming effect straight to my heart, like she's reached inside and slowed down the beats with her grasp.

"There," she says. "You have to be still now. Let your body heal."

"But how can you be here?" I ask.

"I can be anywhere," she says. "But with luck, and some effort on your part, this will be the last time you'll see me."

"Are you leaving?"

"I'll be around, but not to your eyes," she says. "I came to say goodbye, Zak. And to congratulate you."

"Congratulate me?"

"For choosing to live again," she says. "You have important things ahead of you. Worthwhile things."

"I do?"

"Yes. Promise me that you'll do them, the things you were destined to do."

"What things?" I say. "How can I promise things I don't even know about?"

"You'll know soon enough," she says. "And when you do, grab onto them, make them yours. Fair enough?"

"Okay," I say. I have no idea what she's talking about, but she seems so certain of herself.

"What about Celeste and Pogo?" I ask.

She gives me a sympathetic smile. "Ah yes, your friends."

"Are they dead?"

"Dead is a tricky word, isn't it?" she offers. "They came through the yellow door with you. They're here, although you can't see them the way they were. They'll be with you for a while, a part of you, here to help you reclaim your life. But they're no longer in the After. It's a much better existence to be here among your world, I can assure you of that. And maybe, in time, they can even move along from you, to be free to start the next phase of their existence. Do you understand?"

"No."

"I know it's confusing," she says. "Just know that they're okay, and that you're never alone. We'll all listen for you."

"Where's Cause?" I ask.

"Gone," she says.

"Gone forever?"

"Yes," she says. "But others like him can come around. That's up to you."

"To me?"

"Yes," she says. "We create our own monsters, if we allow it. Don't allow it, Zak, or you'll go right back to the After. Shut it out, never to return."

I try to digest the meaning of her words as best I can. "I created Cause?"

"Yes, I'm afraid so. Some time ago, a fragment of you splintered off. Not a physical piece, a spiritual one, a part of your soul. That fragment grew, fueled by your negative energy, into a living being, an extension of yourself. It became Cause. He lived in the After, and he desperately wanted you there with him. As an extension of you, he *caused* problems for you, influenced you throughout your life, ushering you through a self-destructive path. He wanted Zak and Cause together so he could make you both whole again, and then control it all. But you stopped him, with a little nudging."

"I really created him?" I ask. "I didn't mean to do that."

"Of course not," Deena says. "People do it when they experience trauma, never knowing when they do. Your fragmentation came when you were very young, when you first realized that life was difficult. It shocked you enough to shatter a piece away. This is why Cause appeared as a child to you."

I think back to my childhood. As abstract as it seems to subconsciously create an alternate version of myself, it also makes some sense.

"It was when my father died," I say. It had to be when Cause was born. When your father commits suicide and leaves your family reeling and destitute, it changes you forever. "His death dislodged a piece of me and created something horrible."

"No matter," Deena says. "Clear your mind of it now. Cause is gone. It's within your power to avoid creating another, but you really have to work on that. I think you know what I mean."

"I do," I nod.

Someone knocks at the door.

"I believe you," Deena says.

Another nurse opens the door, soaking the room in hallway light again. This nurse seems surprised to see me awake.

I'm far more surprised than the nurse at the door. Deena is gone.

The nurse enters the room. She's all business, the type of nurse who prefers not to speak to patients unless absolutely necessary. She decides that the room is altogether too dark, so she moves past me and opens the blinds behind my bed. Daylight infiltrates the darkness, uncovering an impressive cluster of machines and equipment in the room. Then she returns to the bed to look at me. When she notices a problem straight away, she can no longer avoid speaking to me.

"Where did your breathing tube go?" she asks.

"Breathing tube?" I say. I can think of nothing else to do but play dumb.

"Yes, did you take it out yourself?"

"I don't think so," I say. It's not a lie.

She doesn't believe me. I don't think she can generate any other explanation than I removed it. "You should have waited for me to do that," she scolds. But she has other things to do, so she moves past the awkward moment to check my vitals, adjust my IV machine, and make notes on her computer. Before she leaves, the nurse is forced to speak to me again:

"You have some visitors," she says. "But they can't stay long, you need rest."

She motions to the door, but I've already seen them in the doorway. Maybe I even knew they were nearby. Angie is there, my daughters clutching each of her hands with guarded intrigue.

The girls see me and break free, Lacy around one side of my bed, Kaitlyn on the other. They wrap their arms around my body.

"Are you okay, Daddy?" Lacy asks.

"I'm okay," I say, fighting the pain from their grasps. I remember the imposters of my family. Is this really my children? Yes. How can I be certain? I just know, a simple instinct of truth.

Angie enters and leans over my bed next to Lacy. "Hi," she says, kissing my forehead. "Welcome back to the land of the living."

"Thanks," I say.

I'm sure my wife has no idea the significance of what she just said. To her, this has only been a close call. To me, it's the return from an awful adventure. I don't want to think about it. Instead, I bask in her kiss and the tenderness of her words. Her actions hint that somewhere among our problems, there's still love. I cling to the possibility that she'll have me back, if I just try.

The nurse leaves us alone. Even she knows better than to interrupt the moment, and she closes the door behind her.

Alone with my family at last, their presence soothes me like the instant cure of a long-suffered itch. I think it extends deeper than that. There's a feeling in the room that transcends my family. Others are here, watching. Deena was right, they're all here with me, as real as my own family.

Memories of the After remind me to move forward, to make my future my own.

34

NEVER TO RETURN

I've gone back to teaching. Teaching my students, yes, but also teaching myself how to live. It isn't overnight to reassemble the shards of your life, but I've scratched out a new existence hour by hour, day by day. I've assembled an army to assist, from Alcoholics Anonymous to a psychologist named Dr. Ted. There's marriage counseling, 12-Step, and treatment for depression. I've even joined a gym. Celeste would be proud.

I used to think time passed too slowly among the urges to speed through the suffering. Now I'm content to allow whatever pace is set, since there's little control over that anyway, and there's an enjoyment to just riding along. There's still a long way to go, too many issues yet unresolved, but I'm willing to try to get there.

I enter the empty lecture hall ten minutes early. I descend the steps of the stadium seating toward the podium, rays of morning light beaming across the room. I set my leather bag next to the podium, placing a hand on the stability of the lectern. I turn to face the silence of the empty hall, savoring the final moments of peace before my students arrive. I feel compelled to rehearse my lecture in my mind, but there's no need. I've done this before, the blueprint of my intro class at my disposal like a polished script for a seasoned actor.

Despite my best efforts, fear is still there. Failure, inadequacy, humiliation. Everyone is afraid of something. I used to be afraid more than most, but I'm trying not to be. Real fear is being dead and wondering if you'll live again.

Students begin to trickle in. I can sense the freshmen in all of them. This is the first class of their first day at college, and they tote with them baggage of young apprehension. They hover about the hall before choosing seats, everyone as far from one another as possible, silent except for the opening of laptops and the tapping on phones. Seconds away from start time, more students flood the hall, streaming down the steps like waterfalls, and the seats all fill in. Few have decided to skip today.

"Good morning everyone, let's get started," I say. My teaching voice penetrates the clatter of the room as a hundred sets of eyes focus on me.

Despite my best efforts, I'm unprepared for what happens next. There's something diffusing throughout the room, an intangible gush of feelings, and they react with my own. The moment surprises me, my confidence from only seconds before now retreating.

From deep inside me, feelings I thought were

controlled break loose. I want to run again, to hide, to drink, to wallow, to forget. That was the path to my near destruction before, so why am I so willing to return to it? The memories of the After are still affixed to my consciousness. I know I was there, in a place the living can't imagine, with mountains and deserts, volcanoes and spires, the incessant Shift, demons, Cause. Even now, though, I'm almost willing to put blinders on, to consider it a surreal nightmare, the things of a troubled imagination.

I stand there, unable to find any words, like the English language is less than a rumor, my throat held hostage again. Cause is squeezing it, trying to close my airway, attempting to pull me back. I imagine him standing in the spire dome, straining to manifest my return to him. His contorted face in my imagination tells me he's supremely angry.

I wonder if the students understand what's happening to me. Their teacher should be saying something, introducing himself, presenting a syllabus. Instead of course expectations and reading lists, I have nothing for them. Some of them whisper to each other. They're confused, some even amused, the more empathetic ones alarmed.

I can't even move. I'm dying again, my body closing down. Will there be another ambulance ride, or will I just collapse into the After? I should have known better than to think I had escaped that place. I should have realized that's impossible. Cause will never allow it. I grab hold of the lectern with both hands and squeeze.

Now wait a minute! Stop it! Cause is dead, I killed the little twit. Forget about him.

Never to return. I can hear the words Deena spoke, but this time they're my own words in my mind. My squeezing of the lectern reminds me of my ambulance ride. Denied morphine, I had grabbed my pant legs and squeezed, just like I'm squeezing the lectern. But instead of squeezing due to pain, now I'm doing it out of fear. I stop squeezing and let go. I say the words again in my mind: *never to return.*

I imagine blocking out my negative thoughts, just like I had learned to block out Cause in the spire. I wait for them to recede, to go back to their corral deep inside me, and I lock the door behind them.

I take a deep breath. That's better. Now what?

Something has changed in my classroom, but I can't put my finger on it. My eyes scan the rows of students. They all look as before, at least at first. Then something catches my eye, followed by an incredible realization. How had I missed it before? It was subtle. The mind doesn't always notice when it should.

In the last row of the lecture hall sit two people. Once I become aware of them, they stand out from everyone else, not belonging among the freshmen. There's an aura about them, and something familiar.

They're a male and a female. I've seen the confident face in the female before, pretty but with a glaze of perpetual outrage. Her lips tighten with impatience. She sees that I had struggled for a moment, and it bothers her. Everything about me annoys her, but she's invested in me.

Her eyes are blue, a wonderful blue that I can see even from my distance. I'm surprised by this, almost delighted. When I had seen those eyes before, they were black, the onyx luster of remorseful death. Celeste. For the first time, I see what she looked like when alive.

The male is Pogo. If you could crumple up a demon and shove him into the body of a human, this might be the result. He masquerades as a huge teen, barely squeezing into his seat. His burly arms are folded in front of him, a forked beard flowing down his chest. Somehow he's even more frightening as a person than as a demon.

This might be how it feels to see the miraculous, like a ghost or an alien. You know it's not possible to see what you see, but there it is. Possibilities open in your mind, that there are such things as gods and angels, that maybe heaven and hell exist after all, and that there's a place in between where troubled souls wait and wander. I believe it all now.

I want to call to them, to go to them and embrace them. Celeste knows this and squints a caution at me. She puts her index finger to her lips: *ssh.*

Pogo unfolds his arms and points to the window, the light from outside beaming through. Celeste looks to where he's pointing, to the glorious fall sunlight outside. Summer is refusing to give up yet, stubbornly digging in, fighting for its life. Celeste turns to me, then nods toward the outside. She's reminding me that there's a whole world out there.

I look outside. At first I see the After, in my mind at

least. There are jagged mountains, a wintry valley with demons lurking on hilltops, and an ocean still bubbling from a passed hurricane. Then I look, really look, allowing my eyes to see rather than my memories. I see the campus, the courtyard, the trees. That's a normal day if I've ever seen one, a day of returning to school, but otherwise routine. So why not just let it all happen, day after day?

I look back at Celeste and Pogo. I'm astonished, saddened, because they're gone. Maybe they had never even been there, except to me. But now I'm reassured that they'll never be far, even though I think this is the final time I'll see them.

"Everyone, grab your stuff," I say. "We're going outside."

My students are bewildered by this. They wonder what sort of charade I'm playing. I need my teacher voice to prod: "Come on, everyone up. There aren't going to be many more days like this left. Do you really want to be trapped in this stuffy room with me?"

It takes some more convincing, but eventually I get my class outside. I don't even give them my syllabus. Instead we read poetry in the courtyard, the more morbid and reflective the better. I really think, for once, everyone is enjoying my class. Especially me.

ACKNOWLEDGMENTS

Thank you to those who provided their expertise and assistance with this novel.

Charles Pederson for copy editing the manuscript. As always, his meticulous edits were critical in making the novel what is it today.

Brandi Doane McCann for providing a truly exquisite cover design.

Susie Keithahn for reviewing the manuscript twice and providing countless consultations throughout the writing of this novel.

Simon Tuchman for beta reading the manuscript and offering superb advice for its improvement.

ABOUT THE AUTHOR

Patrick Keithahn lives in Massachusetts with his wife and three children. An editor of over 25 years, he's an editorial manager for a large educational publisher in Boston, where he develops social studies materials. Born in Minnesota, he is a graduate of Hamline University. He grew up in Huntington Beach, California. He has lived in Massachusetts since 2008. *Enter the After* is his second novel. His first novel, *Ring of Ages,* was published in 2016. He enjoys history, football, baseball, and reading fiction and nonfiction. But his greatest passion is writing novels!

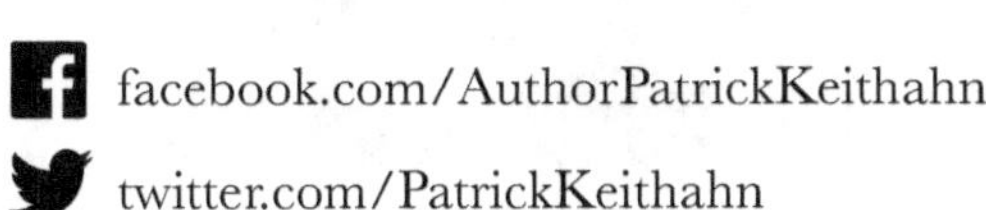

facebook.com/AuthorPatrickKeithahn

twitter.com/PatrickKeithahn

ALSO BY PATRICK KEITHAHN

RING OF AGES, A SUPERNATURAL HISTORICAL THRILLER

A lethal medieval assassin. A magical ring. Two couples across time, from the middle ages to modern-day Boston. A secret is about to be revealed. Two worlds reel as past and present merge. Now available on Amazon.com!